Claretta Street

Colette Barris

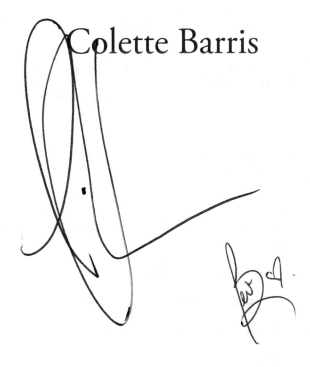

Brown Bear/Barris Publications

This is a work of fiction. Names, characters, business, places, events, and incidents are either the products of the author's imagination or used in a fictitious manner. Any resemblance to actual places, events, or persons, living or dead, is purely coincidental.

Brown Bear/Barris Publications
3940 Laurel Canyon Boulevard Suite 1586
Studio City, California 91604
www.colettebarris.com

Ordering Information:
Quantity sales, Special discounts are available on quantity purchases by corporations, associations and others.
For details, contact the publisher at the address.
Orders by U.S. trade bookstores and wholesalers.

Printed in the United States of America

Claretta Street Library of Congress PCN 2016910703

ISBN 978-0-692-60112-9

Dedicated to my mother Ernestine Moreno Barris who taught me joy,
Love You Infinitely!

For Jackie…Finally!

PROLOGUE

AUGUST 1986

Warm spring night air tickled our faces as the lights of the city defiantly glistened against filled glasses. Sleepy little Pacoima was changing; this refuge of comfort lost now, only a reverberation of a time endless in possibilities and pride.

Smitty moved slowly. Lulia, transfixed in the sky's vastness, busy with the promise of tomorrow, yet confused by the insistence she forget a place and time of great hope.

Lulia filled our glasses with champagne. We sipped slowly, lost in the moment staring into the star-soaked valley sky, contemplating our lives below.

"Pour Deebie a glass. She's here with us," I demanded.

Thoughts of the trial flashed before my eyes, momentary serenity snatched by reality.

"What happened? How did we get here? I've been living a dream. This feels like someone else's life…Moving so fast at times I can't remember anything."

Bev, who had been silent through my testimony, spoke, "Yeah girl it's a trip. How did you ever stay the course, Ne?"

"I really don't know, Bev."

Lifelike depictions danced in my head, a sense of joy embraced me, and I saw my father on the Fourth of July and then David as sadness flooded in.

CHAPTER ONE

THE SOURCE OF MY INTIMATE JOY AND PAIN

My life is a chronicle of contemporary Black America, its triumphs and downfalls…Got a minute to listen?

I have always loved the sun and wind of autumn in Pacoima, a cozy little town in the East San Fernando Valley of Southern California. Dawn's introduction to the day was a special occasion for me, fall's weather crisp, charged with Southern California's famous Santa Ana winds, which gently stroked my face making me feel alive. Pacoima, a refuge for *Negroes* or *Coloreds* (as we were called then), was nurturing, warm and most importantly filled with love.

My home was a modern sixties tract style residence located on a little tree-lined street called Claretta. Middle-class Negroes moved to this Hamlet for its sense of community, beauty and protection. Claretta Street was picture postcard perfect; all the lawns vibrant green and manicured; children played with endless energy and joy, traveling from one house to another surveying each other's existence. Claretta Street will always be my home. When I feel sad, lonely or troubled, I close my eyes and remember…the joy.

Being five years old amongst a vast segment of what I can only describe as Africa was simply amazing. The neighborhood was a cornucopia of African shades and textures, possessing so many different family traditions, cultures and dialects that each home was a different experience. The fact that my parents were the youngest married couple on the block made me part of its *Babies*.

My father Lee worked on the assembly line of General Motors building automobiles. Working on the assembly line was a hard-ass manual labor job, but it paid well, had good medical benefits important to a man with a wife, a kid and another on the way. That summer, my brother Lee Jr. was born. Lee Jr. was very quiet, but extremely intelligent. Even as a kid I was protective of my brother who'd always seemed so deep in thought, yet filled with unknown sadness.

When I was seven and he was four Lee Jr. fell off his tricycle onto his head immediately convulsing. Terrified, I held my dear brother tightly and cried, too frightened to leave him, letting out fear-filled pulsating shrills.

"Mommy, Lee is sick, please come!" My mother ran towards me and snatched my brother out of my arms.

"Oh my God, Lee! The baby! Something's wrong with my baby! Lord, his eyes are rolling in his head! God! Get your keys!" my mother screamed to my father.

We owned a shiny new red Chevy Impala that my father said any Negro would love to have. Daddy popped that Chevy in reverse and off we went to the hospital bouncing back and forth from one side of the wide rear seat to another.

The nearest hospital was ten miles away in San Fernando, another small town blanketed with orange and olive groves made famous by the early missionaries. (Later I learned that these same missionaries forcibly made Native Americans accept Catholicism.) Skidding to a sudden stop, my father began honking his horn. Frantically, my mother opened her door, running with Lee Jr. in her arms.

4

"Got to pee," I pleaded to Granny, who'd come to retrieve me from my long wait in the car. Hurriedly, Granny pulled downed my shorts and panties, directing me to "squat and go potty." Looking down at the small stream flowing from between my legs, the significance of my brother's illness caused fear in me.

"Daddy, what's wrong with Poe?"

Answering in a voice that reflected fatigue and worry, he said in a flat placid tone, "Your brother had a fever, baby—caused a seizure."

I sat in the hospital lobby that evening with my father, holding onto his worn and massive hand, no longer seeking an explanation to Poe's condition, and just holding on, an act I would repeat throughout my life.

Kindergarten is truly a magical place and time for a child. Everything in the world of a five-year-old possesses amazement, awakened each magical morning to my fathers' enthusiastic, "Come princess, school time!"

My mother worked graveyard as a telephone operator for AT&T. She was proud of her job despite its two-tier salary system for Negroes. Staying due to the shares of stock she received in the company, a company that (as she put it) "would be around a while." Affirmative Action had not arrived on the scene and there were massive hills for Negroes to climb in their respective journeys to achievement.

Filmore elementary school, located in lily-White San Fernando Valley, remained segregated by race. Gently shaking me, my father would lift me out of bed, commencing our morning preparatory ritual. Contrary to what the media portrays about Black men, I had a father at home who in my early years was my caregiver. Daddy to this day can out out-comb and out-style many a mother. Preparing my breakfast of eggs and toast with the precision of a master chef, while I played with Poe-Poe, my father would yell the directive, "Don't mess up your clothes!"

Ten to eight, he would load Poe into the stroller and walk me to school. Daddy was a very nice-looking man. Though a mere five feet nine, he possessed a well-chiseled muscular frame, which gratifyingly reflected his rich dark chocolate skin (if the smiles on the morning kindergarten mother's faces were any indication). Daddy would escort me inside the gates holding my hand until I reached the classroom's line, confidently kiss my forehead and pronounce, "Do your best princess." Commencement of the bell, enthusiastic tribal Negro children would follow our teacher Mrs. Stine into the classroom like sheep, where we would fill cubbyholes with our personal belongings and sit on square small brown vinyl mats. Those little brown mats of room ten were magical, possessing the ability to transform my five-year-old existence. Everything Mrs. Stine shared with us was a new discovery. The fact that my mother taught me to read was dwarfed by the knowledge Mrs. Stine was owner to. Mrs. Stine, though White, loved us, eliciting her wealth of knowledge so freely, that even at a mere five years old, we felt strong. Regardless of age, having someone believe in your infinite potential is essential, however as a five-year-old African American, having someone believe in you despite the brown hue of your skin is quite empowering. Providing validation that the middle aged White woman who appears tentative at my approach does not represent all of White America, that others (like Mrs. Stine) exist; whose only measure is ability.

Mrs. Stine leading us in a chorus of "Bye-Bye Bluebird See You Tomorrow," (a song I am sure was her own creation) then bid us a good afternoon, leading the class outside, where we'd wait in single separate gender lines. Looking out into the play yard, I would quickly locate my beautiful ripe Georgia peach mother, uncontrollably waving to her. Mommy's smile was perfect, containing a vast array of sparkling white teeth, shiny long black hair draped over her tiny shoulders. I loved her. Mommy was pleasant to the eyes. Little kids like and know beauty and my mother was beautiful.

"Denise come on," Mommy would say as I hurried to meet her. She would kiss my right cheek and remove the straight-pinned schoolwork from my dress. Commenting enthusiastically, "This is so pretty…you wrote your name perfectly! We have to show Daddy." I do not know…it's just those damn little things I remember and love about my mother—like her compassion.

Mommy loved her bright red little 1963 MG Midget and I relished the times she would pick me up from school in it. My heart raced with excitement, smiling wide. This car was fun! Driving down the road with the top down, her hair blowing in the wind, we'd always take a spin around town. Even then, I suspected that riding in the MG granted Mommy momentary freedom.

My childhood friends on Claretta Street were the kind movies and great friendship novels are based on. Unlike a novel or movie though, they were always there for me. In a time of floss vanity, and what you claim to have, they were the real deal. Smitty Rich came from a family of nine children, of which Smitty was the youngest. Her real name was Janet. She had long straight hair and green almond-shaped eyes which Negroes considered unusual. Smitty was pretty as looks went, but if Smitty was pretty anything she was evil, keeping our young circle in an uproar…you see Smitty kept shit going.

Lulia Gray, also five, was tan or *yellow* complexion with short *kinky* hair which often "BB'd" or napped up on the nape of her head. Lulia lived on Smitty's side of the block two doors up. Her parents (Harold and Olivia) were much older than my own. Mrs. Gray was mother hen of the block, always passing judgment on all its inhabitants.

Deebie Wecks was the home girl of the Babies. She was loud, funny and talked all the time. Deebie was the one amongst the Babies who, if someone pushed up on you, would beat their ass! Most of the time the ass whooping that Deebie put on folks was based on nothing more than a lie of Smitty's creation. Me, Smitty, Lulia and Deebie were the Babies of the block, but I was somewhat different from them all; as the eldest child in my family, I had to navigate solo, forcing me to stand a little taller to protect myself.

Second semester of kindergarten all of the Babies were thoroughly trained to walk home from school together. Our parents would tell us, "Hold hands and don't talk to strangers." Filmore Elementary was just one block away, but for small children it felt like untold country miles.

Deebie, scared of dogs, ran every time a dog approached her, usually dragging the person holding her hand all the way home. Smitty found Deebie's actions funny and often encouraged dogs to come our way just to laugh at her. For a kid fearful of dogs Deebie made the unwise decision to tease one chained to the side of a house.

I uttered, "No," yet before I could even yell, "Stop!" The dog broke free from the chain and began to chase us. Deebie panicked and ran in the path of an older boy riding a bike. He tried to stop but couldn't. Deebie tripped and fell as the boy's front tire ran over her head. Blood gushing from the wound like a fire hose, all of us in shock at the sight of the red liquid running down the sidewalk, in the background the boy screaming, "I didn't mean to...I didn't mean to!"

I heard my father's voice in my head commanding me to get help. Never being a good athlete, I ran until my lungs felt as though they would come right out of my body. My short legs ached but I kept running. Falling as I reached my driveway, skinning my legs, yet so full of adrenaline I did not feel the burn of pebbles embedded in my knees and palms of my hands.

Yelling to my mother, "Deebie's hurt!" Instantly she ran across the street to get Deebie's father Don. I could not explain what had happened; it was all too quick and so crazy. Don and my mother ran to the scene of the tragedy, in the distance his screams heard at the horror of seeing his child's brain oozing onto the concrete.

Everything else was a blur appearing to happen in slow motion; I remember the sirens of the ambulance but not much more. Deebie remained in critical condition for weeks; doctors did not know if she would survive, her life touch and go. Deebie did pull through, missing the second semester of kindergarten. Sadly, Deebie was never the same, having suffered brain damage. And with this rapid change the Babies grew more protective of Deebie and each other.

The summer of 1965 was a riot…no really a riot! I had never heard of Watts or Los Angeles for that matter but witnessed my father kick in our old black and white den television after watching the news. Turning six and seeing Negroes burn up their own neighborhood was disturbing to me. That evening after my father calmed down I asked him, "Why did the police kill the Negro man, Daddy?"

Sitting on the living room sofa drinking a Brew 101 and smoking a cigarette he mechanically responded, "Baby, White folks have never liked us; they always sought to inflict suffering on Negroes." Taking a sip of beer, he pulled me onto his lap where he held me close and confessed in a low pain-filled voice, "Baby…it's that Cain and Abel thing that White folks got backward."

I had no clue to what my father meant thus I sought clarification from my mother on what had unfolded on television. My mother stared at me then painfully exhaled a truth she had not wanted to share, "Sometimes people don't like you because you're a different color."

"But who told them not to like me because of my color?" I asked.

My mother began to cry. She had no answer for my question surrounding this tragedy, and the same is true today. Despite the Watts riots, the summer of 1965 brought adventure, fun and excitement for Lee Jr. and me: *Afro and Black* both terms of identity, which Black people had finally chosen for themselves.

San Fernando Valley summers are extremely hot and brutally dry, little shade was available in our new subdivision; the few mature trees on the block served as refuge for all of the kids on Claretta Street.

Most homes did not possess air conditioning and children improvised using a myriad of makeshift wading pools, water hoses and "Slip and Slides" to keep cool. At night, though the sun's brilliance was absent, the concrete seem to radiate with mirror perfect accuracy the heat of the day.

My parents came from very different places, each carrying their own baggage and passing on the residual baggage to their children. My father grew up in Nebraska, Omaha to be exact. His father was very abusive to my father's mother, beating her and the kids whenever he felt it appropriate. The story goes my father's mother hit his father over the head with a cast iron skillet while he ate, for the blackened eye she'd received for burnt rice. Fearful he would kill her when he regained consciousness; she left with nothing more than her children, purse and clothes on their backs, catching a bus to Southern California where they ended up in South Central Los Angeles. Freedom in hand yet captured raising seven children in a one-bedroom apartment made difficult on a domestic's wage, even with my father and his brothers working to help make ends meet.

First grade was fun as well as challenging; knowing how to read made English and History enjoyable. However, New Math proved early to be problematic and would always be my Achilles heel. Unlike Mrs. Stine, Mrs. Polk never said "Good Job," even when I earned an "A." First grade, despite Mrs. Polk, was an adventure, as I made a few friends who stayed in neighboring blocks.

Longing for the Babies as classmates every year, it never happened. Years later, I figured out why Smitty, Deebie and Lulia never had the same teachers—educational tracking. Students grouped by ability determined by "Powers That Be," those forces (wrongly) believing my block-mates needed a less challenging curriculum. To this day, I know educational tracking held them back; we were a team better together than apart.

As June arrived, my classroom felt like fire and student attention faltered. We needed summer! Not to mention that I was really tired of Mrs. Polk; regardless of the grades I produced, she was never impressed with me, yet alone my ability. Open House my father passionately declared to Mrs. Polk she had a problem accepting Black achievement. What was this new word, *Black*? I was brown! Returning home, I asked my father, "Daddy, why did you tell Mrs. Polk we were Black? Daddy, we are Negroes and brown."

My father angrily directed me to sit down as he began his enlightenment. "You're not a Negro. You were told you were a Negro by the White man. We come from Africa…Brought here as slaves."

Baffled as to the meaning of a slave I rapidly followed up with, "Daddy, what is a slave?"

"Africans were chained, beat and forced to work without pay in this country for a long time, baby, more than three hundred years. All to make the White man's life better…easier, that's what a slave did in America, baby."

At that moment, I had an epiphany, more like an awaking to the reality of what it meant to be *Black* or a *Negro* in America. Staring into my father's eyes, I saw pain, suffering and loss. Now I understood why Mrs. Polk never seemed happy about me doing well in school. My superior grades and determination was not a part of making her life easier. No, I was not supposed to *be like her*, not the way she saw it, I was supposed to improve the quality of her life by *providing her* with service and comfort like a slave. June, the final day of first grade had arrived and not a moment too soon, for all that I could concentrate on (in my six-year-old world) was my impending visit to Val Verde and swimming lessons my mother had arranged.

Gleefully anticipating our summer excursion to Val Verde, where a cacophony of African colors would wash over the lush green oasis. Val Verde, a Black enclave nestled in the hills of Castaic, California, provided refuge for thousands of Blacks. American segregation or Jim

Crow controlled the lives of Blacks on every level. Charlotta Bass and Norman Houston, successful entrepreneurs, sought to create a haven for Blacks when they purchased 1000 acres and subdivided the parcels to make Val Verde the Black Palm Springs of the West. Granny told me the story of Hattie McDaniel coming to the grand opening of the town's public pool. As was the way then, no Black people had the burden of worrying the pool's water would be replaced because a Negro took a lap or two, as this was *their* pool and not Whites!

In the Fifties, my parents as teens made countless journeys to Val Verde. Now it was my turn! Sometimes we stayed in small rented cottages, where cool water flowed from streams and creeks bidding you good morning. Strong quiet breezes propelled you to just be free and reverent in wonder absent from worry.

That evening sitting at the dinner table, preoccupied with planning the details of my summer, Mommy changed gears, shifting the direction of her conversation to me, delivering a fatal blow to my prolific plan for summer.

"You're going to summer school."

Though I loved mashed potatoes, the spoonful I chewed with euphoria became tasteless as I froze in disconcertion and asked, "What is summer school?"

"School you attend in the summer. It is only for a month, Ne, and you are out at noon. You can still take swimming and craft lessons at the park."

She threw in crafts because I loved them. Was this supposed to make me feel better about being locked up in a red hot room with another teacher like Mrs. Polk?

"Mommy, what did I do bad to have to go to summer school?"

"Oh baby, nothing. This is not a punishment, this is to help you become smarter…learn more."

Summer was going to be a drag. Why me? Always me! Who wanted to go to summer school? I wanted to be with the Babies, yearning to walk to Jimmy's produce stand and Toni's liquor store to buy Drumsticks and big glass bottles of Orange Crush (for which my father would not take the first gulp to remove the poison), that I could drink every drop by myself. Longing for jump rope and early morning hikes up Mt. Boom Boom, instead I was going to summer school. Crying an entire hour attempting to get a last-minute reprieve from summer school, my father came into my bedroom. "Be quiet and get out of bed little girl! Got you some new clothes. Look in your closet." Though happy with my new Keds sneakers, I was not looking forward to summer school. Of course, Smitty, Lulia and Deebie did not have to go to summer school; I was the only one of the Babies required to go so, and my life was starting to seem a bit unfair. As I walked through the terrazzo entrance my father had installed himself, I was greeted outside by the Babies who were laughing at me. In unison they shouted with the direct evilness only a child can deliver to another: "Ha your fat butt has to go to summer school!"

Not until their pronouncement of my weight did I realize that I was fat, though Gloria Reilly had nicknamed me Pumpkin because I was so plump and round. I must say, I had never really contemplated my weight, choosing to just accept my fate and move on. As I stared at the Babies, my focus narrowed onto Deebie who as usual was the loudest of the trio. However, today she was especially loud and ugly. Her eyes, which were always big, seemed particularly large and taunting to me. Reminding me of a picture I had seen in Ebony magazine of a kid in Chicago orphaned as a baby, the child's eyes wide and hollow like Deebie's, I thought about the boy who'd run over her, conceding he was responsible for her eyes appearing to bulge out of their sockets. Try as I did to convince myself of Deebie's plight, walking to school at six going on seven, I was resolute that Deebie was a super jackass.

Lulia as expected was sucking up to Smitty, desperately craving the affection of this little elf of a girl so intensely it was now an obsession. Lulia's father, the local trash connoisseur of the neighborhood, worked for Los Angeles City Department of Sanitation, and their home reflected this fact. It seems that every sanitation engineer in America had a home made up of everyone else's junk. Heck, there were days when visiting Lulia she'd come running out of her front door with some broke old toy, bragging as though the crap was really going to work, commencing to show me how it was supposed to work, if not broken. I don't know how I tolerated her for so long. I guess little kids have an in depth sixth sense to see the good in people; unfortunately as we mature that ability is lost.

However, today Lulia had a good plan of action for gaining Smitty's praise, tickets to the circus, which her father had gotten as a "thank you" for dumping some White man's extra garbage in Granada Hills. In possession of only one extra ticket, Lulia selected Smitty to accompany her. Knowing not to invite Deebie's animal fearing self, she hadn't gotten over the dog thing yet, and probably freak out ringside with lions and elephants, eyes big screaming, "Momma, Momma Jesus please help me!" Through her frenzied laugh, I put all three of the Babies out of my mind, as I was off to summer school to maybe make a new friend who was not so ridiculous.

"Please be seated in a chair of your liking," Mrs. Weeks requested. "Summer school should be fun. When you leave here in August you're going to feel good about yourselves and what you've learned. You'll know more than anyone else on your street that didn't come to summer school…so let's have fun!"

That summer I did feel good about myself. My reading improved, as did my printing, yet math still made me physically ill—I could not grasp its twists and turns. Praying intensely each evening that summer *it* (math) would be revealed to me; everyone understood math, even Deebie, what was wrong with me? My little brother Poe counted my change for me. I was truly a fool. Seven is when I learned shame; shame was embarrassment that clouded light, darkening your joy regardless of the happiness present. No matter how hard you tried to shake or hide it, shame was always in your damn face. Just like being Black or Negro in America.

During the afternoons, we took swimming lessons and swam in my Doughboy. Yet the best part of the day was simply just being together and exploring our universe—together. Talking about what Smitty's fast sisters were doing. Smitty (as all children) was inquisitive or *busy in grown folks' business.* She was a mess, hiding in a bedroom closet secretly listening in on her sisters' conversations. (Looking back though most of what she heard at seven was ass-backwards). Smitty was the first one to tell us about boys and girls "doing it." We were both amazed and frightened by her accounts. Yes, Smitty was the grown one of the group, sharing some wild stuff about stinky girls' *privates,* which her sister referred to as "pussies." Smitty was our direct line to what the Big People's world was like, and at six and seven we did not like their world nor were we in a rush to get there.

Summer seemed endless yet brief, joyous but troubling about what was to come. The Fourth of July, 1966, when my father savagely beat my mother. My fathers' crazy brothers and sisters had come to celebrate with us. Daddy's family was an interesting lot, all in need of serious psychotherapy. His older brother, Spenser, stabbed a man through the heart, killing him, for flirting with his wife, Diane. Diane stuck to the story, laying on extras of rape and intrigue, Uncle Spenser did five years in state prison for his crime of passion.

Uncle Spenser was very smart, it would be fair to say he was a genius; he built ham radio systems for a living. Daddy said he was one of the best in the state, though he possessed no formal engineering training outside what he had picked up in the Korean War.

My mother said Uncle Spenser was a little "touched," attributing his behavior to the war, probably shell shocked. Uncle Spenser said American and Korean troops left over a million land mines in Korea; he'd even lost a couple of his friends who stepped in the wrong spot. Granny was not as kind. She said my uncle was "crazy as a road runner, just like the rest of the Burelfords." Uncle Spenser had two kids by his second wife, Diane, and five from his first wife, Bonnie.

Then there was my Uncle Egan, the eldest of the brothers, who for the most part was normal. Uncle Egan married a Korean woman (Chung Li) he met during the Korean War, without the drama that besieged Uncle Spenser.

Uncle Frank (my father's youngest brother) was also normal, except he was a compulsive borrower—no, stone cold user. Despite this rather large shortcoming, Uncle Frank loved Poe and I.

"Just never lend him a dime or God forbid your car," my mother would say. Once he borrowed her 1962 white Ford Falcon; after his use, the car had to be towed home with a blown engine.

Aunt Betty and Mary were my father's two sisters. Aunt Betty was the youngest of the family; an unsuccessful young marriage produced two kids by a man who never gave her or the kids a cent, forced her to live with her mother in an unincorporated portion of San Fernando. The house my grandmother (her mother) owned was built in the 1920s; the basement always scared me for I believed she would permanently lock me up in this dark and dreary place. This section of town had no sidewalks and it was years before a single streetlight existed, lent to the house's eeriness, which always seemed to smell like a mixture of pepper trees and old newspapers.

Marrying young, my Aunt Mary had six kids, electing to be a full-time mother wishfully ensuring their well-being and futures, a noble gesture considering all but two are now doing time in San Quentin.

Helda Burelford, my grandmother, was always an elusive character to me, as I never really connected with her. Helda Burelford was one-quarter Sioux Indian, one-quarter Negro and one-half Irish, a true Octoroon. My grandmother was a fair skinned Negro woman with long, sandy brown almost red hair (that I had the misfortune to inherit). Helda was a *"passer,"* Negroes who for the most part are unrecognizable to Whites.

My grandmother bore a common Midwestern look. Possessing strong, high cheek bones, large often-wide eyes (which followed all with embedded suspension) and a weak smile, providing her an odd almost peculiar sort of beauty. I think Helda never got over the fact that she was Black and therefore sentenced to such humble aspirations due to her unfortunate connection to the Negro race. Truly ironic as she married a true Negro man (who was as dark as furnace coal); she carried with her a particular bitterness that transcended her daily being.

Helda was no fan of my mother, and as young children, my cousins let me know right away that Aunt Helena's (my mother) kids were at the bottom of grandmother's list. One Christmas, I received a nylon scarf and a box of waxy crayons. Do not get me wrong, it was not the gift but the thought (or lack of thought) which upset me. Each year Helda gave Poe and me the absolute worst gifts of all of the grandchildren because of the dislike of our mother. As Helda saw it, we were an extension of our mother. It got so bad that my mother told my father, "Lee, the kids and I are out of the Christmas celebration at your mother's…she can strike out at me but not my kids. I'm done!"

"At six years old I learned to keep secrets, and be a good soldier…"
Denise

CHAPTER TWO

AWAKENING OF DEMONS,
WHICH WOULD CHANGE MY LIFE

Fourth of July 1966 was so much fun, bombarded with an abundance of barbecue, fireworks and swimming, what more could any child desire in a day! That evening, exhausted from the day's frenzy, Poe and I dressed in light blue cotton pajamas, kissed our parents good night, and recited our prayers, falling into the surreal. Dreaming about the day's events, only to be abruptly awakened by the hollow screams of our mother.

"Lee, please stop, you're hurting me. Please stop!"

Attempting to protect her face with her hands as my father slapped solidly across her mouth, knocking my mother to the floor. I stood petrified with fear, Poe through tears begging our father to cease his attack, this only redirected the rage upon me and Poe, grabbing Poe's plastic baseball bat he began to strike us with it.

"Get your asses in bed now!" Our father shouted.

Enraged, defiantly, my voice made its way out of my mouth proclaiming, "No!"

Receiving several more hits from my father. Making our way to my bedroom, Poe and I huddled, statuesque stillness gripping us. This act though had allowed our mother to escape the vortex of madness created by our father. Mommy ran out the sliding patio door scantly clothed, void of shoes, scurrying out the gate down a darkened alley, assured that whatever lurked in the darkness was a far safer bet than what she faced in her home.

"You better keep your butts in that room damn it!" Professing that our mother embarrassed him in a game of *Scrabble*. We did not know what *Scrabble* was; all we knew was that the demons residing in our father had surfaced. Dazed and confused, I cried for hours unable to console myself. There is a state of surrender you embrace when wroth with fear and confusion; young children usually reach that level of surrender with hyperventilation, the undeniable rapid exhale and inhale identifying childhood panic. By four the next morning our little bodies surrendered to it. There was no other choice, we had no clue to our mother's location, we did not know if she was safe, all we could do was pray for her safety. We slept to replenish our souls, to figure a way out of the nightmare, believing that the morning would free us from this horrific dream.

Unfortunately, we awoke to the realization that the bad dream experienced the night before was not a dream but our reality. That we had in fact watched our mother guard her face, screaming as our father beat her. Since this was real, then our father could have killed our mother, or she had escaped never to return to us.

Poe Poe was crying, "Ne Ne, Mommy, where's my Mommy?"

Slowly we walked into the living room, praying our father had left, since he'd not attacked us, yet there he sat drinking, swaying his head from side to side to the Four Tops, shielding his shame with dark sunglasses, inharmoniously singing, "Still water run deep, still waters."

We backed away, never letting our crazed and drunken father know we'd seen him, taking Poe into my bedroom silently crying in each other's arms.

Our mother's absence felt like an eternity. Smitty, Lulia and Deebie all knew about my father beating up my mother; hell, everybody on the block knew. Summer school went from great to awful, reliving the events repeatedly, literally feeling the blows of the plastic bat, the sharp sting of plastic against my flesh repeatedly. What had we done wrong?

"Denise, will you read page one hundred three please? Denise, did you hear me?"

"Oh Mrs. Weeks, I…I…forgot my glasses."

She knew I was lying. I was always prepared, she continued staring at me; despite my profession of misplaced glasses, and Mrs. Weeks was determined to make me read aloud. I was locked in the teacher stare of "right now!" Surrendering I began to read aloud, "I will protect you, you can't go." Filled with pain in the word protect and my lack thereof I pleaded to be excused.

Sadness was in my teacher's eyes. Could she feel my pain? Did it show? Did she know of my father's deed? I was so embarrassed, laden with shame. I had to be all right, had to hold in my pain and not cry. I would finish this passage.

"No that's alright I can see the words well enough," as I began to read, the recess bell rang, saving me from my own tears.

Walking home from summer school in a state of total confusion and fear, why did this happen to my mother? Why me? Was I bad? Desperately wanting to run and tell, but to whom? Granny. All I had to do is call my grandmother; she would rescue us, how would I do this? Daddy was on the phone quite frequently Friday evening; I was unaware as to whom he was speaking with. Suddenly a knock at the door, we prayed the knock was our mother, opening the door with immense anticipation we were quickly let down, it was Gloria Reilly coming to babysit.

Could we trust her enough to tell her about what Daddy did to Mommy? Was he standing outside listening? Would he hurt Gloria if we told? So many things went through my head. I decided that doing nothing was best. This would be the first of many secrets my brother and I would keep. The next morning, while Poe and I played with Fella our dog, Mommy returned home. Running to greet her with unbridled excitement, our wide grins conveyed answered prayers. We would behave better so Daddy would not get upset. We would listen more intently, so Daddy would not scream at her. Gleefully waiting in the doorway with arms outstretched, we ran into their safety as her tears fell on our faces.

I will never forget that moment for it was the first time I saw pain in my mother's eyes. I saw her anguish and her frustration in the reality she was owner to. What do you say at seven to make your mother's eyes sparkle again?

"Denise please come to me," my mother requested.

Hurriedly I responded as not to upset my father entering the family room, Poe and my mother sat embracing on the sofa, Poe crying in her lap.

"Ne-Ne, I am so sorry for what happened to you and Poe. It had nothing to do with you. I'm sorry you kids had to see us behaving in such a horrible manner."

Confused, I asked, "Mommy does Daddy love you or us?"

"Yes, your father loves you; he has a lot of things that make him angry."

"So does he hit you because he's angry?"

"Mommy...Mommy doesn't know what your father feels anymore." Extending arms around our mother, we silently cried. As in all good armies, each solider knows that they may be a causality, as Poe and I would be in Mommy's war.

Fall of 1966 seemed to sneak in from nowhere, in a way I was glad, wanting to forget the summer of 1966. September and the start of school was just around the corner, JC Penney and Sears were visited by the Burelfords, as layaway boxes arrived the first Tuesday of

September. As usual, I had the standard attire consisting of Brogans, Health Tex dresses, Red Goose shoes, Keds sneakers and one coveted pair of 501 Levi jeans. Poe always looked better in his clothes than I did; his clothes provided a handsome and neat image while my own attire always seemed to fit too tight and without fail made me look like a beach ball, round and colorful in appearance.

Sucking up my immense dislike of my wardrobe, elated Lee Jr. would attend school this year with me. Providing his big sister (me) the opportunity of showing him the ropes. Forget Deebie's crazy behind, Smitty's trouble making and Lulia's sucking up, now I had Poe to share the school day with. Poe, however, had other plans regarding the formation of his own crew with Maurice Reilly, the baby of the Reilly clan. Maurice over the summer befriended my brother; instantly became Poe's best friend. Maurice knocked on our door every summer morning by eight to invite Poe into his world. The Reilly boys (two out of ten children) were true Louisianan sportsmen like their father who lived to fish and hunt every chance he got when he was not working to feed his brood. Thousands of Black people dreaming of streets paved with opportunity made their way to California from Louisiana in the Great Migration. The Reilly family was one. Their backyard was a Bayou menagerie, from egg-laying hens and geese to pigeons. Wade, the eldest son, laid claim to some of the most beautiful birds that spectacularly rolled when he clapped his hands. One occasion, Poe, believing he was on Mutual of Omaha's *Wild Kingdom with Merlin Perkins,* stuck his hand in the guinea pig cage, almost losing the tip of his finger; to this day Poe's love of nature was a gift from the Reilly boys.

Who was I kidding? I did not have a chance in hell to have Poe as my confidant as Maurice had won my beloved Poe's heart. God only knows what they did during those daily absences, as is the case with most little boys. Therefore, in the end, Maurice would be Poe's companion. Fortunately, everything we truly love and release we gain in another manner. In my case, a twist of silly kid fate would bring Bev Reilly into my life.

As we (the Babies) played in Smitty's front yard, I would watch Bev with her friends, studying how confident and assured she was. Only two years older than myself, Bev towered over me; all of her sisters were Louisiana tall and big-boned beautiful.

"Ne-Ne, your turn, I'm going to take all your jacks!" Shouted Lulia.

"Alright, don't think I'm going to just hand over my jacks…what's wrong, got those from your dad?" I laughed and bounced the tiny red ball.

Smitty in her usual start shit and hide mode, told reactionary Deebie in a sly quiet voice, "Tell Bev she is stupid."

I stared in disbelief that Smitty could be so crazy for she knew her family was outnumbered; even if the Reilly's were Pentecostal and the church-going type, they could kick some ass! What could she possibly be thinking about? Lulia snickered as if a sly rat as I started to tell Deebie, "Don't say it!" It was too late; the words left her mouth at lightning speed.

Deebie blurted out in a high-pitched voice reminiscent of Butterfly McQueen in "Gone with the Wind,"

"Hey you big ass stupid girl!"

By this time, Smitty took her slick butt into the Johnson's yard some twenty paces away from the scene now evolving in front of me. Lulia and I were boxed in. Deebie, still laughing, head cocked back, eyes the size of silver dollars, just did not comprehend how much trouble she had created.

Bev stopped, she was so tall her shadow blocked out all the hot August afternoon sun as she stood over Deebie, slowly uttering to the giggling fool, "What did you say, you little big eyed girl?"

Finally, reality hit Deebie, her intoxicating smile and wild laugh turned into a frantic frown of fear, she began to tremble, her voice shaking she said, "I...I...I wasn't talking to you...I...I was talking to Smite-itty!" All the while Deebie pointed to an evacuated space, a space she believed Smitty stood backing her up in madness. Deebie turned to seek support from Smitty, tears began to fall down her cheeks upon discovering that Smitty was nowhere in sight. Bev was now walking forward, her fists clenched, Deebie was hollering her "Oh God Jesus" routine as Bev got up close and personal. Once again, I thought about the boy who had run over Deebie and came to her defense.

"Please don't hit her, she does dumb stuff like this all the time. You see that little girl running home?"

"Yeah, so what? She gets on my nerves laughing like a hyena all the time!" Bev said.

"She told her to say bad things about you, Smitty loves to see Deebie perform, still the trouble maker...Smitty saw this dog and Deebie was scared and...well it's a long story," I shared.

"That bad Smitty! I'm going to tell her sisters on her!" Bev stared at me while Deebie and Lulia took off like rats on a sinking ship, leaving me to settle with the towering giant. Bev's gaze softened, recognizing me.

"You're Pumpkin. My sisters babysit for you and little Poe, right?"

"Yeah and we like them...all of them too!" My remark quick as not to upset her present mood.

"Do you want to walk to Jimmy's with me? I've got to get lettuce and tomatoes for dinner, we're having tacos," Bev asked of me.

"Yeah." In that instant, my loss was replaced.

Running home to ask my mother for permission, I could not believe the strange turn of events, replaying them in my head, over and over again. With permission, off to Jimmy's, walking along the wooded rural path, Bev seemed patient and protective, reminding me to watch out for gopher and snake holes. She told funny stories about herself and her family, sharing her world with me during this short walk. She was not mean like Smitty, Bev did not seek to divide like Lulia, and unlike Deebie, Bev was really smart, but best of all she sought my friendship. The journey to and from Jimmy's felt so different from the many times I had traveled it with the Babies.

"Thanks for taking me along," I said to Bev.

"Tomorrow I'm going to T.G. & Y and pick out some patterns for school clothes, do you want to come?" Bev asked.

"Yeah that'll be fun."

"Ne, take your bath and come help me with dinner when you finish," my mother yelled to me.

Given this was my weekday ritual she had no need to remind me of my duties. Cleaning out the tub, the scent of Tide engulfing my hand towel, finishing as my father yelled, "You're going to have a baby!"

I didn't know what to think, was he happy or mad? Would we get a beating or a hug?

Poe met me in the hallway, "Ne-Ne, Mommy is going to have a baby and I'm sad."

"Why?"

"Because I won't be the baby anymore. I can't sit in Mommy's lap!"

Why was Poe sad? We were going to have another sister or brother; there would be three of us.

"Poe, Mommy will always love you, you can still sit on her lap," I explained to Poe, trying to stop his crying.

However, he seemed more upset with my explanation. "How can I if her stomach is popped out!" Poe shouted, sobbing loudly.

Our mother entered the room to comfort her son. "Poe, Mommy will always, always love you. You're my special little boy who writes beautiful notes and gives me special Poe hugs that only you can give!" Poe stopped crying, tightly gripping our mother's neck in glee, convinced he still owned her heart. My parents once again were happy, Poe felt secure, and I had an older friend. Eating dinner, Aretha

Franklin's "Natural Woman," played in the background and for the moment everything that warm August evening seemed right.

Labor Day signaled the end of summer; Bev's mother busy sewing her children's clothes as did many a Negro mother in Pacoima. One of the things I miss is the *inheritance* of skills, skills that passed down to children, knowledge which saved and enriched our lives. Mothers sewed their children's clothing, everyone knew how to hem a skirt, replace a button or fix a flat. Black children prepared for life on every level, as our adult providers knew a battle awaited us in the world beyond Claretta Street. Watching Mrs. Reilly sew darts onto a blouse was magic, but more importantly I had a new friend. Bev and I stood looking out of her den window. Smitty was riding Lulia's bike up and down the block. Lulia, her usual crybaby self, was begging Smitty to get off her bike, with Deebie engulfed in full gutbucket laughter, and I was glad not to be caught up in their moment.

"King Solomon was a Black man, his skin was dark as coal.
Why don't they draw him that way?"
Lee Sr.

CHAPTER THREE

"Come on, Precious, time to get up," feeling a light nudge on my shoulder as my father's soft baritone voice delivered my wake-up call.

"Wake up. Your clothes are at the end of the bed, go in the bathroom, get yourself washed up." What? Was this a change in the system?

"Mommy, why can't Daddy or you wash me up and dress me?" I asked.

"Because you're in third grade now. Poe has to stay with Mrs. Hackmon and your father has to help Poe. You're a big girl now, Ne."

Dressing myself just did not feel as special as being dressed by my father, understanding (sadly) things had to change, there was two of us now. Placing the bar of Ivory into the lukewarm face towel, I imagined how it would be when the baby arrived.

Quickly as my thoughts formulated, I was jarred back to reality hearing my father prophetically pronounce to my mother, "The White man in America will never allow the Black man to rise above the ghetto. Look at Dr. King protesting, marching, people dying, houses and churches destroyed, blown up by the Klan! Elijah Muhammad at least has a plan for the Black man in America, a plan for us to have what the White man has…but on our own terms, and I am not going to pray to no White Jesus! Hell Helena, Jesus was not White. You know that! Woman, they messing with Jesus!"

"Lee the Witnesses preach equality of the races, what are you saying?"

"I'm saying it's still a White man telling you about you! Look at the drawings in this book…look at King Solomon, he is drawn as a White man! You know King Solomon was a Black man, read the scripture. White man wants to control everything from God, his son to your life…Allah help us. I'm joining the Nation of Islam!"

What did all this mean, the Nation of Islam? 1967 and we had just stopped attending the Methodist church, switching to the Kingdom Hall, now what? Putting on my socks, then strapping on my shiny black patent leather Mary Jane's, Daddy was still on a roll.

"And you might as well get use to not cooking that swine in my house."

"What are you talking about, Lee?"

"Pork, that bacon you're cookin' for my kids, from now on buy beef bacon; pork is filthy, contributing to the Black man's health problems."

With that, my mother threw out the bacon and made us oatmeal. I loved bacon, why did we have to suffer from all this new stuff? Finishing the unpleasant porridge forced on us, Mommy instructed me to hurry so my father could comb my hair, providing time to discuss the whole Black Muslim Nation of Islam thing.

Sitting between my father legs holding barrettes and Dixie Peach, I asked, "Daddy why do you want to be a Muslim and do I have to be a Muslim too? I thought you said they got Malcolm X killed. Remember you said that, Daddy?"

Finishing my right ponytail, he said to me while tightening my barrettes, "Daddy is now a Muslim baby. Black Muslims believe that being Black in America does not mean you have to accept less, that our families do not have to suffer. We can have what the White man has for his family."

"Does Mommy's Kingdom Hall tell Black people they can't have things?" I asked as he finished my left ponytail.

"No, not exactly, but the Jehovah Witnesses don't stand up for Black people getting ahead."

By this time, I was very confused. I needed to shut up and think about all my father had shared. In a home with a Jehovah Witness and a Black Muslim, I never really recovered from the experience, but I did learn from both.

"Ne, my name is now Lee X."

"No, it's not, Daddy, your name is Lee Burelford the first. You like to play tricks on me," I said to my father with a wide grin.

"Baby, that's my slave name; you see the White man took our names when we came to this country. So the X tells me and the world I am a man with no true last name."

Lee Jr. eagerly strutted goodbye holding the hand of his one and only and made his way next door to Mrs. Hackmon. Yeah mean old Mrs. Hackmon, who would sit in her window and watch everything on the block, telling on you in a heartbeat. If caught in childhood madness you would get it from her, and once again when you got home. Mrs. Hackmon was the CIA and the FBI rolled into one; no one got out clean. She (and all of the Claretta Street adults) was there for us ready to give us the praise and the pain when we needed to be better.

All right, I was ready, with the Babies in sight waiting for me in Deebie's yard all dressed and *greased up.*

"Come on Pumpkin, we gotta go!" Screamed Smitty.

Crossing the street, the excitement of the first day of school hit, Lulia as usual was bragging about her stuff, holding up all of her school supplies, all along knowing that Smitty would own them before we arrived at school. Deebie commented that my dress was cute but laughed at my shoes.

"You going to church? Looks like you going to prayer service. Why you got on church clothes?" Deebie postulated.

While everyone laughed, a voice called out, "Ne…Ne." It was Bev. "Wait for me."

"Dang! She's going to kick my butt!" Smitty said.

"No, she's not. I'm going to wait for her."

The Babies decided after their last mess up they'd better wait as well. Bev caught up with us, and I began to feel different again. Even as a child I was keenly attune to emotions, the way something *felt* to me from a smell, a color; regardless what it was, I connected emotionally.

"Hey Ne, Smitty, Lulia and oh stupid silly one Deebie, are you ready for school?" Bev said.

"Sure, it's just like last year," we said in unison trying to seem mature.

Entering the gates of Filmore elementary, things seemed different—in a good sense. Hopefully I would gain control over math this term. The bell rang, and all of us headed towards our lines from the previous year to meet our new teachers.

Lulia, Smitty and Deebie happy, laughing clapping about their good fortune in teacher selection. Looking around a wave-like moan rang out, hopefulness for the school year quickly faded for me. Entering Mrs. Bulcher's classroom, order was clearly the business of the day; color-coded bulletin boards with alternating corrugated paper borders. There was a *daily event* section, a *gold star* section; everything had a section.

"Boys and girls, please find your name card and stand behind the chair where you find your card."

Mrs. Bulcher, surveying our progress, passed back and forth, waiting for everyone's undivided attention. When whispers diminished, she spoke.

"Good morning boys and girls, my name is Mrs. Bulcher. I will be your third grade teacher."

"Good morning, Mrs. Bulcher," we responded.

"Third grade is very different from second grade. You're going to learn new things. First, I am going to teach you how to write in cursive. You will learn to write like your parents, you're going to learn your multiplication tables, so that you can become better at doing math."

Why did she say that! Everything was going so well until that point.

"You see class, numbers have a certain way they behave or act. By understanding the way they behave or act you can work out the answers really fast," Mrs. Bulcher proclaimed.

I was dead! Overcome by a feeling of sickness at the thought of numerical computation! I could barely add or subtract, now I had to learn multiplication?

"We're going to learn so much this year!"

Everyone cheered except me. I wanted to run home and cry. However, I would not be destroyed by this math thing, never! Mrs. Blucher had placed in our desks ruled paper. No more fat wide lines and pencils with erasers to anticipate mistakes. Copying from the front board the alphabet in both upper and lower case cursive and this was only day one!

Studying Mrs. Bulcher, she was tall, extremely wide yet not fat, appearing older than my mother. Mrs. Bulcher looked to be the age of my grandmother who was fifty-two. Her short graying brown hair was not styled in any great fashion. It was plain and orderly just like her.

"Follow the tallest line up, Denise. Hold your pencil in the middle not the top."

Very good, here we go, just single me out! What was it, my weight? My church shoes? Adjusting my grip of the pencil as I copied the board, Mrs. Bucher circulated around the classroom telepathically conveying the need for deliberate detail; there was no room to be free, only exact. "Class, it is almost recess, please leave your handwriting samples on your desk, and place your pencils inside your desk. When you put your pencils away…fold your hands and show me that you are ready to line up for recess."

"Denise, you may line up at the door." My heart danced at her pronouncement.

One by one all the children made it to the line as the recess bell rang. We walked hurriedly outside to visit with our friends. Since it was the first week of school, we had no play areas we could use this time to forget our collective disappointment. Chabell Taylor and I exchanged glances of disappointment in getting Mrs. Blucher as our teacher. Why did it feel like another year with a White teacher who was angry with Black kids not making her life easier? I had no answers. Wanting to see all the happy brown (no, Black) faces so I could laugh a little and play a lot.

Looking through the crowd of kids, I spotted Bev with her friends who seemed so much older than me. Fifth graders appeared particularly statuesque, some of them had breasts and wore bras, as did Bev. Their world seemed so different from my own.

"Ne, come here!" Bev said.

Oh no! I could not go over there, they would peep I was still little and sometimes wet the bed. I only wet the bed when I had the dinosaur dream, the one where Tyrannosaurus Rex peered into my room. Screaming for my parents, but no sound came out of my mouth, and as my family slept, I was eaten. I summoned the giant reptile when worried, usually after my father would beat up my mother. Bev stared me down, and began her march toward me wondering why I had not high stepped to her.

"Ne, come here little girl, you got an ear infection hard of hearing, what? I'll come get you for lunch, get with it!" Bev snapped.

Recess concluded. Once again dejectedly I went to my number on the blacktop to await Mrs. Bulcher. Single file, walking in military lock step, we made our way to the classroom waiting for her command. "You may take your seats now, quietly, no dragging of chairs." I whimpered softly, disturbed by this boot camp sergeant.

Uncovering a large chart on the west side of the room in a Houdini-like fashion, the chart attached to the front bulletin board (maybe I was confused by all her order or maybe she did have special powers), Mrs. Bulcher directed us to copy all the *Ones*. What is a *One* I wondered?

"Class look here," approaching the chalk board she wrote, "1x1=1, the x means multiply which means to multiply the number. Therefore, 2x3 would mean 2+2+2 equals six. Or 3+3=6."

My eyes crossed, tear puddles gathered on the corners of my desk, feeling as though I was in a foreign country unable to speak the language. Damn, why did I need math? Maybe if I paid real close attention I would get it. Oh no! My head ached. Mrs. Bulcher's' lips moved, but I heard no sound. I wrote but did not understand. I copied the board praying the answers would be delivered to me. It was over for the moment, the spirit of New Math caused the day to cast a dark hue on school, now truly I was in need of Bev's comfort. As we lined up outside our classroom, my reoccurring "yuk" feeling returned with the realization I did not like Mrs. Bulcher (and it was only day one). As she approached us, quietly waiting with an insistent demeanor for all to cease talking, able to deliver her demand with only a silent death grip stare. "Remember stay standing behind your desk and chair."

3:00 pm, school ended, the Babies talked about the day without my input about being mortified by math. With the exception of Lulia the rest of us were Latch Key kids; we unlocked our own doors and took care of ourselves. No big deal, lots of kids had keys around their necks, just a rite of passage. However, for a child an hour and half felt like hours. I could not express my unhappiness with this extended segment of time our parents needed us to uphold our responsibilities. Mrs. Hackmon in her mid-sixties was an Amazon of a woman, standing a robust six feet in bare feet. Cocoa covered, possessing sculpted large hands which though beautiful were not delicate. Mrs. Hackmon's solidly placed hips formed perfect mounds delivering excellent body symmetry. She did not look like my grandmother, but she was easy on the eyes for kids to trust. Laboring long and hard as a house domestic, saving her nickels and dimes to buy land in Texas (holding oil) which she sold at a hefty profit. Just as she began to enjoy the fruits of her labor, Mrs. Hackmon's son was killed in a traffic accident, bleeding out on the way to the Colored hospital some thirty miles away. With his tragic death, the Hackmons left Texas and southern Jim Crow prosperity, moving to Claretta Street. Hurriedly arriving at her door, she quickly appeared, causing my words to be ill-paced. Now I felt what it must be like to be on my own as Poe and I entered the quiet unassuming living room, entering the kitchen, climbing unto the stepladder, dialing from memorization my mother's work number.

"You reached Helena Burelford, supervisor, speaking."

"Hello Mommy?"

"Hey honey how was your first day of school?"

"It was fine," dishonest in my response.

"That's good, where's your brother?"

"Changing his clothes, I'll get him. Poe, Mommy wants to speak to you," I shouted.

Poe came running, happy, almost glowing with satisfaction of a great school start, grabbing the phone from my bent and disgusted frame. Why did he get to be so happy?

"Hey, Mommy, how are you!" Poe said.

"How was Mommy's baby's first day of school?" she asked Poe as I listened in on the living room phone.

"It was so much fun, Mommy," Poe said through child happiness, which always pleased mothers. "Ne, Mommy wants to speak to you." Poe yelled.

"Ne, I left sandwiches in the refrigerator, pour you and your brother some milk. I'll be home in an hour. Don't go outside or answer the door, alright?"

Taking the sandwiches out of the refrigerator, I thought about the days ahead…about the baby being born, about my father now being Lee X, and about my dreaded fear of math.

Removing my homework from my notebook, fear griped me, taking out the ditto sheet, slowly reading the instructions to myself, repeating simultaneously the affirmation, "I can do this, and I can!"

"Ne you want to play cards?" Bev asked.

"Yeah, coming now, are we playing War?" I asked Bev.

"Well, Ne, how's Mrs. Bulcher?"

My mouth elongated as I answered, "I'm not well...happy. Mrs. Bulcher she seems real mean; math is not my best subject, I just don't get it!" I cried.

"I can help you, just come to me after school. I de-clare—war, I win!" Bev exclaimed.

"Where are they from, Mommy?"

"Wala-Wala Washington. About seven hundred miles from here, their Daddy's second cousins. You and Poe have to share his bedroom."

"Hey now!" A nervous stout little man hollered into our front screen door.

Daddy happily greeted an older, dark-complected man who looked like he worked outdoors, his skin buckskin tough, frayed and wrinkled. Behind him stood an older woman whose red dyed hair fore-dated her. Arm step from the woman stood an older teenage boy. He was willowy tall with a coy demure manner, which seemed to peek out from his large natural.

Studying the scene playing out, watching teenage girls across the street reviewing him with wild bubble gum grins. He was cute but not that cute, I thought. Maybe I felt this way because they were just some of my father's relatives.

"Hello, Lee, what's going on cat!" The man nervously said.

"Just trying to make a living, just trying to make a living man!" My father responded, happy to see his clan.

"Lee, this is my wife, Sandra, and my son, Fred."

Daddy, as all men instinctively do, presented his family in exchange. "This is my family, my Helena and my children, Denise and Lee Jr."

Mommy was now three months pregnant and the wear and tear of work, running a house, caring for two kids and a crazy husband had taken its toll, this evening she seemed tired. Dinner was reserved for adults at the Burelford table with children relegated to a Q&A session only when prompted. My father stared at my teenage cousin then asked, "Son, why aren't you in school right now? You're how old?"

"I'm sixteen."

"But he's taking a little break for a moment, had some trouble in school, you know how these kids are," his father nervously interjected.

"Poe and Ne, there's no school for the next two days due to the Integration boycotts. If they do not want little Black kids to go to White schools we will teach you at home and get you a tutor if necessary. Los Angeles Unified must follow the law with Brown 1954, why does everything have to be so hard for White folks?"

What was *Integration*? What was a *Boycott*? We had many questions for our mom.

"Mommy what is Integration? Why can't we go to school?" Poe and I asked.

"Integration means you can go to schools that are not all Black or all White; hopefully have more choice, prepare you better, get you into college. If my kids cannot attend integrated schools, you won't go at all and we will continue to fight. The Supreme Court gave you the right, that's what your father was talking about," our mother angrily responded. Possessing a bit more clarity with her explanation on integration, I was able to draw upon my own experiences with segregation. Recalling the many occasions my mother taken us to visit her best friend Mona who was White. Playing jump rope with her daughters, neighborhood kids would chant, "How does it feel to be burnt toast, Nigger?" Laughing, running away, empowered by their destructive hate-filled actions. What prompted such cruelty about something as basic as my color?

My cousin shared his stories of racism in Washington, vividly reliving the incidences, telling us about men coming to his home and burning a cross in their yard, because of my cousin's White girlfriend. Confessing this was the reason he was not presently in school—the family had received death threats. Insisting he'd been lied on about "doing things" to her. Because of Smitty's information about *doing it*, I rather knew what he meant.

Adults sat comfortably perched in the living room, my father, his cousin and wife drinking scotch and soda. Fatigued, Mommy lay asleep on the sofa. Daddy invited neighbors over to play *Tonk*, his favorite card game, as our home rustled with conservation. We displayed board games to Fred, he settled on checkers. Soon Poe and I grew weary, fighting fatigue, succumbing to sleep.

Fall had begun, yet the weather still lingered with warmth; windows opened, allowing a soothing Indian summer breeze to visit, Poe dreaming atop the bedroom carpet. Leaving Fred playing Solitary while listening to Wolfman Jack on the radio, I crawled on top of Poe's bed, unable to muster another second of focus.

"Good night little cousins," Fred said, excusing himself from the room and closing the bedroom door. As I began my descent into sleep, a warm and heavy breath on my face, the likes of which I had never experienced. Abruptly opening my eyes to a large Afro blocking the light in the room—it was Fred!

Animalistic, evoking the voice of depravity, he asked of a seven year old, "Do you like me?"

"Why are you in my bed, Fred?"

"Kiss me."

The only people I kissed were Mommy, Daddy and Poe. Smitty's tales flooded in, fear forced panic.

"No Fred!"

"Then touch me here." Here, his unzipped pants.

"No Fred this is wrong…You're bad…no!"

Fred hands began forcibly roaming my body as I pleaded for him to stop; he used his forearm to cover my mouth.

"Don't you want to know how to get a boyfriend?"

Traumatized to silence, I could not talk. Confused about all my ill-twisted fate, I fought to get up, removing myself from this horror. Fred's large right hand with cobra-like speed pressed down on me so intensely that I could not move. While his left hand pulled my shorts down, I began to cry. Feeling like I'd been caught in a landslide, trapped, buried alive gripped in the agony of suffocation, gasping for the last bit of air remaining in my lungs, insignificant for life. Oh God, why was this happening?

The same hand ripped into me with great force, so painful death seemed eminent. Waves of molten fire shot through my body, Fred, oblivious to anything but his sickness. In shock, yearning to faint, my head spun flashes of white light dancing in my head. Suddenly, as I could stand no more he moaned in accomplishment of his vile deed. Someone should have heard my cry for help—but no one did. He lay on top of me with a sense of accomplishment, as he uttered with a stale voice, "Uh good."

Pulling my hair, Fred demonically said, "If you tell anyone, I'll tell them you wanted me to do this, and your father will beat your ass!" Slithering away in the cover of darkness, never detected by adults, perched comfortably in the living room, and my little brother lay next to me on the floor; he would never have any knowledge of this horror. In great pain, filled with fear and confusion, why had this happened to me? If I told my father, he might beat us all. Mommy was pregnant; I did not want to evoke one of my father's evil visits and hurt the baby. I had no choice but to keep this from everyone for I knew what deeds could be summoned by Daddy's demons; I needed only to recall July.

The next day, Daddy took his relatives to Los Angeles. Both mentally and physically sick, the only time I left the bed was to use the bathroom; even that was a nightmare, burning with each drop of urine. Declaring to my mother I was too sick to accompany them to Los Angeles, conjuring up a fake cold and cough. Mommy called upon the Reilly girls for babysitting duties.

Entering my bedroom, Bev sat on the end of my bed. "Do you want to play cards?"

Suspecting that she was on the search for a cause of my malady, I deflected.

"No, I don't feel like it," I said, covering my head with a pillow. "I'll look after you and make sure that no one hurts you, we'll share our secrets always." Removing the pillow from my face, I hugged her neck tightly. I never told a soul what happened but I always suspected Bev knew.

Eight years later, my parents discussing old relatives, quickly mentioned our cousins from Washington. My father informed my mother cousin Fred was serving a life sentence for rape and murder. I was not surprised, thank God or Allah my spirit had not been broken.

"There are no knights in shining armor."
Granny

CHAPTER FOUR

The Integration Boycott of 1967 was a success. Los Angeles Unified School District had been humbled by the will of the people. Supporters of the boycott hadn't all been Black, some were White, Asian and Latino. Collectively this diverse consortium brought the district to its knees. Mommy explained that now Poe and I could go to any public school we wanted to, and not just the school for Blacks. Maybe returning to school I would stop having the bad dream with my cousin on top of me.

Monday morning as Poe and I dressed for school thoughts of why things had not been so good for me abounded, questioning why Poe had Mommy to shield him, where was my protector and shield? I learned in short order my protection and life dreams would rely on God…. As I always ended up figuring my way with God.

I was glad to go back to school; sadness haunted me, my air heavy, hard to expel. Sadness that each time I rinsed my face continued to cloud any attempt at happiness I conjured up.

"Cat got your tongue this morning?" Daddy joked.

Instantly flashing back the words Fred uttered concerning any form of confessing his despicable crime to my father, fear sealed my mouth from releasing vowels and constants of truth, so I lied, "Yes guess the cat does this morning, Daddy, I'm just thinking about school, and I love it." My response sufficient for him to inquire no further. Just then the doorbell rang. It was Bev. Having her here this morning had to be God's way of giving me the courage to push through this new wave of awful.

"Hello, Mr. Burelford. Ne, you ready? We can walk together, you don't have to put up with the Babies," Bev said.

"Ne, what is Bev talking about? What did I tell you about picking up a brick or rock and knocking them straight in the head!" Daddy angrily pronounced.

"See Bev...Let's go!" I whispered.

Working to keep up Bev's pace and not seem like my legs were five inches shorter than Bev's, the Babies shouted. "Ne, Ne! Wait for us!" in unison they chanted. Any other day, they would have left me in a heartbeat, but today I had Bev; now they wanted to be my friends. "Every day they make you run to catch them if you're late, today you're gonna leave them fools behind. Keep walking!" Bev said.

Behind Bev and me, the sound of frantic little scuffling feet running to catch up, "Pumpkin don't look back, don't you dare laugh! Just act like you can't hear any of it."

Nodding instructively as we continued to walk, turning slightly to my left to see the Babies approaching.

"Wait...Wait!" Deebie said.

Smitty in front with her minion, Lulia as expected trailing her, carrying everyone's books. Running at our heels, we heard a loud thud, then rumbling like a runner attempting to steal a base, "You're out! And pull you dress down, looks like you're wearing your church panties," roared Bev, as Lulia had fallen in their mad dash to catch up.

"Lulia, are you all right?" I asked. She was embarrassed, and even if she were hurt, Lulia would never admit it.

"I'm okay...damn my new socks...leave me alone!" As we gathered Lulia up, the blue tone that filled my present mood was gone...The day would be good.

Making my way to the classroom's line, I wondered what math was going to be about today. Mrs. Bulcher appeared like a giant blob in front of us, she really just excluded your view of everything but her.

"Good morning class, let us enter our room now." Standing behind our chair and desk waiting for the command to be seated I sensed some anger from Mrs. Bulcher, whose face provided no clue to the severity of her words.

"Children, integration for you means that you can go to any school you want to. This right was hard-earned and a long time coming. Use it to your full advantage."

Was this the same teacher that treated us as if we were in the Army? Could it be that the teacher, who never smiled or was satisfied with your work and thought you could always do better, really had a heart for Black kids?

That morning changed the way all of us viewed Mrs. Bulcher; though her demeanor never softened, we grew to understand her desire for us to be strong—better than own expectations. Third grade remained difficult, but she never quit pushing me to meet all challenges, and finally math did get better. Funny how things are not quite what they appear to be on the surface; guess you cannot judge a book by its cover.

"Your Granny is coming over tonight," my mother said while setting the dinner table.

LeAn Valinda, lovingly known as "Granny," was colorful and fun. Mommy's side of the family were all very interesting. I once read children inherit their intellect from their mothers and I believe it, for all my mom's folks were unbelievably intelligent. I could not figure out how my parents ever got together. My father did not enjoy school, but my mother did, and to make matters worse she possessed a vast wealth of knowledge about all kinds of stuff; she just knew more. Granny was vibrant, a mere five feet tall, the hue of decadent butterscotch. Granny paraded her West Indian and Creole roots in loose ebony ringlets that glistened in the sun, which she kept impeccably styled in a short bob. Her clothes were elegantly tailored like Lena Horne or Joan Crawford; my grandmother loved and lived the good life, which was even more incredible considering Granny's upbringing; life had not been easy.

Her mother, my great grandmother, whom we called Nana (I did not know until adulthood that all Black folks had a Nana), worked as a domestic. Nana was away from home five days out of seven, leaving Granny to read romance stories about White damsels in distress and White knights who came to their rescue. She dreamt of a life fostered by such stories where there was chivalry, romance and glamour. An impossible if not difficult task to accomplish due to the continuation of racism on Negroes. Colored men in the forties lacked real access or opportunity. Everything achieved through unimaginable will and God, Jim Crow segregation was real, both a ruthless and sociopathic continuum of oppression experienced by Africans in America.

Nana, a calm and patient woman, was the direct descendant of Reconstruction ex-slaves (if there ever was such a thing as an ex-slave ,since Black people in America have truly never been free). Coloreds as we were called during Reconstruction were our ancestors of note, in possession of the living memory of the Middle Passage and the plantation. Nana was such an ancestor, a true African direct from ancient Kimet, inherited master of the stars and the land, she could grow anything from seed and fish with just a pole and a line. She came of age at the turn of the 1900s. Nana possessed the physical strength of several men; strength obtained growing and chopping sugar cane and picking cotton from sun up to sun down. Nana, unlike many Colored women born in the late 1800s, was literate, having completed high school in the mayhem of Louisiana.

In her early twenties, Nana's only brother died of a heart attack. Her mother wrought with pain and despair died a month later, leaving Nana alone in the midst of the hatred and oppression of the South. Nana awoke one morning from a dream clouded in destruction, a voice spoke to her instructing her to leave; that death was near. The next day she informed the Baptist church who ran the one room school in Coushatta, Louisiana she was going to Chicago. One week from the day she left Coushatta, the Klan came in and burned the town to the ground, killing twenty men who tried to protect their families and town. Nana told Poe and I this story a hundred times and each time we asked her why her answer never changed.

"Denise, White folks thought three hundred years wasn't long enough; the Civil War took it all back, and we still owed them," Nana told us.

Making her to Chicago, Nana, (as were most Colored women) had been trained as a maid; being able to read and in command of impeccable King's English she sought work as an estate maid. Nana was hired by the Janewalds, Midwestern industrialists. Working in Chicago, Nana met the man of her dreams—James Johnson, but he was only a figment of the imagination; in the midst of prohibition and Al Capone, James was a Moonshine alcoholic. With the birth of her child (Granny), Nana left James as the beatings increased, never to see him again.

The Janewalds provided Nana with a one-room apartment in a building they owned. Granny, during the week, was cared for by Nana's Great Aunt Haddie. This didn't lend much to the development of a viable mother and daughter bond. My grandmother for most of her childhood knew very little about her own mother, who worked to keep a roof over her head and food on the table, a common occurrence for African Americans living in America in the 1900s.

Due to his wife's frail health (caused by Tuberculosis), Mr. Janewald elected to move the family west to Santa Barbara, California. Land was plentiful in California; other industrialists were already here staking (exploiting) empires and so would he. Nana was asked to accompany his family west to Santa Barbara, where Mr. Janewald purchased a small bungalow in the Mexican portion of town for his prized domestic.

My grandmother had a difficult time, for the West was not free and being a little olive-Colored girl wasn't easy. Reading by five, Granny possessed the best social skills and manners of any child regardless of color. She was cognizant at an early age that more existed in the world and she wanted it…Well, where was her prince?

Colored schools in California were few in the 1940s, and my grandmother dreamed of college and a business degree as she methodically studied the goings on of the Janewalds. Granny's burning question: How would she achieve her dream? Absent of money, her mother a maid with no real family to speak of in California, my grandmother used determination and ancestral will, insisting that Nana buy her a used typewriter necessary to attend Business College. Four years later, she finished her bachelor's degree in Business and got a job working for the Federal government as a stenographer. The start of World War II, Granny was transferred to New York City.

Arriving in New York, excitement covered every space of the city. New York bustled with life, packed pulses of humanity, city lights, nightclubs, and oh all the Colored folks! There was an entire section known as Harlem, where everything seemed to burst at the seams with hope. Artists, musicians, writers, Colored attorneys and doctors; everything was there! Women and men all wore beautiful clothes, and for once in my grandmother's life she believed she could really find her, "knight in shining armor."

Granny worked long hours in an all-White stenographers pool who didn't take kindly to the little high-yellow Nigger gal in their midst. Granny existed in a world of racism before Affirmative Action but she would not be deterred from her dream. After years of just surviving, she had a chance at bringing a level of security to her life. Granny's attitude was, "The hell with those Crackers!" At night, Granny and her girlfriends went to Colored clubs, listening to the likes of Billie Holiday, Duke Ellington and Count Basie. Good-looking men abounded. One night she met hers, Herman Fineste, a smoldering Adonis of a man who, even in winter seemed tanned and beautiful. Dreamy green Asiatic eyes glistened with enthusiasm and hope for life. Mentally gifted and handsome Herman came from a family reflecting a myriad of aspirations; yes, she'd found her prince!

Free and loving bonds did occur between the ancients deemed outcast by America's founding fathers and settlers. You cannot discover a nation if others were present and Indigenous and Africans were here, despite denial. Free and loving bonds did occur between Native Americans, Africans, Chinese, (and later) Filipinos on both the East and West coasts of America. African, Asian and Latin cultures fused, creating a vast array of traditions and beliefs. Herman Fineste was a product of such a union. In Herman Fineste's case, his father was an attorney from Trinidad's upper class of *Coloreds* or *mixed* race people, his mother Filipino and Creole. Herman was a fourth-year medical student at Meharry Medical College when he enlisted for military duty as one of the "Tuskegee Airmen." Herman's mother was outraged that he would leave his studies for the military. Herman viewed his enlistment with pride, because he could defend his country with honor, like a White man.

Married in March, Herman left for Europe in April; during his absence, my mother was born. Herman demanded that Granny stay with his mother and father, who he called Mommy T and Poppa Martinez. Mommy T (as Granny tells it) thought her son a god.

Herman and his wife selected the name of their child before he left for basic training, Helene Illena Fineste. Mommy T was certain that Granny's high-slung stomach held a girl, backed up by a dream, the scene covered in pink. After the birth of my mother, Granny began to miss her own mother in California. She was eager for Herman to return to finish his medical residency and move to California, where he could set up medical practice.

My grandmother told us she began to worry when she had not received any letters from Herman in over a month. This was not like him. He wrote because there was little else to do besides waiting between sorties. Colored soldiers weren't allowed to mix with White soldiers. As Herman wrote, "When Lena Horne came, she performed separately for the Negro troops, and very quickly." Something was wrong. She began to lose focus of her life with Herman one day at a time until she surrendered all hope of a future with her new family, "Baby your Granny just knew bad was coming."

A telegram arrived on a cold, placid morning and my grandmother's fears became reality. Poppa Martinez took the telegram from the Western Union courier, his hand shaking, closed the door, falling backwards onto it for support. Head bowed, Poppa Martinez handed the envelope to my grandmother. She slowly opened the envelope, reading the words to bring finality to her future, "Lt. Herman Fineste has been critically injured in France." Herman's unit encountered incoming shelling; Herman was hit with shrapnel, blinding him.

Returning to the states, Herman was never the same. His dream of becoming a Colored doctor who had served his country with valor like a White man had been destroyed. He never got to see his child (or anything else for the matter) again. Herman was forced to work at menial jobs supplemented by a small veteran's pension. He cried all the time, and when he wasn't crying Herman sat quietly, listening to life pass him by. My grandmother asked Herman to leave New York City, go to California complete school. Herman told his wife (my grandmother), "I can't. I have nothing more to offer you," in a low broken voice.

She tried to tell him this was not true, frantically reciting a litany of merits Herman possessed. He stood perched in front of parlor doors. As my grandmother continued to speak, he opened the doors, professing one last time to his wife, "I love you baby, just have nothing to give you and my child." Herman turned and jumped to his death.

The train ride back to California was silently long; memories of my grandfather jumping off the fire escape lingered in her mind. In

California, Granny had her adoring mother who loved her, and right then she needed that. Returning home with a toddler, no husband, no knight in shining armor still haunts my grandmother.

Helena grew up in a juxtaposition of privilege and poverty; nevertheless, for a little Colored girl her needs were always satisfied. The only child until the age of sixteen, my great grandmother spared no expense regarding her Helena who had the pony rides and walks along the shore. Helena was immersed in a collage of diversity, able to live vicariously through Santa Barbara's elite.

But when Nana went to work as an estate maid things changed. Granny, a bookkeeper, returned home early one evening, noticing a little girl in a dirty sleeping shirt with a piece of corn bread in her hand on Main Street. Reminding my grandmother of Louisiana, the little Colored kids scrapping to survive the horrid pains of poverty and oppression, my grandmother commented to herself, staring at the children, "God bless those little dirty-nosed nappy-headed children, thank you, Lord, I can provide for my baby."

As she approached the children her heart dropped, realizing that one of the Reconstruction ex-slave looking children was in fact her own. That did it! My grandmother reapplied for work in Port Hueneme, told her mother (Nana) all she wanted her to do was take care of her baby and to stop raising White folk's kids. Nana stayed home and took care of her baby; my grandmother kept her promise, providing for her mother and her child, working six days a week for the next ten years.

Granny possessed style; she loved jazz, instilling in us a great appreciation of the art form. As kids we got lost in Coltrane, Wes Montgomery, Sarah Vaughn and Billie Holiday. In fact, we preferred to listen to jazz instead of rock and roll, as the feeling of the music seemed to make us come alive. My grandmother would place us next to her in her large white leather-tufted high-back bed, ordering us to "sit back and be still" while sipping scotch and milk introducing us to song selection and melody. My grandmother had an intoxicating force about her; you just wanted to be around her, to follow her existence.

Granny never liked my father much nor his family, commenting little about them not to give away her disdain of my father, as my grandmother had an opinion about everything except ignorance and chaos (my father's family the Burelfords had both). Granny blamed herself for my mother getting with my father, as an act of defiance, conceding her love of scotch and milk forced my mother away from home. This always kept Granny from coming down hard on my mother.

Nana remarried Mr. Moles, a Filipino citrus farmer up the coast in Santa Maria. Granny also remarried, just as my mother turned seventeen. (This was also the year my mother married my father.) Granny too married a Filipino she met at Port Hueneme, named Samuel Valina. Samuel was a Longshoreman. I do not know what the connection was for both of my grandmothers to Filipino men, but if I had to guess, it probably was each other's silent strength and the knowledge of oppression. They had a son, Uncle Junior. When Junior developed asthma, Samuel and Granny moved to San Fernando. Despite both Nana and my grandmother's collective dislike of my father, they traveled to Southern California and purchased a little house (in San Fernando as well) for my parents so they could at least start right.

When Granny entered a room, she was electrifying; she was good-looking just like her daughter, but unlike her daughter, she loved drama. Men just went crazy in her presence. Damn, I can never remember her not having a man or a husband, for that matter.

"Hello Lee. How are Grandma's babies? Grandma's going to take her babies to May Company to shop, Darlings," Granny said with a wide frown on the left profile of her face and smile on the right. Granny's visits to May Company with us in tow happened only a few years out of segregation, but Granny didn't give a care; she walked into that high-end department store daring anyone to question her (and her revolving credit card). It was hilarious.

Poe was little and cute, he was magnetic like Granny; you just wanted to touch him! Despite the fact my grandmother only stood a mere five feet, she inevitably ran to pick him up, while I had to settle for a hug. My grandmother giddily released Poe then said to my mother, "Helena what did I tell you…stop feeding that child so much. Cut down her portions."

"I don't, Momma. She just likes to eat."

"Never let a man control your entire life!"
Granny's Pearls of Wisdom

CHAPTER FIVE

October 1967, my parents named their beautiful baby son David. Daddy seemed happy enough about the baby. He had been particularly nice to my mother during the pregnancy; hopefully the birth of my little brother had conquered his woes.

Our mother stayed home a year after the birth of my younger brother, during which time our lives seemed more connected. Children do enjoy order and direction, and with our mother home we had an abundance of it. Right as we began to feel secure in our mother's presence, my father's demons returned. Standing at the kitchen sink with our mother, Poe and I watched as she bathed David. My father arrived home earlier than usual, entering the room with immense anger, oblivious to all, slamming the bedroom door behind him. Poe and I looked at our mother, wondering what we had done. Maybe we had been too loud after his long day at the plant, both of us contemplating what could have triggered our father's anger.

Mommy never commented on my father's new eruption, deferring instead to the enjoyment of bathing her new baby. I now understand that my mother's lack of reaction was a way of denying the reality she was owner to. Instead, my mother sought to reaffirm love in a man who had betrayed her with adornment of symbols; those symbols (her children), provided my mother the will to go on.

Mommy took special attention putting on the infant's nightgown and wrapping the baby warmly in his blanket. April, the weather was still quite cool, which is why bundling David so carefully should have been adequate warning for me to prepare for an immediate evacuation.

"Damn it, Bitch! What the fuck is your problem!" Erupted my father.

"What is your problem Lee…What did I do to you?" My mother answered with whining disheartenment.

My father eyes, now bulging, shouted, "You made me come home tonight to be with you…these kids…what about me! I need time for me!"

My mother began to cry; Poe and I were frozen in disbelief at my father's words.

"I came home from work instead of playing cards for this bullshit!"

The baby was now crying as my father's voice resonated across the room, shaking it like thunder.

"Bring your ass here now!"

"No!" Our mother declared, fearful of the next act to happen. She could not go into their bedroom, we had to leave, and I knew we had to run!

"Did you hear me? I said come here now!" My father demanded.

"You and Poe get Mommy's purse by the couch in the living room…go wait in the car," my mother whispered.

In one fell swoop, I grabbed Poe and my mother's purse, dashing to the red Chevy Impala, quickly jumping inside the car I loved so much. Mommy, barefoot, clutching her new bundled infant, raced out of the house into the car, turning the key in the ignition, when a booming voice seem to rattle the world shouted,

"Where in the hell you think you go'in? Bitch you think you leaving here!"

The sound of breaking glass greeted us as the brick entered the windshield. "Go Mommy!" Poe screamed as my mother jolted the car into reverse.

Terrified, I sat holding my brothers, confused and angry. Anger, which can only be described as murderous; wishing my father dead; shamelessly wishing he would suffer, agonize for all the pain and sadness he had inflicted on his family. Wanting him to be run over by a big rig and kicked by a mob repeatedly until he called out in pain for mercy.

"Go Mommy! Let's just leave and never come back!" I pleaded to my mother.

"Helena, Momma told you to leave his crazy ass when Ne was a baby, come home and go back to school." Granny said, as my mother sobbed.

"I'll take the kids into Junior's room," my grandfather said.

"Helena, divorce Lee, he can't be any better than what he is! That entire family is crazy. I told you that when you married that fool. You come from an entirely different background, why do you fight me so, child!"

"Momma, I've got three children and I'm not working! What, how I am supposed to make it with these kids? I don't have any money. Lee has all the money in his name!"

"From this day forward, never and I do mean never let a man control your life! I am going to give you two thousand dollars right now in an account; every month your grandmother will put a couple hundred dollars in. Helena, don't you ever as long as you live let this man push you down on your face! Don't you let him hit you or your children! Money should not be your jail; use it for your freedom!" Granny held my mother protectively in her arms, "You are my child, you deserve better."

1967 was pretty much a potpourri of the same events repeatedly frequently. My parents fighting then making up, the Babies making me the butt of their jokes while I sought solace with Bev. Needless to say I was glad when 1968 arrived. Hope quickly diminished. While sitting in class the day King was assassinated, I wondered why Black people seemed to suffer more. When I thought about Dr. King's struggle, how people supporting him jumped ship when he spoke out about the war; calling him unpatriotic; the people who'd been killed, beaten and destroyed for freedom; I began to reaffirm that much of what my father said about White people was undoubtedly true. Why did he get the bad shit right? It was a hard time for Pacoima and America. Cities from Newark to Los Angeles burned to the ground. Why God, was being Black so hard? A few months later, Daddy, motivated by anger and disbelief, volunteered to help Robert Kennedy run for president. He told us over dinner that even for a White man Kennedy felt the Black man's sorrow and just maybe because he was White he could really change the rule of law for Black folks. My father dressed in his tight black shiny suit and headed out for someplace called the Coconut Grove, in a downtown Los Angeles hotel ballroom. The next morning my father returned home, his eyes fire red, "Somebody killed Robert Kennedy last night, and everybody had to stay in place. No one's left to help us."

Daddy, now a fully-fledged Muslim, prayed every morning towards Mecca at dawn. I had no idea where Mecca was and its significance, nor did I want to know. Nevertheless, because he was so involved in the Black Muslims he left us alone more; now, for that I could thank Allah. Being a Black Muslim meant pledging your allegiance to Elijah Muhammad as well as being proactive in the community, involved in helping other Black men straighten out their lives, for my father this meant selling Muhammad Speaks or bean pies, all of which Daddy was a failure at, but I'm sure Brother Ralph at Pacoima's Mosque number nine didn't know, as my father talked a good game. Purchasing hundreds of Muhammad Speaks newspapers (which were supposed to be sold or passed out in the community) that stayed stacked in our garage. The situation got so out of hand we could no longer open our garage without neighbors commenting that our garage was a warehouse for the Muslims! Daddy would give the newspapers to local Black business owners. He stopped though, afraid of being discovered, when one of his Muslim brothers caught him out one evening at Foster Freeze with us in the car.

"As-Salamu-Alaykum Brother Lee."

"Damn it!" mumbled my father. "Wa-Alaikum-Salaam Brother Steve, what brings you here tonight?" Daddy replied.

"Just to get my wife an ice cream cone, you know how women can be when pregnant."

"Yes, I do brother," Daddy sincerely remarked.

Why did he lie? Daddy knew that this was never his way of showing our mother love; he'd never bought my mother an ice cream, I thought to myself. Daddy sighed and threw the bundles of newspapers in the back seat with Poe. Looking back at my father's stint at Islam made me realize he was trying to find himself in a spiritual sense. However, in order to find yourself spiritually you must acknowledge the good, the bad and all your fears, something Daddy was never willing to do.

David grew rapidly, 1968 turned into 1969 and David turned two in October. On the surface, we looked like the ideal American Black family. Possessing the good-looking, hard-working father married to the beautiful and intelligent wife who produced three talented children and kept a lovely home. Nothing could have been further from the truth, but we sure looked good on paper. Nevertheless, in the classic Lee Burelford spirit, he brought her home a new shiny navy blue Chevrolet Malibu SS. Mommy had not wanted this particular car, she longed for an Impala station wagon, for which my father adamantly said no, confessing, "station wagons were for old people."

Being a Jehovah Witness, my mother did not celebrate birthdays, but my father did. Refusing not to forget his son's second birthday, he organized a huge party to force my mother in a corner. It was weird watching my father with his super 8mm movie camera filming everyone singing "Happy Birthday" to a toddler as my mother sat stoic.

Mrs. Hackmon informed my mother she was going back to work as a maid in Encino. Mommy quickly scrambled to find a new babysitter for David. Helda volunteered for the job (with pay). Mommy broke the news about my new responsibility. "Ne when you get home from school, I want you to leave Poe at the Reilly's and walk to your grandmother Helda's to pick up David."

"Yes Mommy," I answered. Youth is an essential mechanism, for if I fully understood the scope and nature of the task given to me at such a young age, I surely would have objected.

Bev's morning knock signaled the start of my new routine and test of maturity as I had become more comfortable with Bev and her friends while less concerned with the Babies.

"I've got to get home quick now. I have to walk to Lake View Terrace to pick up David from my grandmother's." I shared with Bev.

"Ne-Ne you're really growing up; look at you, lost your baby fat taking care of the baby on your own! And you don't let the Babies push you around anymore…I am proud of you."

Bev made me, as a boring fourth grader; feel as though I were ten feet tall, despite all the clouds in my life.

Being ten years old and crossing Van Nuys and Foothill Boulevards was a big deal. Directly on the corner was Rucker's mortuary. We joked as kids if you messed up crossing that's where you'd end up; as there were no stop lights several children had done just that! Walking past tall Eucalyptus trees, gentle breezes pushing fragrant branches softly, while exploring this new section of town was exciting; horses stared, dogs barked in unison, all of it unfamiliar for me. Ranchers large and very White, without my knowing kept sniper focus on me. Pushing the empty stroller, my passive steps accelerated to a rapid trot, it was not complexion that sparked fear to rise in me, it was indifference that scared me. It said if I were to disappear, it would be all right.

Breathing a sigh of relief at reaching Helda's, I possessed a sense of accomplishment at completing the first leg of my expedition. Entering the waist-high chain link gate into the walkway of her home, children (my cousins) were running all around screaming and playing with such schizophrenic intensity the scene was straight-out scary.

"Hey, Ne, come to ge-get Da-Da-vid," stuttered Aunt Mary's son, Frankie. My cousin made me nervous, as without provocation he was capable of rapid mass destruction, quick!

Entering the house, Uncle Egan stood trying to convince Helda to give him one hundred fifty dollars for a new battery and tires. David sat in his high chair, a patch of oatmeal from breakfast intertwined in his curls. He sat resolved to the madness, still and quiet, his stillness an admission that something was not quite right with these people.

"Hello," Helda said to me. "I didn't know you'd be here so fast, I would have the baby ready for you… I said no Egan! You're a grown man, I'm tired of this."

"Grandma, did David eat lunch today?" I asked.

"Yes! What are you trying to say, that I didn't feed my own grandchild?" She snapped back at me.

"No, I just wondered…" I mumbled.

"You're just a child!" Helda declared.

Did she think she was fooling anyone? Quickly changing David, I packed him and his belongings, thanked Helda, and took David outside where I hit the wall of madness. My cousin Jerry, in possession of the stroller, was tearing through the front yard as though the stroller was a formula-one race car.

"Give me the stroller, Jerry! Dang, you crazy!" I said as they laughed at making me mad.

"Here…at-take the str-stro-oller u-ug-ugly," Frankie stammered to get out. Quickly taking the stroller, placing my brother in it, we ran out of the yard away from the madness.

"The only time things change is when they must."
Daddy 1969

CHAPTER SIX

PEACE ON THE HOME FRONT

Abruptly one day I noticed my chest was no longer flat. Little knots had taken flight overnight. Were these breasts? Would a bra be down the road soon? Boys in my class teased the girls in possession of such knots, and they were even crueler to the girls in fourth grade in possession of such knots. Was it because nothing had grown quite as rapidly on their bodies?

I had just gotten over being fat and suffering through Weight Watchers. I could not handle this right now. If it meant I had to press these knots down with Poe's undershirts, I would. Despite spring's beauty in the East San Fernando Valley, a tinge of unhappiness rolled over me. This was my last year with Bev, in June, I'd have no confidant to confess my thoughts or feelings to. Sharing my front porch with Bev, we watched the football game going on in the middle of the block, across the street stood Lulia hoping for an invitation to join us. "Look at her, she really thinks I'm friends with her. She really is off! Let me put my head down and play jacks with you so she can keep her goofy self away from me…she's still a nut!" Bev said to me.

"Just going to leave her staring at us like she's been orphaned after a flood? Maybe Bev you should at least wave at her, then take your turn; she'll get it."

"Ne, if you are wrong, I going to be upset. I try to look after you, not them. I love you, they just annoy me. Remember your family. Naw, let me tell her to get on!"

Bev stood up armed with fake rage and as expected Lulia ran off (probably due to flashbacks). Lulia's Wilma Rudolph departure made Bev giggle.

"Ne, I started my period!"

"You started you period? What's that?"

"I was sitting down at my desk when it happened. I got up and Mrs. Winston told me to sit down until the bell rang."

"Why did she do that? I don't get it."

"Ne, you really don't get it living in a box. I take you around, teach you, and you're still like Alice in Wonderland… I bled through my dress, that's why."

"How, what did you do Bev?" I asked.

"Waited for my mother to pick me up. What could I do, Ne, parade around everyone?"

"Do you bleed every day for life?"

"No, just for three or four days. Pretty soon you'll get your period, Ne. I saw your chest, you need a bra!" Bev laughed and gave me a hug. We realized our worlds (once again) were changing.

The summer of 1969 was full of change. Neil Armstrong walked on the moon, and everyone was into space travel and the moon. My father, he was consumed by the ideal of outer space. I really believed Daddy was claiming the moon on behalf of humanity. Maybe that was his problem; he wanted to stand out as some sort of pioneer, be it the moon or the current state of the world, something was wrong with him. There was turmoil all over the country, and Pacoima residents seemed to have their share of it as well. San Fernando Valley College erupted in civil unrest; several of Pacoima's best involved in the upheaval took over the administration building demanding to be heard regarding admission of Black students. Years later, Pacoima residents Barbara Rhodes would become college president of the university and William Burrell a tenured faculty member of California State University, Northridge.

The Vietnam War raged on. Many Black guys, some of them just seventeen years old, were sent to *Nam*, as my father called it. I overheard him say Vietnam was a White man's war. He believed that the Black man in America had no business fighting with the Viet Cong when we did not have our freedom in America. He professed that young White men had a better chance of avoiding the draft because most had money and knew people to aid them in getting out of duty. He said he did not have to go because he took care of his family, but was sad as Black men always ended up on the front line of the war, and most of the time came back in body bags. I did not understand all the politics of the war, but it did seem like all the people that went (to Vietnam) in our community either did not come back at all or came back junkies, crippled or both. Jimmy, Sherry Reilly's boyfriend, served in Vietnam. They had planned to marry when Jimmy returned, but when he came back he was not the same. Sherry said, 'Jimmy's head was not right anymore; that all he wanted to do was shoot heroin.' Ear hustling an adult conversation, my father said of the heroin that it came in by the American government, oftentimes in the coffin of soldiers.

Jimmy took all of his *war* money from the military to purchase Smack, walking the streets so high at times you wondered how he stood upright. There were a lot of Jimmy's in Black communities of America. I saw it on CBS Evening News. Why go fight a war where you had to kill people you knew nothing about for a country that still called you a Nigger? When they came back their lives and girlfriends never really welcomed them back home, and many became drifters.

I just thought the war was dumb, and could not see how we were helping anybody by fighting the Viet Cong.

Jimmy overdosed six months after he got back from Vietnam. His mother found him dead in his room with a needle stuck in his forearm. Sadly, no one today talks about what happen to the Jimmys who went to Vietnam.

The moon represented for my father a place where the presence of White men was not a factor, where the fabric of racism had not been woven into the planet's surface. A place where Black men did not have to die without reason, where the word "Nigger" did not exist—not yet. The moon represented freedom.

August, I heard my mother say she was going to divorce my father. Daddy acted like an infant, falling down on his knees, crying and begging for acceptance. Although my mother sounded strong in her resolve, in the end she gave in to my father and did not file for divorce. The summer of 1969 Daddy really did appreciate his wife and children. It was nice to be in a quiet environment where my father behaved, as he if he truly loved us. I try to remember him the summer of 1969, because he was an apparition of a man who never really was.

"We hugged our father, in all his damn madness,
seemed like a daddy in deep pain."
Denise

CHAPTER SEVEN

HOPE AND THE POWER OF BELIEF
SOMETIMES ARE NOT ENOUGH

David came down with the flu in October 1969 and was sick a month, mending just before Thanksgiving, only to be ill New Year's Day.

Dr. Washington, our family physician, prescribed the usual pink antibiotic liquid for my brother. "Give him cod liver oil and he'll be good as new," Dr. Washington told my mother. Mommy followed Dr. Washington's instructions and David improved slightly. Possessing a beautiful bright smile, David's warm smoky hazel eyes were perfectly framed against his golden curry-toned skin. Granny said David looked like Herman spit him out, professing that he had that Fineste Adonis look about him.

I hurried to pick up David up from my aunt Chung Li's. Today was his birthday and he looked forward to the party that awaited him. As I lifted my brother up to greet him, I saw a large lump, which I pointed out to my aunt.

"Aunty, did something bite him today?" I asked

"No, he just sleep a lot today, he not want to play. Let me see him," she responded. Checking David, she found another lump on the left side of his neck. My aunt was now upset she had missed it. On the way home, David, as are all children regardless of the degree of illness, was happy and upbeat it was his birthday, smiling and singing. Reaching home and lifting him out of his stroller, he felt warm despite the chill of autumn. Quickly telephoning my mother about my concern, a familiar voice on the phone answered.

"Hey, baby, did you pick up David?"

"Yes, Mommy, he seems warm to me, how can I tell if he has a fever?"

"Take your right hand and feel under his chin and cheek, does he feel warm?" My mother asked, trying to hide panic, her words rapid and void of patience.

"Yes."

"I'll be home in fifteen minutes."

I never contemplated why David seemed to keep a cold, never gave a second thought to the reality about to unfold.

"Davey, let Mommy see your neck," my mother said. She touched the right side of his neck, her face frightened and alarmed. By now, the intensity of my mother's concern osmotically channeled to me, worry consuming my young being.

Dr. Washington saw my brother within the hour. Unanswered time accelerated rapidly. As Poe and I sat watching the afternoon sun in October trail away, there was no sign of our mother and beloved brother David. Poe had fallen asleep when our mother appeared, tears in her eyes.

"Mommy, what's wrong?" I asked worriedly.

"David has to go onto the hospital so Dr. Washington can run tests…see what's wrong with your brother," my mother sobbed.

Entering the house, my mother burst into tears, declaring to my father, "David is sick—the doctors don't know what it is;—they're performing a biopsy tomorrow—we have to be at Pacoima Lutheran Hospital by eight in the morning."

"When did the doctor tell you this...right now?" my father shouted.

"Yes! I came home early from work went straight to Dr. Washington's with David."

"Why didn't you have the doctor call me?"

"Does it matter? Your child has to go into the hospital!" Mommy angrily stated.

"You and Poe have to stay here until your Granny comes for you." Lee Jr., though distraught, inherited our father's silence. He sat motionless, not speaking, but I knew my brother was deeply troubled.

"I'll get the baby's things ready," my father said.

My parents solemnly in lock step gathered my mother's small brown overnight bag, systematically packing David's pajamas and favorite teddy bear. In this brief moment and space, fear was triggered in me, believing (once again) that something ahead of me was incredibly sad, praying another bad thing would not dampen my family.

"Mr. and Mrs. Burelford, David has Valley Fever. You know all the construction of the freeway has brought up some spores that cause some nasty things. I am going to prescribe a regime of antibiotics. He should be back to full speed in a few weeks." A collective sigh of relief erupted over us, and we were all happy that our lives could return to normal, whatever that meant.

Riding his Big Wheel with the skill of a NASCAR driver, David seemed to sputter out quickly as the days drew on, growing weaker. April, during spring vacation, I was old enough to babysit David while my parents worked. David loved watching television, clapping his hands wildly and laughing as Bugs Bunny beat down Wiley Coyote. But this was short-lived. His smile weakened before climbing back into his bed. Something was wrong. I telephoned my mother insisting that she come home. When she did, I once more witnessed fear in her eyes.

"Something is wrong with my baby. Ne, get my phone book and find your father's number at the plant."

"Paint shop," a man's voice answered. The sound of loud machinery roared in the background.

"I would like to speak with Lee Burelford badge number 26789 please—this is his daughter, sir—his son is very sick and he must come home"

"Ne, what's wrong with David? Where's your mother—is she there?" My father said. Despite the noise, panic could be detected in his voice.

"Yes, Mommy wants you to come home right away."

"Lee I want to take the baby to U.C.L.A.—he's not getting better—I don't care what Dr. Washington says!"

My father arrived home at noon.

It was now ten in the evening but I was determined to stay up until my parents came home with David.

An array of thoughts raced through my mind. Maybe it was taking so long because David had some type of surgery, and maybe he'd died. I was terrified.

It was now midnight, and abruptly Mommy and Daddy entered the front door, tears cascading down her face and Daddy possessing a hopeless stare of frantic despair caused me to search the room.

"Where's David?" I asked my father.

"Ne, your brother is really sick, Ne." My father told me while dialing Dr. Washington.

"This is Lee Burelford. I need to speak with Dr. Washington—this is an emergency. Look, Bitch, do you have a cure for cancer? If you don't know how to cure lymphoma then shut the hell up and get Dr. Washington!" My father venomously shouted.

The words emitted from my father's mouth almost twenty years ago feel like yesterday, clear and so final. The Carpenters played in the background, "Close to you," my mother lay sobbing, rolled up in the fetal position in the corner of the living room. I knew what cancer was. Lulia's cousin Jeffery died of cancer last summer. David was going to die.

"Dr. Washington, this is Lee Burelford. Dr. Washington, David has lymphoma. Don't know how much time my baby has. I have a question doctor, how in the hell did you not see David's cancer? You stole some of my child's time damn!"

Going into David's room in possession of the same overnight suitcase both he and my mother previously filled, this time Daddy solely selected David's attire and favorite stuffed animal. Folding his child's clothes ever so carefully, my father silently wiped his tears from his eyes, holding his pain in, as was his way.

Lee Jr., though distraught, sat motionless, but I knew my brother was deeply troubled. Lee never asked about cancer. Instead, he asked Maurice Reilly to bike ride to the public library. I found the book under his bed.

Our parents spent the next week at the hospital, returning only once. They instructed us to get ready, that "we were going to see David." In no time, cards purchased, pictures drawn were carefully bundled as we waited patiently on the living room sofa.

"David is very, very sick. He has a form of cancer called lymphoma. He is doing better but he is still very sick. Your brother's face is swollen from the medicines given to fight the disease, called chemotherapy, so don't tell him he looks different."

We didn't understand all the new terms like chemotherapy and such but our mother did not have to tell us not to make fun of our sick brother, Poe and I were somewhat confused by her last comment, but possessed her fear.

Reaching the hospital, Poe and I stood in total disbelief of the hospital's massive size, all red brick and very advanced, appearing to go on for miles. We knew our brother was somewhere inside this large smart place, but where was the mystery. Waiting for the elevator an image of David in a coffin came to me, and I forcibly squeezed my eyes shut, removing the coffin from my memory. The elevator ride transported us to a different place and time, to a secret world of sick children in seemingly metal cages and wheelchairs that became our reality. Families, all expressing fear and worry, lined the corridors, all possessing distinctive stares that focused on the brightness of the outside. Maybe all felt if they could leave this place, their lives, and above all their children, would return to normal, free of sickness.

David's large hospital room was shared with another sick child that I did not focus on. I was only interested in the little golden brown boy lying in the bed in front of me now tinged and yellow with tubes and needles in his arms. Clapping his hands seeing Poe and me, like his namesake, David was a warrior. The image of my brother in a coffin resurfaced once again. I pushed back, sensing my brother's will to live.

Two weeks into his hospital stay, David underwent another spinal tap to determine the progress of the chemotherapy.

"I don't want another needle, Mommy. Daddy, kick his butt, don't let him give me that needle!" Pleaded David.

"Little Man, Daddy loves you. Do you think Daddy would let them do this if it wouldn't make you better? Just one more, Davey, and I promise no more little man. Do this for Daddy," my father asked, his voice deep as he choked back tears.

David stopped crying, having embraced belief in our father's words. As Dr. Feldstein and his nurse turned my brother on his stomach, David never moved nor cried. My father stroked his head and within minutes it was over. Daddy kissed his child and handed David to our mother.

"Go to your father," our mother instructed us.

Daddy was standing in the hallway, crying like a baby experiencing their first fall, the cry long and heartfelt. We hugged our father for who in all of his madness was a father in real pain.

A few days prior to David coming home, Mommy lived at Lindberg's health food store. She'd quit working so she could be home with David.

"David is coming home; Mommy needs to make sure that he gets well."

"How long will it take for David to get well?" I asked.

"I don't know, but he will get well…he must," my mother said.

At that instant, I knew my mother was determined that my brother would beat cancer. My father told us that we had to wear surgical masks like surgeons to protect my brother from infections. We had to keep people away from our home. Questions bombarded my mind as we made our way over the hill from the valley to U.C.L.A. The Carpenter's "Close To You" ironically played on the radio. Life-like depictions raced through my head; I saw my mother huddled in a ball, sobbing, my father's smoldering rage at having a sick child, and tears pooled in my eyes. In that moment I realized all that I had known before was gone. I couldn't get it or my brother back as they were before cancer.

"Lee, he gon' be alright, the Lord gonna let us all have him.
I know he will."
Mr. Hackmon

CHAPTER EIGHT

THE NEED TO BELIEVE IN SOMETHING

Entering the hospital lobby with my family, I prayed this would be the last visit to this vast Pandora's place, waiting for one of the dozen elevators to descend from the sickness above, praying God would forgive me for all the bad things I had ever done, blaming myself for David's illness. I was older and my parents would not miss me as much as their cherub. David symbolized a future filled with love, a family whole. On this beloved child's shoulders rested a family's salvation; he had to get well, the Burelfords for once worked as a team.

"Hurry Mommy, get me dressed, today I can go home! I want to ride my Big Wheel fast! I want to ride Poe's motorcycle, let's go, Mommy!" As the elevator chimed, we waved goodbye, off to seek our destiny.

"Mommy, I'm out of this place!" David shouted, exiting the lobby as light rushed in.

Mr. Hackmon came quickly to greet David. Many an afternoon he sat holding David on his lap, playing gently with him, telling stories about his own son, and my brother's chance as well.

"Let me see that boy!" I thought it would fall out if his voice got any higher. "Davey, where that little boy of mine!"

He loved Mr. Hackmon, who for practical purposes was his grandfather. Grandfathers have special relationships with their grandchildren based on things that should have happened with their children.

"Poppa, my Poppa!" David shouted.

Mr. Hackmon cried, "Lee, he gonna be alright, the Lord let us all have him. I know he will."

My father mustered a weak smile and I prayed this would be true. My hair fallen into what Black women refer to the as the, "Nappys." Mommy was far too busy to care for my hair to her normal perfectionary standards. To make bad matters worse was my own inability to comb it correctly. This was a task my mother took pride in refusing to allow me to practice on my own hair styling. Luckily, Granny took over the duties and she in turn passed the assignment on to Pacoima's most famous Black beauty shop, Town and Country. I was the third generation of Rose West patrons, servicing both my mother and grandmother's hair. Town and County was an experience. There was energy in the shop, a mixture of old and white-glove classy, with a tad of street. Ladies left their chairs coiffed, just like in Ebony and Sepia magazines.

Despite the onslaught of the Afro, pressing your hair bone straight was still popular. Kinky hair still viewed as a symbol of shame and unkemptness. That is the message all Black women and girls in America were indoctrinated into believing, taking a hot metal comb that when it touched your head made the oil implanted sizzle, affirmed it was the correct thing to do.

The first time my mother pressed my hair, I told all the Babies about my pressing experience. They'd been through this Negro female rite of passage. The pressing comb carefully guided through my head by my mother who, as all Negro mothers, told you not to move or risk the chance of being burned as the oil crackled. For Black women, the display of cocoa butter plastered across your forehead or face was the equivalent to earning a Purple Heart, signifying bravery, one of the many factors contributing to a Black woman's strength. European's commercials glorifying beautiful blondes and brunettes swinging luxurious straight hair were outright criminal and cruel; they'd never sat their assess in a kitchen chair next to the stove in the middle of July with scalps set ablaze with hot oil running down your scalp. Maybe if they had, applause and respect would ring out for all those who dared this brutality in the pursuit of beauty.

One of the beauticians in the shop was named Connie. On most days, she looked like a tall, dark big-boned Alabama woman. Connie was impeccably dressed and fashionable, but her voice was deeper than my father's, which I did not get it. Watching Connie as I waited, she applied a greasy white cream that smelled like rotten eggs into a customer's hair. Applying the cream in sections to the woman's hair, I watched the customer fidget wildly then scream.

"Connie, it's starting to burn my scalp, finish the last section and get this out of my hair!"

"Wait just a second or two more, I need to get back in your kitchen, Honey," Connie shrilled.

"Please get this shit out of my head now! I can't take it. Oh my God, please! My scalp is on fire. You're going to make me lose all my hair!"

Three beauticians helped Connie hold her down and wash the smelly stuff out of the woman's head. As she cried out in pain, I vowed never to put whatever it was in my own hair. I was a bit confused about the lack of concern patrons had for the woman crying at the shampoo bowl. Even at eleven, I knew grown people showed more concern for an injured animal, so I must have not gotten all the information I needed on this matter. I asked my grandmother, who was sitting under the dryer, to explain what I'd witnessed.

"Granny, why doesn't anyone help that lady crying?"

"Oh honey, she scratched her scalp before she permed. Connie asked her if she had scratched her scalp and she said she hadn't," Granny said in a plain, "it was her fault" tone.

Sitting in Connie's chair, panic began to creep into my being as I thought about the white cream, feeling the heat, hearing the pop of grease hitting my scalp with the pressing comb, just a trifecta of horrors awaiting me. No, I'd not receive white pain in a jar today. I couldn't take the torture—nope not for me, this was my protest. If I had to run up and out of the salon, I would. As Connie walked towards me with the jar of white phosphorus in hand, I blurted out, "Connie don't put that stuff in my hair. You won't burn me alive. Nope! I'm telling my grandmother. Granny!" I protested, turning my chair to alert Granny.

Connie drew back in animated laughter. "Baby, you think I'd do something to hurt you, pretty girl? Don't worry, honey, Ms. Connie would never hurt you."

Relieved that Connie had no plans to infuse my hair with pain, I began to settle down, looking up at her as she leaned over me. Studying Connie's face, I saw a beard like my father. My curiosity heightened. Why did Connie have a beard? Was Connie really a woman? Hanging under Bev acquiring valuable life information, I knew about "Little Richards." Bev's older sister called them homosexuals. Was Connie a homosexual? As Connie finished the last curl of my bone-straight ponytail, my staring was so intense now Connie seemed concerned.

"What's wrong child? You don't like your Shirley Temple curls? Tell me now, what's wrong?"

Uneasiness filled me. I desperately wanted to ask Connie why at ten o'clock in the morning she had a full beard, but I'd been drilled on correct child etiquette and rule number one Mommy taught us: only speak we spoken to…So, since Connie asked this was my opportunity. "Why do you have a beard like my Daddy?"

Connie's face seemed to take on new features, previous playfulness left, and she forcefully pursed her lips, confessing,

"Baby girl, I am a man. They call men like me homosexuals, and men like me do not want woman as a girlfriend, we desire the company of another man."

"I know, like Little Richard?"

Connie's smile still wide and full lost some of its light, the possession of sadness apparent. "Yes, baby. I think you have it right. Baby is you mad at old Connie?"

"No, I just like you for you. You're always so kind to me and you always make me feel special."

Connie seemed relieved and brightness returned to her smile, "Let me give you a little height to those curls, add some teenage style for you."

"…How could God be a loving God and let this happen to Davey?"

CHAPTER NINE

LEARNING TO TAKE A PUNCH

The end of May, David began having trouble keeping his balance, Mommy, worried, made an appointment for David to see his doctors. Daddy returned home by himself later that evening minus my mother and brother, entering the living room unemotionally pronouncing, "Your brother has a brain tumor, they're giving him a new medication and radiation to stop it from growing."

Waiting for the news as well, Granny sat motionless, at a loss. We as a family had the wind knocked out of us. She sighed and uttered in a low, drawn-out voice, "Ne you and Poe get your clothes for school tomorrow. You're spending the night with me."

Riding silently on the way to Granny's in the back seat with Poe deliberately lost in the distraction of traffic images to block out what was going on, the image of David riding his Big Wheel at lightning speed in a mean spin out played out in my head. I had a difficult time praying that evening. Why did God allow this to happen to such a beautiful creation? My faith as a child to comprehend imperfection (as Mommy taught me) was difficult; did the same loving God that I believed in allow this to happen?

I was afraid to share my lack of understanding with another soul out of fear the Devil would hear me, making matters worse, even after being told by Nana the Devil could not read your mind, it was only when you expressed thoughts aloud.

After six days of radiation and chemotherapy, David was discharged from the hospital. The family was elated he was home and the brain tumor shrinking, and he was behaving like his old self. I asked my mother if this was a sign from God that David was going to be cured from cancer. She tearfully answered, "Yes…Thank You, Father."

Fifth grade was a strange time for me: no Bev and suddenly breasts, and the weight I had lost returned, resting neatly in my face and stomach; I was back to the cuddly "Pumpkin." Summer came and Daddy became more distant. He worked hard, and strayed away from the streets and his family. When my father held his son, uneasiness and joy were co-occurring emotions. On one occasion I overheard a loud horn-locking conversation between my parents. My mother was bitterly indignant at my father's audacity, "What do you mean you're numb and have no feelings for any of us, Lee?"

"Helena, I'm fearful of pain, loss. The only way I can deal with it is not to, that is how I survive." In the midst of her baby's cancer, my mother who fought to stay with her oppressor was summarily left to her own emotional devices, icy all over again.

Mr. Davidson opened a barber shop on Foothill Boulevard. The new shop drew attention from Pacoima's men. This was Pacoima's second Black barbershop. What made Davidson's "House of Style" different was he really knew how to give you a natural. Mr. Peters, the owner of the Elequentville barbershop on Glenoaks, always gapped up your haircut, so much so it was a standing Pacoima joke that if your hair was messed up Mr. Peters probably cut it. He never had a line of customers waiting. A Saturday ritual in the Black community was visiting the barbershop, as it was where all knowledge on all things could be derived. Sometimes graced with Griotic wisdom or troublesome foolish bullshit, this day it was my father and Poe's turn to experience it.

"Who needs a haircut?" Mr. Peters asked of the morning crowd.

My father liked Mr. Peters and without fail accepted his invitation eagerly, unaware that people were engaged in laughter at him and his son, who exited Mr. Peters' chair with the worst flattops one could imagine. Poe always had tears streaming down his face leaving the shop.

Shauna Davidson frequented her father's shop. The Davidsons were new to Claretta Street, and Shauna was nothing like any of the Babies. Unlike us, Shauna was stacked, possessing breasts as big as most grown women, and shapely hips without comparison. Next to us, Shauna looked like a Girl Scout while we were Brownies; physically, she was already a woman, hourglass figure and all. Teenage boys (and sneaky men) whistled and hollered in her presence. What were we to do with Shauna? Invite her to play with our Easy Bake ovens and our add-water packaged cake mix attempts at cooking? Moreover, Shauna was not interested in us. While Smitty performed Olympic gymnastics trying to gain her confidence, Shauna would not take the bait.

To my distain, Bev began to forge a friendship with Shauna. I was more than a little bit annoyed, Bev was my partner in crime, why did Shauna have to show up now? Bev and I shared everything, cherished walks and RTD bus rides down Van Nuys Boulevard, experiencing momentary independence to local hang-outs like the *Chicken Shack*, *Frosty Freeze*, and *Joe's Swing Shop*, where 45s rhythmically put bounce in your stroll down the Boulevard. Allowed to experience the hub of our community with Bev, as my parents trusted her with my safekeeping, Pacoima's public housing project (Pacoima Gardens) surrounded the boulevard, forcing everyone to have his or her game faces on, and Bev always did.

"Dang!" I said while glancing at Shauna, who stood in the way of my pink cardboard box from the Chicken Shack, and filled with mouth watering fried chicken, fries and coleslaw. Now I would never get to step inside Joe's Swing Shop to bop my head to the latest records. Shauna really put a damper on my life, interfering with my vicarious learning of *Superfly* and *Sweet Back*. Now I'd miss out on what the drug connection to hustlers and Italian gangsters and Vietnam really was. (That's what Shirley Reilly said of it.) All I knew was there had to be something to it, as all the teenagers and young adults sure thought it was happening. Things began to change, and my connection to understanding that change was being destroyed by a fast ass girl who could not spell or knew the meaning of any damn thing. All she could shout was "Ice Berg Slim." I hated Shauna!

Shauna looked far older than her years so Bev could take her to visit her crew. On one such excursion, Bev invited Shauna to her cousin Pam's to listen to records. Pam lived on Mercer Street. The street was known to be somewhat out of bounds in terms of acceptability. On Mercer resided the criminal element of the community. Not to say that everyone on the block was a thug, but Mercer had more than its share of riffraff. As luck would have it, along the way to Pam's, Bev and Shauna ran into the Brewer Boys from Chicago. The Brewer Boys were Pacoima's genuine thieves and robbers; if something was stolen, they were usually behind the crime, with the Brewers experiencing countless police visits.

"Dang, he's cute!" Shauna yelled at Phil, the oldest of the Brewer clan. At fifteen, Phil was truly a thug, having seen the inside of Juvenile Hall several times. Phil was a teenage boy to the tenth degree, translated to mean Phil was a dog in heat, and Shauna for a twelve year old was beyond fast. There was no stopping them, and the rest, shall we say, was history. After school, she would ditch us and meet Phil in the park. Lying to her parents, saying she was playing softball with Bev, when in actuality Shauna was doing her thing with Phil.

Not until Shauna began sneaking out of the house at night to see Phil were we forced to spill the beans on her. But Smitty being Smitty was not happy with letting anything go, and an episode in shit was about to take stride.

"So, Shauna, you doing it to Phil yet?" Smitty asked Shauna as we sat on Deebie's lawn.

"Whatcha mean doing it, Smitty?" Shauna said, embarrassed that Smitty had asked so directly. Smitty smirked, proud that she had created and gotten Shauna's full and undivided attention. Despite the ugliness of her words, Smitty continued, "You know, are you given him pussy?"

Lulia, Deebie and I were ready to run, anticipating Shauna's impending eruption, but ferret Smitty had no common sense. What did she expect her to say, "Yeah?" Smitty stood upright stupidly proud in the release of her poison and planted her feet, arrogantly awaiting Shauna's response.

"Smitty, I should kick your little flat-chest ass, don't you worry about what I'm doing, you little yellow baby-tooth elf!"

Yes, the grown folk had shown up in Shauna; one too many Bid Whist parties in the company of Jack Daniels-filled adults for her. Smitty was silent. For a group of twelve and thirteen year olds, this was exciting stuff unfolding in front of us.

"Smitty, I told your little ass to stay out of my business!"

Shauna's right hand caught Smitty dead in the mouth, knocking her on her butt, her crying mouth bleeding. All of us in shock it had come to this. Maybe just maybe, Smitty'd keep her mouth shut and stop the trash-talking.

"I was too young to understand the concept of free will…"
Denise

CHAPTER TEN

NOW I UNDERSTOOD THE MOTIVATION OF DADDY'S COOLNESS

November arrived and the family rejoiced in another thirty days of remission for David. I'd overheard my mother telling Granny that the new drugs were effective in controlling his cancer, sharing with Granny that the doctors were optimistic about his full recovery, even though the lymphoma David had was difficult to control. My mother was determined her child be freed from his death sentence. Before encountering the Jehovah Witnesses, she would have entertained thoughts of taking my brother to see a faith healer but now she reduced this to an act of desperation.

"Only God had the power to do such things and faith healers are not God."

"Mommy, what do you mean they're not God? If they use their powers to heal David why is it bad?" I asked, confused how faith healers were not good.

"Witnesses believe that miracles of the full flesh like curing David's cancer are not pleasing to the word of God." What did this mean?

"What is wrong with Kathryn Colgren putting hands on you to make you well?"

"God says in the Bible that the day of miracles have passed, today we must walk in and on faith, regardless how imperfect or unfair this world is, Jehovah asks us to rely in the power and strength of his plan for us."

"So would it be wrong for us to take David to a faith healer, because we would not walk in the faith of God?" I asked my mother. "God stopped the presence of inspired healers thousands of years ago, Ne. We don't know where they get their gift from but it could be from a source other than God."

I stared at the Bible in front of me, reflecting on God allowing his son to die a painful mortal human death when God could have stopped everyone and thing in their tracks, forcing all to see the error of their ways. So was my mother telling me that she being a mere human had to endure as perfect entities as God had in the loss of his son? I thought about the lesson that I was to gain from David's suffering and found Mommy's belief a little unsettling.

December of 1970 arrive and my spree of happiness was about to change.

Santa Ana winds were peculiarly cold and harsh, which should have been my cue what was to come. I spent the last Friday before Christmas vacation from school in the library dreaming about things I would do over the two-week break. My parents did not allow Poe and I to participate in the Christmas program so there we sat with the other outlier children. Reaching home, something felt amiss. The living room drapes were pulled shut. Mommy's car was gone. Immediately my mouth dried, trying to convince myself that my mother had only ventured to the market and was just late.

"This cannot happen again..." I mumbled.

Poe and I realized that something familiar and tragic was happening again to us in a cyclical destructive manner. Opening the front door of our home, a sheet of paper from our mother carefully stuck to the entry mirror.

"David had a seizure today. Have to go back to U.C.L.A with your father. Do not leave the house. Your grandmother will come for you... Mommy."

CHAPTER ELEVEN

HOLDING ON

December 21, 1970, my brother's war with cancer raged on. He was back in the hospital again, trying to defeat this thing that had consumed our lives. I had begun having the casket dream again. Attributing it to fear did not make it any easier. Walking with Granny was different. She walked as though on a mission, her steps short and smooth, never varying. My grandmother told me the story of how White men taunted her, calling her dirty names, insisting they would rape her. Terrified, she kept walking, suspecting that if she stopped, she would have appeared fearful and been killed. Accompanying her this day, I felt her will, her ability not to show fear, and I felt safe. The dreaded wait for the elevator, massive number plates, the people fearful of sickness, stale disinfectant and the call of doctors; I hated this place.

When I reached David's room, his eyes opened. David smiled weakly and rose up to greet us. Looking at my tired mother, I was worried. She was David's light but now Mommy seemed dim. David was pale; three intravenous lines covered his left arm, the arm now swollen and darkened, frightened my grandmother.

"Helena, did the baby's veins collapse?" Granny quickly asked.

"David's relapsed. The cancer is back—chemo stopped working," Mommy painfully confessed. Granny tightly hugged my mother, staring blindly into the air, not caring about anything, just lost in the space of their existence.

"Ne, come sit here," David asked of me. Though young, we were seasoned veterans of heartache and the pain that went with it. Our beloved brother was going to die.

"I want my baby at home, David is coming home," I heard Mommy talking to the doctor. She said if David could not be helped, she wanted her son to die in his own bed.

Looking weaker than he had just a few days earlier, he'd lost more of his beautiful brown coloring. David bore his suffering, his color mustard yellow. This child knew time was everything and he wanted to exhaust all the time that remained for him.

"Daddy, I want to ride my motorcycle."

"David, you're not strong enough yet, man. Wait a day, okay?"

David peered into his father's eyes, stating his demand, "No Daddy, I want to ride my motorcycle now!"

At four and half years old, he knew death was imminent; nothing could wait until tomorrow; all that mattered was right now, the ride his last chance to feel the wind in his face, the rush of speed he loved so much. As the engine revved, Claretta Street residents assembled, wondering what was going on at the Burelford residence; my father, his young son, and all those watching with tears streaming down their faces.

"No, I don't want the helmet, I want to see," David insisted.

"Hold on, man," my father said. As he and David began their last ride together as father and son, Daddy's flaws were inconsequential and meaningless. In this moment, my father was perfection. David's smile was faint but full; through the horror of cancer his beautiful smile was still unique. Back and forth, David and my father rode. Uncle Sheldon filmed their ride until tears made it impossible for him to see through the camera's viewfinder.

Families are strange and wonderful entities, yet family is always supportive, and at this time of need, we were no exception. David required a full-time nurse; Granny spared no expense for David's next journey. Paula, Granny's eccentric friend, a registered nurse, informed my grandmother she'd have it no other way. Paula was noble. Most people would have stepped out of the situation, unable to deal with the agony surrounding the loss of a child, as parents are not supposed to bury their children.

Helda hadn't come to greet David, instead electing to send her sons to assist in the care of David, with the exception of Uncle Sheldon. My father's other brothers couldn't handle the scene, making their visits mere drive-bys. Funny thing about family, it is not solely DNA. Family represents an internal connectivity regardless of bloodlines. Claretta Street residents were our family; as family they never left our sides and our lives.

Though weak, David did not seem to be in much pain, and if he was, Paula made sure he never ran out of morphine. David fought to maintain his dignity in the face of death. Even now as an adult, I vividly remember the intuition David possessed. What is the mechanism of a human's experience when they are nearing God? My brother knew he was nearing the essence of all.

It was clear time was short. Nana never left my brother's side, her eyes never closing, following the rise and fall of his chest. My mother lay beside her child, cuddled as she had at his birth, reminding each other of cherished moments that began in the womb, she would soon say goodbye to her baby, something loved and nurtured in her; never again on earth would she hold her child, only in her dreams—or when God called for her. David could no longer get out of bed. This was the first time in all my years I had ever seen my father change a diaper, yet he did it with so much care and love I felt that he was trying to make amends for not having done so before. Despite all the crap my father put us though, whole-heartedly this was the one instance where love prevailed. I guess this is why my father had nothing left; he had used it up. Everyone's emotional quotient is different, with some possessing endless supplies of love that last the duration of their lives while others have enough for one of life's great events. For my father this was it.

"David's urine excretion rate is dropping. I'm worried about kidney failure… yes I understand, increase the morphine, hold the discomfort to a minimum, thank you I'll call when there is a change," Paula said, taking a great sigh, her eyes scanning the family room bar, coffee mug in hand pouring a long non-pausing stream of scotch.

Evenings proved infinite in their duration. It is true when ill or dying night is the evil to conquer. David spent the night tossing and turning, sometimes asking for my mother or Lee Jr. or me. In and out of consciousness, he'd awaken asking for Fella, seeking comfort from pain. I was losing my baby brother, the one I loved to bathe and dress whose flowing black locks reassured idyllic childhood happiness. Poe and I, annoyed the extended family that gathered were extracting from our time with David as we sought to recount our antics: how Poe stuck him in his bicycle basket riding to T.G & Y, or how it hurt when David hit me in the head with a hammer when he was two.

Sitting on the bed next to David, his eyes opened, "Ne Ne, play my song."

I searched through the tapes on the dresser, finding the Jackson 5 album, which contained David's favorite song, "I'll Be There." Our little brother provided us an assurance he would always be with us.

"Davey, do you hurt anywhere?"

"No. I just feel tired. Ne Ne, I'm not scared. Just stay here with me, just stay with me."

Eight-thirty in the evening, the family assembled around David's bed. My mother held her baby in her arms, my father at his feet,

Granny and Helda sobbing the cry of every African parent's ancestral loss of children taken from them, surrendered to helplessness, my grandmothers carrying out prayers.

Holding her cherub, David's breathing labored, "He's going."

David opened his eyes, urgently uttering, "I want Mommy, where's my Mommy?"

"I'm here Davey. You go baby… go to God."

Taking a last gasp of air, David was gone. With the tragedy of childhood death time slows to a crawl, memories bombard the mind, the impact of pain laborious and crippling. Dr. Washington pronounced David's death. Nana washed his body, my mother commenting her child was cold. John Rucker backed his black hearse into our garage, my mother, crying; spoke to Mr. Rucker, "Take care of my baby. Mommy has to let you go now." Then fainted.

"A Chance for a New Start, a Chance for Love, to Be a Family."
Helena

CHAPTER TWELVE

GEOLOGIC MOVEMENT

New Year's Eve 1971 was a sad one: the funeral having taken place for David, guests were all but a memory, and the Burelfords were up close with the tremendous reminder of their loss. Each of us retreating to our own camps to lick our wounds and grieve, it was a quiet time in our home. Daddy chose not to be there, often spending a great deal of time at card games and hanging out with his friends and at old hangouts, leaving our mother to grieve alone. She spent time with us but we could not absorb her pain, we were just children.

Laying on the den sofa with Poe watching Dick Clark counting down from Times Square in New York, our little brother was not between us, only empty space. "Ten, nine, eight, seven…four, three, two, one…Happy New Year!" Dick Clark shouted as we slept.

I was glad to get back to school, to get away from sorrow, elated to see Bev. She smiled and I hugged her neck tightly. The Babies were early this morning, but passed on rushing me, I greeting them at my front door. "Hey, Ne Ne," Deebie said in her crazy, shrill dog-whistle voice.

On any other occasion, I would have refused them entrance, but today was different. I felt their need to help me and I needed them. Deebie parted my hair, Lulia held the hair barrettes, and Smitty held the grease. Curious to witness their creation, I checked myself, my part was crooked just like Deebie, I had too much grease in my hair like Smitty and my barrettes were just like Lulia, regardless of our ragamuffin exterior, we loved each other despite our shortcomings.

The ninth of February 1971 would be my learning tree. Daddy aroused by four each morning to be at the plant by five-thirty, slow to dress, vanity possessed, changing work clothes several times before his departure at five o'clock in the morning. As Daddy's work orchestration concluded sleep returned, suddenly what felt like the motion of an atomic bomb blast violently pelted the room. Unable to get out of my bed, knocked down by another wave as my bedroom walls met the floor in ebb and flow motion. Tossed around and free of toys, I was not hurt. Attempting to stand up only to be knocked down by another wave, reminding me when I was five at Zuma beach, Mommy holding my hand along the shore, as a large wave and heavy undertow snatched me off my feet away from my mother's grasp. I kept tumbling in the water pulled deeper into the current by the undertow—I was drowning. As I tumbled, a man grabbed me, saving my life. Suddenly as I was tossed across the room, my mother grabbed me.

"Come on Ne, Poe hold on to Mommy."

As we fought to make our way down the hall, the house began to come apart, glass breaking, the hiss of gas coming from the hot water tank, we ran for our lives. The water heater pilot ignited the escaping vapor. Wearing only our pajamas, within seconds flames shot high into the early morning sky, followed by a loud explosion. Neighbors running with hoses desperately tried to extinguish the fire, the water stopped, then resumed as Claretta Street fought to save one of their own. "Call the fire department!" someone screamed.

"I'm trying but the phone don't work!" shouted Mrs. Hackmon.

Mommy left the car out so we had refuge as we watched our home burn to the ground; as the scene unfolded in front of us, our father ran straight up the walkway of the house flames licking his face.

"Where's my family, my kids? Helena!"

My father shouting as Mr. Hackmon restrained him, "Lee everybody got out, car in the driveway!"

12442 Claretta burned fiercely before a fire truck arrived to apply what water they could in an attempt to extinguish the flames. "We cannot do any more, the city is on fire all over, and the flames are out. Keep water on the rest with your hoses, this is the best we can do; have to go, everything's real bad now."

My mother told my father, "I have to get the kids pictures, that's all I want...I've got to find what's left."

The 1971 Sylmar earthquake measured 6.9 on the Richter scale, killing 140 people, destroying a wide section of the San Fernando Valley.

Making our way to Granny's, the damage blanketing the area was immense. I felt lucky; some people stood on sidewalks crying without trapped love ones. Reaching Granny's, happy her home was still standing, built on a raised foundation, faring better than the new tract homes constructed on a ground level slab.

"Helena, I tried to call but the lines are down, on our way to you, are you alright?"

"Momma, the house came apart and burned to the ground...the hot water tank, everybody's alright." My mother said.

"Where's Lee?" Granny asked.

"He stayed to salvage what he could, insurance, pictures, everything else is gone; Momma give me something to put on, I'm going back, keep the kids."

Once again, the earth began to move like a large series of linear dominoes in a wave-like manner. "Aftershocks. We're going to have them for a while, let's stay outside; Junior get the patio furniture in the backyard, so glad Sam didn't put up brick fencing, look around they all came down, always go with wood or chain link," Granny said. My sadness left; yes, I grieved for the loss of my brother but now I was transfixed with the Burelfords' survival; once again all that I had known was no more, strange how trauma can cause redirection instantly needed for survival.

Rebuilding took eleven long months. I was glad when our home finally was completed, we had good insurance—but no earthquake insurance; until now Southern California had not experienced a major earthquake since the 1900s. Thank God for strange blessings, however; we did have fire insurance, making the rebuilding of our home possible. The contractor hired to rebuild our home probably hated my parents, as every penny saved was counted, enabling the Burelfords to travel across the country in a new Winnebago motor home.

Each time we reached a new state or amazing natural landmark, my brother and I would shout, "Wow, look!" In an instant, it was gone, as though my father was at the helm of an Apollo rocket; if you blinked you missed it!

"Helena, we got to make time," my father would say. "Got to get to the KOA campground by nightfall."

I just didn't get it. Why take a vacation if you could not see anything? I thought we were supposed to experience America. Arizona, Texas and most of the South was just a flash of light. Truthfully, Daddy did not want to stop, said the South brought him too much anger, too much rage. My father shared that his father's people had been "free people of color," that they were not slaves and he was very proud of this fact. He had a hard time with true southern Negroes because he said they, "Yes'um boss" too much. Nevertheless, we were awakened to the vibration of the motor home's engine, transmission-turning axles with tire friction on the highways of America; half of it, mind you, we never got to see. Before leaving California, my mother discovered she had a sister in New York City and wanted to make her acquaintance on our cross-country odyssey. The East Coast was different from California; everything was old, even dirty. People packed like ants seemingly coming from every direction; there was movement all around. Poe liked New York because the city was alive full of human energy. As we waited for Mommy's sister, Black folks jutted out of the woodwork to inspect our vehicle.

"Hey man, look at that house tractor!" someone shouted as people gathered around.

"Hey brother, you from California?" The questioning voice asked.

"Yeah man, we are," Daddy said while reaching under the seat for his gun.

"Man, this thing is out of sight! You sleep in it, shower, use the bathroom in this thing, man?"

"Yeah, we can," affirmed my father.

"Man, you better be careful down here with this, you know how folks can be! Hey man, I lost my job last month, got put out by my girlfriend, you think I could use your restroom right quick?"

"Yeah, brother I will be careful, but man you can't use my bathroom…now move the hell back!" My father demanded.

"Helena, we got to get out of here, these people are crazy and I am not into killing Black folks."

Just as my father turned the key in the ignition, a car horn sounded from behind the motor home.

"Oh good, it's my sister and her husband."

Christine was my mother's half-sister; Herman gotten busy in New York; prior to Granny, Herman dated a woman from New Jersey. Before leaving for medical school, his New Jersey girlfriend got pregnant, she never told Herman. (After Herman's departure) Mommy T found out about the baby, offering to care for the infant so the Jersey girlfriend could finish her degree at NYU. Mary never went back to New Jersey; she did finish college, but had no room in her life for a child. Mommy T convinced Christine's mother she was too young to raise her child alone, instead raising Christine.

"Hey, sister, I'm Christine."

"Oh my God, I really do have a sister, come closer let me look at you," my mother said.

"Christine, we need to leave here and go where it's a little safer."

"Follow me back home; you can leave the motor home there, we'll take the subway to see Momma T and Poppa, they'll be so glad," Christine shared.

Granny's stories about my deceased grandfather came to me when I met Momma T and Poppa. Now I understood my mother's Nefertiti-like beauty roots; they were stunning. Mommy T was statuesque and tall towering over Poppa, he did not seem to mind probably enjoyed having a stallion of his own; my great grandmother had the duality of West Indian exoticness with the familiar pretty of a Georgian southern beauty. I'd never seen a city building like the one Mommy T owned before, my father said that it was a Brownstown walkup; nevertheless, it felt like I'd stepped back at time, the architecture right out of 1800s, massive and regal, beauty loud with subtleness, every direction I turned intricate and ornate. Holding Poe's hand, standing behind our mother, the woman (my great grandmother) studied us.

"Helena, precious, I haven't seen you since you were a five-year-old, come here give me a hug!"

"Momma T, you are as I remember when Momma brought me to see you; I feel the same as I did at five, loved. These are my children, Denise and Lee Jr.," my mother said as she released us from her, grip directing us into the arms of our great grandmother.

"Come to me children, Momma needs to feel her family, you must remember me…Come to me my precious ones," Momma T directed. Mommy was right, our visit with Momma T and Poppa Martinez magically became a part of our being, the essence of their existence engrained by mannerisms and sensory memory, and I still can feel her embrace to this day.

What was the subway? I was curious as to its purpose and structure. Entering the subway station discovering the subway was an underground train which ran the length of the city—in this case heading for Harlem. New York's rapid pace and energy lent to its animated non-personal feel. The air smelled like garbage. Hustlers jumped out at you like characters in a children's popup book. A young man of twenty wearing dark glasses begged for spare change, my father gave him a dollar, commenting how sad it was to be a young brother reduced to begging. Just as Daddy finished his statement, I turned to capture his face in my mind again, when I noticed he had removed the glasses and was busy counting the money he had wrangled.

"Daddy, look, that man is not blind," I said in disbelief.

"Baby the brother is lost, he would rather beg than fight; don't ever lose your will to fight."

Christine possessed the Fineste intellect and good looks, her good looks unlike my mother's had to be carefully examined and sorted. Christine's inherited green eyes appeared buried in deep thought. She, like her father, was a doctor. Christine's smile bright and wide, coupled with a bit of uncertainty, "Helena when I was a child I prayed for another sister."

"The nation's capital where the laws which governed and oppressed us were made." Denise

CHAPTER THIRTEEN

COMPLETING THE JOURNEY

"We've got to make it to D.C. by tomorrow evening," my father said while smoking a cigarette and drinking coffee in an attempt to ward off exhaustion. My mother, now keenly aware of fatigue, not wanting a Colorado repeat, when my father refused to stop adhering to his *schedule*, too tired to go an inch further for the night, unknowingly parked next to a waterfall that by four in the morning began to inundate the motor home, completely frightening.

We did reach Washington D.C. the next evening; pulling into a Howard Johnson's hotel it became clear to me this was going to be a different type of experience. This was the nation's capital, a city ironically designed by Benjamin Banneker, a Black man, where the laws which governed and oppressed us were made.

Mommy wanted to visit the Washington and Lincoln monuments before going to the Smithsonian Museum and Capitol Hill. I really did not care to visit the Lincoln and Washington monuments because I did not see them as that important to my future let alone my freedom. Besides, I really did not want to stand in the sweltering heat and humidity of D.C. listening to lies, but we were on vacation, and maybe my obnoxious life as a teenager was beginning to emerge.

Looking around, the Lincoln Memorial sparked an internal duel of ideas; visitor's sorrowful, reflective solitary moments of genuine praise for Lincoln in the formation of America. I was unable to understand why Lincoln and Washington got so much credit for the development of America when Black people gave four hundred years of free labor. Africans (Blacks) were the country's greatness and what about the Indigenous who never were seen as the original inhabitants, their land stolen away as Christopher Columbus laid claim to discovery? Odd, how could he discover America if there was a civilization already in place? Where was the monument to them and to the Africans who built America on their backs? Nowhere.

"Hey, my man, where's the brothers' part of town?" My father called out to a Black man crossing the street.

"Make a left, go about a mile, and you're there; this is Chocolate City."

What we saw was disturbing, forcing me to tell my parents I was ready to leave; the Black portion of the nation's capital was old, dirty with a prevailing aggregate of poor folks, how could this be here? Nothing had really changed since Lincoln and Washington, nothing.

"Mommy, why does D.C. look like this?"

"D.C. doesn't have statehood; the economic base of the city is controlled by the federal government."

Contemplating if the government truly wanted to do right by Black people, then why was the District of Columbia so impoverished? As a kid, I realized that in the not too distant future Black folks would grow weary of the cabal of crazy put upon them.

"Let's go," my father said in disgust.

We were all ready to leave Washington D.C. Making our way back to California, my family seemed to relax and take in the scenery a bit more. Even my father was amenable to a few stops on the road home. "We had a great time; it was beautiful! I really enjoyed this trip. Man, it made me realize that I don't want this big ass house on wheels anymore! Yeah, going to sell and save for a trip to Africa next year," Daddy shared with Mr. Johnson.

Africa? Where did my father get these ideas? Why did he always have to go to the extreme! We knew no one in Africa; I didn't even have one Nigerian pen pal. Why not the West Indies, say Trinidad or Barbados, where we had family?

Bev walked over to greet me, I realized that despite my fun, I had really missed her; she filled me in on all the Claretta Street happenings that had occurred in the last month. Shauna was sent to Oakland for the summer to get away from the Brewer boy, after her mother came home and caught them in her room getting *busy*. Bev said Shauna's mother was going to put her in an all-girls Catholic school. However, even I knew that was not the answer, the girls I knew in Catholic school were faster than public school girls were.

"Bev, do you think she is pregnant?" I asked.

"No her cousin said Brewer always used a rubber," Bev answered.

"What's a rubber?" I asked.

"Keeps a guy from coming in you," Bev answered

"Coming from where?" I confusedly asked.

"Oh Ne! I mean that a guy can't get you pregnant because no sperm gets ejaculated in your vagina; sperm is the fertilizer that makes the woman's egg grow," Bev explained.

"I knew I had to focus on knowing me, an endeavor
I would continue all my life; the quest to know myself."
Denise

CHAPTER FOURTEEN

MY FRIEND PUBERTY AND JUNIOR HIGH

The summer of 1971 came to a rapid close; I would start Maclay Junior High as a seventh grade scrub. Being a scrub was a crappy title to have. Demoted a scrub meant you had to take direction from upper classmen; if they told you to move, you did, if they asked you to buy them lunch, you bought it. It was a time-honored tradition in junior high school to *crumb* on the scrubs, who were rather odd looking at this stage of life, sort of like a picture out of focus because of puberty. During puberty you still had the innocent baby face and voice, still wore preteen dresses and slim pants; puberty made you an oddity in need of time for nature to formulate your ultimate adult physicality. The best thing about junior high was I had Bev! This kept the whole scrub thing down to minimum.

The rest of the Babies on the other hand seemed involved in being major junior high players. Deebie had almost pressed out all of her hair, trying to tease it up high in the back with short-cropped bangs. Deebie's profile looked like it had been ironed and slicked in varnish and scorched to the core. Lulia insisted on elastic waist skirts made by her mother; after she left the house, they were easy to pull up high and expose her racehorse legs. Smitty was a wreck, worried sick, lacking the physical body she desired, looking more like a fourth grader; she felt cheated. Here we were on the first day of school, attempting to be *together*, unable to cut mustard, just spring lambs following Bev, instead of catching up with her (in terms of physical development), Bev just lapped us. In possession of flawless olive brown skin, dyed Auburn perfect hair (a Reilly tradition), tall legs attached to pear-shaped voluptuous hips that swayed gently, swaying in perfect stride all at fourteen; yes we were just spring lambs.

"Denise, baby, wake up, I wanna talk about a few things this morning, before you start junior high; wow Daddy's getting old…I want to tell you how proud I am of you, Ne, your growing up, married your mother when I just nineteen. Baby I want you to have what I and your mother couldn't…keep your head in those books and remember what we've taught you and you'll be alright." My father confessed at four-thirty in the morning.

"Ne, time to get up first day of junior high, oh my God you're a teenager, your outfit is on the bed." My mother now shared.

Did she say my clothes for the first day of school were on the end of my bed? My goodness could I at least pick out my own clothes? White cable knee socks, penny loafers, blue wool skirt and white polo pullover, where did she think I was going? Obviously not the Black school in town. The girls at Maclay wore miniskirts and halter tops, had large Afros, teased hair and make-up. Why did my mother dress me as if I just stepped out of the little girl's section of JC Penney's? I swear my outfit was on page seventy-eight!

Reaching the campus, a sea of brown surrounded us; I had never seen so many grown-looking kids in my life. Some of the ninth grade girls were getting out of their boyfriends' cars, hugged up and all, and here I was in knee socks! Oh well, could be worse, keenly aware I could not hang and was not ready for much else. "Well this is it,

Maclay Junior High, and you're all scrubs!" Bev told us, laughing at all our goofiness.

I realized Smitty, Lulia and Deebie were about to go into stupid mode and I wanted no parts of their drama, walking the exterior hallways made me think about how little I knew about a community I thought I knew everything about. Even if I wanted to, there were just so many kids to get to know.

Joining the mob of kids in the corridor would take a lot of getting used to; choosing not to stop and experiment with my locker combination, I saw several victims just lose it when their lockers would not open. Kids would laugh and point; it was embarrassing.

I met up with the Babies outside of the gym gate as we began our journey home, ice cream trucks in front of the school anticipating the collection of nickels and dimes. Walking home, sucking on Popsicles, listening to stories from Bev and her crew, trying to hear and slurp at the same time, instantly in the mist of the pack I tripped on a rock, falling, my Popsicle now history.

"Are you alright?" A tall bronzed boy asked me. Extremely embarrassed, questioning why this cute non-scrub wanted to help me.

"Yeah, I'm okay, thank you," I said, walking home with my legs scratched and ego bruised.

"What happened to your skirt and socks?" My mother questioned.

"Tripped over a rock and fell."

Daddy arrived home and for the first time in months he was mad, causing me to shake in fear, praying he would not go into monster mode.

"Helena, I'm going to play cards, not eating with you and the kids tonight, put my dinner on the stove."

Once again, my father started the madness; I really did not care if he stayed out all night long, but he hurt my mother with all of his mood swing polarity. No sooner had she begun to feel somewhat better about her future, my father's resurrection of madness resurfaced. Daddy's absences from the family became commonplace.

Saturdays in the Burelford home was a time to catch up on sleep, watch early morning cartoons and do chores. Poe and I loved it; Mommy took our Saturday morning reprieve to let my father have it, sharing with him the continual pain he'd inflicted on her and his kids; she sat motionless, her lips tight, eyes pensive, me and Poe would not leave our mother's side, fearful of what could occur. Sitting like a grandmother at a Greyhound bus station, we sat for hours waiting for my father entrance. We grew tired only to be awoken by the sound of breaking glass.

"Bitch, I told you to stay out of my business, I don't have to answer to you!"

"Lee, I am going to leave your silly ass this time if you don't stop your mess!" My mother yelled, entering her bedroom, quickly locking the door behind her. Daddy stood motionless, caught off guard and embarrassed (for once) that his kids had lost the newly found respect held for him as a caring virtuous father; moreover my father knew his wife meant it this time, it was the feel of her vocal intonation, she was tired of it all.

The rest of the weekend, our home was church mouse quiet. Monday rolled around and my father seemed somewhat remorseful, from that moment on my father stayed home, with my parents spending a great deal of time in the bedroom. January, my mother took ill, I thought she had the flu or God forbid she was getting sick like David. Did she have cancer?

"Mommy, what's wrong with you?" Poe asked.

"Mommy's going to have a baby; you're going to have a new brother or sister soon."

"Lee, it's time to move on with our lives."
Helena

CHAPTER FIFTEEN

FRESH START

My mother was exceptionally quiet at dinner; her pregnancy had not been as easy as she figured. Suddenly my mother grabbed her stomach, screaming in pain, "Lee, I'm bleeding, something's wrong."

Looking on, frozen in disbelief at what had unfolded in front of us, something was wrong with Mommy and the baby; one problem after another for the Burelfords. Recuperating a few days in the hospital after the miscarriage, my mother stared at us, then said, "Lee, it's time to move on with our lives, I want to move to Northridge, we've got the money, let's make this our time to start fresh."

"What about our friends here on Claretta Street, they're our family, Northridge ain't got nothing but Honkies anyway…Why should we put up with them? They do not want us next to them anyway! We have worked hard to get ahead, Helena, I don't believe the White man's water is colder, our neighborhood is just fine!"

"Lee I need a fresh start from all the bad, we'll always have Claretta with us, we carry this street and people in us, inside Lee. They'll never leave us. We can visit, call, but it's our time to move forward. Just us, it is our destiny, this is God's plan for us."

"Okay, Helena, we'll go, you're right it is our time, just fear of the unknown, I need to let go of my bad habits."

Northridge was a predominately-White community where the houses were large, perfect and all seemed right in the world except for us. The home my parents selected for our move seemed massive—five bedrooms and four bathrooms. Both Poe and I were overwhelmed by the girth of this new space we would call home.

True to their word, my grandmothers saved twenty-five thousand dollars (their promise to my mother), combined with my mother's several hundred shares of AT&T stock, which she sold for a tidy sum. Our father continued to operate his part time janitorial business of which every dollar made was saved; he did not pay Poe or me when we worked with him; in fact, we had to beg for a shared Slurpee, while Daddy always purchased a large for himself! During weeks of house hunting, I learned my parents owned three other homes, when they had acquired them remained a mystery but they had them. Sadly, if my father truly loved us undoubtedly, we would have been quite the wealthy bourgeois Negros that Granny spoke of, whatever that meant.

Withdrawing money from San Fernando Valley Savings and Loan turned into a Burelford ordeal once again. Why did everything have so many angles? Just once, I wished we could walk in a straight line, level and smooth. Sitting in the cool square sand-filled chair watching Mommy remove a slip of paper, she huddled close to my father almost as if a clandestine meeting was taking place, whispering to one another, writing ceased as they waited in the line of customers. Daddy nervously held the slip of paper, repeatedly glancing at the clock on the wall ahead, my father turned toward my mother declaring, "Helena get ready; always hard never easy."

"Lee, please don't jinx us, let us get up to the teller first and see what happens, please!" At the teller window my father slid the encrypted slip to bank teller, there was quite a bit of back and forth, my parents handed over their driver's licenses and savings books, more conversation ensued, my parents were instructed to "wait for the manager," my father's voice began to carry inside of the savings and loan.

"Why do we have to wait? Wait for what? You've looked and asked for everything but my children! Listen, I want my damn money… just give me my money!" As the branch manager appeared, he seemed determined to put the show out of the purview of other customers.

"So sorry, Mr. Burelford, we'll have your bank check ready immediately. Is there anything else I can do for you, sir?"

"No, just give me my damn money."

Next leg of our new adventure, the real estate sales office. Walking into the sales office the agent who had shown us the house approached, looking a bit confused as to the nature of our return. "Oh, you're back, did you have more questions—oh I know you left something behind…right?"

"We like to purchase the house we saw early this afternoon," my mother said.

Instead of a smile, he began to frown, "Well that home requires that you close escrow in thirty days, is that something you can do?" Questioned the sales representative.

"Yes… Sir, is there, well, a problem? HUD does have laws in place; it feels as if you do not want us here. Best as I figure it would take at least thirty days to purchase a home in this track, so are you helping to sell us a home or you're trying to discourage us?" My mother asked.

"No…No, I just didn't know you, well, had that type of money," proclaimed the salesperson.

Al Green's "I'm so tired of being alone" played on the radio, my father lit his third cigarette as my mother hummed, making our way north up Van Nuys Boulevard. I turned, studying our journey, focused and linear I could see all the way to the red light at Glenoaks, everything looked and felt of home. As we made our way to Claretta, sunset was apparent, the streetlights seemed to put a gentle yellow glow onto everything. Children playing with a rapid pulse trying to squeeze out every second of the sun's long narrow shadows, signaling the end of the day and the end of our time on this beloved street.

The Burelfords would be the first Claretta street family to depart. Our moving sent ripples throughout the block as its inhabitants looked cautiously at each other, seeking support that this would not upset the Hamlet they called home. The big forest green Bekins moving truck made its way up Claretta Street, while I sat quietly on the front steps harboring a potpourri of emotions; the excitement of this new adventure and the sadness felt with the loss of security and a loved one, but there was no turning back. Seeing the truck's arrival, I went inside, informing my parents our move was under way.

"Ne, you and Poe go check your rooms for unpacked last minute things," my mother demanded.

Sitting on my bed, a montage of images once again surfaced; I saw David running back and forth down the hallway, Poe throwing Chinaberries at Mr. Hackmon and the brutality of my parents' fights. With all of our possessions and memories loading unto the burgeoning rig, Claretta Street convened upon us, the Hackmons (through tears) gave Poe and me a farewell kiss. Mrs. Reilly navigated her way the front of the growing crowd to bid my mother, her "daughter," goodbye, appearing the most moved by it all, concerned about the absence of her presence, keenly aware of my father's demons. Lulia, Deebie and Smitty struggled back and forth with a large dog-eared photo album, "Here, Ne, for you, this was all my idea," Lulia confessed, collectively handing me a going away scrapbook.

"We want you to have this," Smitty said for the group. Once again, my life was changing, and I began to cry.

"Ne Ne, why you crying, we got the weekends for each other, besides you're still going to Maclay," Deebie shared. Laughing through my tears, turning the jagged and worn pages of my past, for sure this was something Lulia's dad found on his route; the scrapbook's inside jacket was signed 'To the best dad in the world, Love Julie.'

"Wow, thanks you guys, let me guess this was your book, Lulia, right? You think of everything!" I said to the Babies.

All that was left was my goodbye to Bev, what was I going to do? There was no one but her, Bev loved me when no one else even knew I was alive; fat, shy or a bookworm, Bev made me feel complete.

"Bev, I'll miss you, you have always been my best friend."

"Ne, it will be fine. Nothing will ever change for us, you gotta believe that in your heart," Bev said pointing to the center of her chest.

"Your heart is not there, move a little to the right," I said laughing. "Smart ass!" Quipped Bev; laughing, she extended her arms to hug me, squeezing me tight.

Daddy sat in his new living room drinking his usual elixir, a Brew 101, and smoking a cigarette, blowing his much-hated smoke rings while inspecting his newly acquired purchase. He had a lot to be proud of, he was a young Black man not quite thirty-six years old with cash, owned property and, above all, had a stunning and intelligent wife that bore him exceptional children, while surviving the death of a child, his vortex of self-inflicted madness, he had risen to the challenge and was still upright. Staring out into the stark evening calm of the turquoise blue water absorbed in the stillness of the pool he mumbled, "Pray I can keep it all together." My father sighed, continuing his blank stare as beams of light danced against the water.

There was no welcoming committee to greet us; a short balding rotund White man with a sunburned head watered his yard, affixed to my father's every move, peering directly at us, absent gestures of hospitality.

"What the hell are you looking at?" Daddy shouted.

The man continued eyeballing my father; it was clear he was not happy with our arrival; his face constricted, he began to voice his disapproval until my father's shirt opened, revealing the gun in his waistband, startling the man breaking his stare. Weeks later, the man's house was for sale.

"That's good because I won't have to shoot his dumb ass when he tries to burn a cross in my yard," my father said.

Sheldon passed me in the corridor, I quickly remembered how he'd helped me off the ground, laying face down, panties exposed, skinned knees, and ego crushed.

"Hey, Denise, how are you?" Sheldon asked.

I stood there looking up at him like an idiot, thinking about my yellow cotton panties he had been privy to, yet realizing I needed to respond.

"I'm fine, Sheldon."

"I heard you moved to Northridge."

"Yeah, we did. But I'm going to stay here and finish junior high," I stuttered, replaying the spill every time I looked at him.

Sheldon exposed his perfect smile, his natural long but shapely and neat, wearing a beige double knit shirt and 501 Levi's perfectly cuffed; and then there was me on the other end of the spectrum with the little girl in knee-high socks thing. What was he smiling at? My hair was still in two braids, just plain-ass ponytails!

"Look, asked Bev about you, she's some friend, wouldn't share anything about you, no phone number, your address nothing! Told me to get it myself."

Sweating and it wasn't even P.E. I asked, "Why do you want my phone number, Sheldon, I'm a scrub?"

"But you're a fine scrub, that's why."

"Sheldon, you don't know my world; I mean my parents, I can never pass out my phone number, I can't have phone calls from boys my father does not know."

"We'll let him know me then! I'll have my brother Larry ask him at the plant. Larry works with your dad at General Motors. We'll see about that phone number."

As the school year ended, Sheldon called, as did my period. Awakened one morning to small traces of blood in my panties, startled, naïve I had wiped myself too hard. Regardless of the knowledge you are taught as a woman, the day a girl begins menstruation still feels out of body, like the surprise party you truly were not expecting. I showered, put on white jeans, then realized I had bled through my jeans; hell my period had come a calling! Why couldn't I have one more year without it? Now I had to tell my mother and have her gush with maternal pride because her only girl was becoming a woman! My walk down the hallway seemed to take forever, my mouth dry and stomach bloated. "Mommy, could you come in my room please, I started my period, need the Kotex now, please…please."

This was the hardest thing I had ever shared with my mother, as expected we revisited the woman lecture about babies, boys and sex, all rather daunting for me.

My father arrived home and I knew Mommy was bursting at the seams to tell him about my new component-ripe ovum. "Lee, Ne started her period today!"

My father lowered his fork and stared at me; it was a blank stare but not frightening, "Denise go upstairs and get dressed, I'm taking you to dinner. I'm going to be the first man to take you out.

"Daddy already laid down the law
when it came to boys and dates... None."
Denise

CHAPTER SIXTEEN

SUMMER OF CHANGE

Having no friends to speak of, the summer of 1972 was really uneventful and boring. That boredom allowed me to become an excellent swimmer, but the downside to improving my aquatic skills was my hair turned clown red from the sun and chlorine.

Sheldon called regularly during this time, allowing us to learn a little about one another. Our discussions lasted for hours (when I was allowed to talk to him). His father died of a heart attack when Sheldon was four, his mother was very sick and unable to care for Sheldon, his older brother and sisters were his guardians. He wanted to be an engineer. Sheldon believed playing basketball was his ticket to college in the form of an athletic scholarship, Sheldon to his credit never pressured me to be his steady.

Back on Claretta Street the Babies spent the summer of '72 practicing French kissing and monkey bites, while I was left to concentrate on losing ten more pounds and passing Algebra II, all not the least bit exciting. Certain the reason why Sheldon never pushed up on me he deemed me a square (as I found out later); square or not I enjoyed Sheldon.

My parents planned a party and barbeque for Lee Jr., inviting all of Claretta Street. The Saturday of Poe's barbeque our house and backyard was full of guests; all ages, shapes and sizes. The swimming pool was so crowded only the tops of bushy heads bobbed on the water; if you tell Black folks' free food and liquor the rest is history, we will come out of the woodwork! Daddy was already uptight at the grill for two days, sick of looking at chicken, links and ribs, my mother suggested in the eleventh hour he pay his brother to finish the barbeque and save himself; Daddy being "Lord Cheapness," refused.

My mother strategized wisely, enlisting the services of Mrs. Reilly and Hackmon. This turned out to be a wonderful decision. My father was, on the other hand, now moderately drunk, having downed more than a few beers and burning up more than few pieces of meat, trying to cope with the excessive valley heat. When Uncle Frank arrived and asked my father to relinquish his duty at the pit, everyone was relieved.

"Work out now; show them what you can do!" My father ordered of me, now drunk in full Soul Train mode. Guests full of barbecue and booze danced, but my lit-up father wanted the entire party to know his daughter was a dance master. Insisting that I put on a dance exhibition for all, not letting me stop until I got the crowd behind me, I hated this dance trip thing. Sheldon was supposed to be coming, he'd think I was a fool trying to finish my dance moves with the Brown Sugar, and there was Sheldon. Why did he have to see this? Here I was finally thirteen, embarrassed like a four year old by my father.

"Wow, Denise, didn't know you could dance that well, where did you learn how to do those moves girl!" Sheldon said.

Dejected and embarrassed, I hung my head, feeling that Sheldon thought I had no real-life *Black folk knowledge*, this hurt my feelings.

"Denise, I'm not trying to make you mad, I just thought you were really good out there dancing with your father." Sunset and the flicker of surviving light hit Sheldon's face, being close to him I noticed above his mouth a very light mustache like a man, which confusedly drew me to his perfect lips.

"Let's try again just to be friends," Sheldon said.

Moving to shake his out stretched hand in a gesture of friendship, but instead he hugged me. I'd never been hugged by a boy other than my family, and after the incident with my cousin from Washington, I feared all men. Sheldon was different; fear did not engulf me, beanpole tall and muscular, he even smelled different in a wonderful sense. My awareness of these differences overwhelmed me and I released him, hoping no one had seen our exchange. Sheldon stuck around the summer, gaining my trust, he saw me whole and not in parts, as boys his age normally did; Sheldon wanted me complete; regardless of age, women seek relationships with men who value them as the sum of all parts.

CHAPTER SEVENTEEN

FRUIT NEVER FALLS FROM THE TREE

My parents were getting along pretty good until the end of November when *he* started the madness again, personally loathing his relapse and the craziness, which came with it. Missing dinner with the family became commonplace for my father; I never figured out what his triggers were to his descent into violence, however what I did know his fall always climaxed with a grand crescendo of craziness. Coming in at four in the morning with the wildest stories I had ever heard in my life, rustling everyone out of bed, turning on all the lights, walking through the hallway forcing us up to hear his mythical creations.

"Helena, Ne, and Poe, I just pulled someone out of a burning house, took me four hours, I had to give a statement to the police and wait for the ambulance, the guy really had bad burns, he was on fire when I pulled him from his house!"

"Wow, Daddy, are you okay? You could have burn your 'fro right off!" I sarcastically said, sick of the madness, praying my mother would leave my father. Okay, if my father pulled a man out of a burning house, why weren't his clothes singed and smoky? Better yet, why hadn't he suffered any burns? This had to be, *"Phony Heroism 101"* rule number one, force everyone to believe you out of fear and intimidation. I was sick of this! This would be my last time opening my eyes in the wee hours of the morning. Poe listened to this madness with glee, wanting to believe my father, yearning for his mentor to be honorable; our mother had little choice for if she did not engage him an argument would surely have ensued. Why did he put us through this masquerade? We would so appreciate our father just telling the truth: I was chasing women and drinking with my dudes—plain and simple.

AAU track and field season for Poe and I began as did our father's indiscretions with Lorie Standard whose daughter Rochelle ran track with my brother. Unbeknownst to me Rochelle knew my father was messing around with her mother, home visits and all. She went to great lengths to make my life miserable, ridiculing me daily, you name it, Rochelle was insistent on inflicting mean kid bullshit. So sick of her taunting I deliberately loosened one of her starting blocks causing her to fall flat on her face.

Not until Mrs. Jones's seventh period music appreciation did I truly understand where Rochelle's animosity came from. The large classroom felt like an arena, rows of chairs in this acoustically soundproof room vectored at the ceiling, packing sixty loud teenagers in one room. Ms. Jones my music teacher was a tall, slender Irish redhead, Gershwin loving aficionado who looked like a cross between Carol Channing and Lucille Ball, played breathtaking piano so well students were never tardy; eagerly awaiting her daily tickle of keys, we loved Mrs. Jones' class. In the midst of explaining Scott Joplin's use of syncopation and his contributions to Ragtime, out of the blue Rochelle shouted from the bottom row of class, "Your father took my mother to Las Vegas." Mrs. Jones, who had forged a relationship with my mother from PTA, rolled her eyes at Rochelle; in anger, biting her bottom lip, Mrs. Jones began playing louder in order to minimize the buzz of disbelief and gossip making its way around the room. Realizing Mrs. Jones wasn't going to stop, chatter subsided. Mrs. Jones struck the keys so hard the walls vibrated, but it didn't matter. I was ashamed and embarrassed, unable to understand why Lorie had to be so ignorant and humiliate me. Mrs. Jones, who frequently expressed enamorment of my mother, angrily stared at Rochelle, played louder, striking the keys with rage; the buzz of gossip and disbelief making its way around the room neutralized.

It wasn't me bragging or flaunting about anything! Why did the Willie Lynch thing, which Nana spoke of, have to be so destructive? My father said the story was made up but Nana said she'd seen White people put it into practice, made me believe my great grandmother. Nana said there were lots of White Willie Lynch's that traveled through the Deep South, indoctrinating other Whites how to keep the "Niggas in order."

My body went into shock from both shame and humiliation. My heart raced, my eyes began to water, and tears ran down my cheeks. What was I to do? I didn't have the strength to run out of the room, my legs felt like rubber and my head was spinning, only five more minutes of class remained. I could leave, pull myself together before my mother picked me up, and she was never on time; my mother had begun to sell real state and was out in the field inspecting homes. As a realtist she made it her mission to highlight that she was a realtist and White agents were realtors. Mommy with pride hung on to the realtist title. I needed to dry my eyes, compose myself and once again hold another eternal secret. No, I would not be the cause of my mother losing this child, there was no doubt what Rochelle said was true: my father was in Las Vegas, he'd driven our brand new 1973 Monte Carlo...hold the pain in, keep it together.

"Denise, are you okay?" she asked.

Mrs. Jones' eyes welled up with tears, I could not cry, I was a Burelford, this was a minuscule horror, I had to suck it up get on with it. "Yes, Mrs. Jones, I'm okay."

Walking the corridors, I felt detached from my body. I heard nothing, saw no faces, what just occurred in my teenage world?

As my luck would have all things negative, the convergence of crazy collided at once, and this was one of the rare days my mother was on time, motioning for me to make way to the car; walking in denial mode, I had to play this off.

"Hey Ne! What's wrong…you look like something is wrong?"

"Nothing, I'm just tired and have a headache."

Mommy went into *nurturing* mode, feeling my forehead. "No fever, must be your sinuses again, want you to get some rest when you get home." Making my way straight to my bedroom, pulling off my pierced armor, crawling under my blanket, I knew I could not forget what had occurred; maybe through sleep I could remove the countless eyes that were staring at me.

My mother returned several times to check in on me, worried that I was coming down with a cold, she gave me the new big thing, *Tylenol*. Her conversation became louder and more disgruntled in the adjoining family room; I wondered what was the cause of her unhappiness but was stuck in the gloom of the afternoon and stayed buried under my sheet and blanket.

"What Yvonne, Lee took that Standard whore where?" My mother questioned.

Oh no! I had forgotten she was in the class, I should have caught her outside the room and told her not to tell, I was just shell-shocked, unable to think clearly, now my mother was mad as hell.

"I'm carrying this fool's child and he's off in Vegas with that ignorant piece of crap…. The last straw, I must leave him."

My mother was very angry, telling Granny if my father hit her again she would kill him; I prayed my father would not die tonight upon his return home, for I saw blood in her eyes, my father's blood. Mommy came into my bedroom, I pretended to be asleep, knowing what was about to be unleashed.

"Ne, I heard what happened at school today, guess that's why you're so quiet isn't it?"

I did not want to talk about this, I felt so bad for my mother, such a loving person undeserving of my father's disrespect.

"Mommy, I couldn't tell you because I didn't want to hurt you, it was so horrible."

My mother held me in her arms, "Baby, it's not your fault, I'm not mad at you, I'm sorry. I wish I could take the pain away but I can't."

Friday evening as we watched *Good Times* on television with Poe, laughing at James and Flo trying desperately to escape the complication of being Black in America (aka getting out of the ghetto), I realized we had not escaped either. Exiting the ghetto did not mean all the crap that went with it did not follow you, unable to understand why Daddy, who had everything for a Black man (or any man for that matter), treated his family with such disdain. Poe drifted asleep, though exhausted from the day I dare not sleep out of fear what might happen when my father came home.

The front door opened, my heart began to pound, my father entered the kitchen, which sat off the family room; my mother stood staring at him, her stare cold and piercing.

"Lee you took that Standard slut to Vegas didn't you? Here I am carrying your child, and you're out with her! What is it, Lee…I don't kiss your behind enough?"

My father's enlarged eyes appeared to bulge out of their sockets, aware how his rage could manifest when caught in a lie, cognizant of the beating he was capable of, I shouted "Mommy, please!" It was too late.

"Bitch, I can do what I want to do." Grabbing a coffee mug off the table my father hurled it at my mother's head, hitting her lower jaw. Blood ran down my mother's face, she began gagging; rushing to help wrapping a dishtowel around my hand, holding it to my mother's face.

Blood spewed from my mother's face, only able to make a gurgling sound she could not speak. Poe and I rolling her on her side, holding her head in my arms, while Poe hysterically dialed Granny, his little fingers paralyzed with fear, he cried, forcing him to dial the correct digits, "Granny, Granny come now!"

"Oh my God, Ne, Daddy didn't mean to hurt your mother, Oh Lord what have I done!" My father whimpered, carrying my mother to his car and speeding away.

My grandparents frantically searched area hospitals for my mother, Granny running into Granada Hills Hospital's emergency room. Reaching the triage, Granny let loose.

"You no good son of a crazy bitch, I'm going to kill you if you don't leave my daughter and these kids right now you no good coward, why isn't this man being arrested? He beat my pregnant daughter, almost killed her!" Granny protested to the nursing staff. My father backed out of the treatment room, "Get your cowardly ass out of here, God I wish you dead!"

"Helena Burelford your daughter?" One of the physicians asked my grandmother.

"Yes." The doctor informed Granny my mother's jaw been shattered and she required emergency surgery. Granny knew my mother's life was at jeopardy when she inquired about my unborn sibling.

"Will this affect the baby?"

"We hope not, I am bringing in a specialist to perform the surgery. Her jaw will be wired for a few months so it can heal; there will be a slight scar, but cosmetic surgery can fix that."

We sat in the surgery waiting room for hours, my father's whereabouts unknown; after four hours the surgeon reappeared tired and angry.

"Your daughter has come through the surgery very well; she won't be able to eat solid food. This will be a big problem with her being pregnant. We're going to give her protein and nutrition supplements that can be made into milk shakes until the wires are out…I will need to show you how to use pliers to keep her from choking, she was very lucky."

Anger flashed onto the doctor's face. "Tell her to leave that garbage alone if she wants to live. Never seen anything like it—what's wrong with him?"

"Had I not been born, this—*it* would never happen to my mother."
Denise

CHAPTER EIGHTEEN

Granny wanted my father at the very least arrested; ask Granny what she really desired, she shared with a friend my father needed to die. My grandmother retained a lawyer to start divorce proceedings against my father; Granny did not hold her feelings back about my father, he was public enemy number one.

I had not known that my mother married my father at seventeen a year before planned because she was pregnant—with me. Granny in her rage blurted this fact out immediately I felt responsible for my mother's pain; if I'd hadn't been born, my mother would not have had her jaw broken or buried a child.

"Denise, your mother never told you any of this, oh baby your loud-mouth grandmother is so sorry, Granny would never hurt you baby. This is not your fault, baby, you remember that. Your mother loves you more than she loves herself, a tall order for a Burelford my love."

Was this admission by my grandmother intended to inspire me? The fact was my mother married my crazy father because she was pregnant—with me, I hadn't brought happiness only pain; without me, my mother's dewy fresh beauty would joyously leaped out at the world, and most importantly she would have been free and happy. My mother would have captivated the world with her assurance, instead of being a woman now devoid of confidence, harboring a blackened and bruised soul. "This was your fault," I told myself. How could I return my mother's self-esteem, make her see that she was still the breathtaking and intelligent woman people loved to watch and listen to for hours? I was a child powerless to change the state of her existence, created in the nebulae of chaos, cursed.

Granny vacillated between having my father arrested or killed by the Stewardts. The Stewardts, a family my grandmother known forever, were Pacoima's true gangster family. Whatever was illegal, they were into, book making, hot or stolen goods, car theft, robbery, even "*offing*" someone, the Stewardts had their hand in it.

Back in the fifties, the matriarch Old Lady Stewardt borrowed money from my grandmother to buy a home. Two years later, Old Lady Stewardt came to repay the money as agreed on, Granny refused to take the money, "Florence you still broke and alone with those kids; money no good if it doesn't help one another." For the two women loyalty became their bond. Granny believed if she accepted the money, she would have severed their bond, as money could not buy friendship and loyalty. Granny and Old Lady Stewardt remained close allies through the years; Old lady Stewardt and her family viewed Granny as family, both protecting and respecting her. This made me so mad about the way my father treated my mother; it would have only taken a word to the Stewardts by Granny, and my father would have at the least been beaten to a pulp; my mother never told my grandmother all of the things my father did. It was January 1974, Poe and I both were pretty disconnected from all that we had known as normal in our lives. We had lost our brother to cancer, home to fire, and now our father had almost killed our mother and unborn child. Though young, I was aware that my life would never be the same again, having completed the remnants of a fairy tale now living in the reality so many others were owner to. The day of my mother's discharge from the hospital, concerned about the whereabouts of my father, I worried he would try to finish the job and kill us. Getting dressed, flashbacks of weekend family drives with my father at the helm up the coast, driving so fast the car shimmied, vibrating as though with just one more increment of speed the car would pull apart. On the other hand, the countless times the family tooled around the Valley forbidden from putting the windows down as he chained smoked, feeling as I would pass out, shaking, quietly gasping for air. Now suffering from chronic bronchitis, my lungs damaged by my silence as not to upset my father. Praying silence would keep the driver from wrapping us around a highway light post at one hundred miles an hour, changing lanes, cutting off other drivers. We were just like the men who'd come back from Vietnam—shell shocked.

"Ne Ne, hurry up!" Granny screamed to me from downstairs. Closing my eyes tight pushing this twisted memory out of my head, as not to jinx the day.

"I don't care if she wants to give him the house! Let his Black ass have it, that nigga! I'll get her another one, her life means everything to me. Samuel, you got me all worked up now the kids have heard me!"

"Me, woman? You upset with everything!" Samuel said.

"That Burelford family never been right, helped them get that house his crazy mother lived in on Borden, them people is nothing but users and fools. Helena should have never married him! I knew they were crazy when I saw the chain and lock on the refrigerator in the bedroom. Samuel, I blame myself; if I would have been present, been a parent to Helena and drank less, she wouldn't even looked his direction!"

As we made our way into the hospital lobby, we saw a shadowy outline of a well-dressed Black man wearing a navy blue suit—it was my father. "What the hell is this son of a bitch doing here?" Granny's short legs began making her way towards my father, mad beyond words. "Lee, stay the hell from my daughter, how dare you show up here; Lord he done showed up at the hospital!" Granny said, shouting at the top of her lungs, prompting everyone to look at the drama unfolding before them. Poe and I stood staring coldly at our father in disbelief.

"Look, I don't want any trouble, just came to take Helena home where she can be comfortable," my father said.

"Be comfortable, what the hell are you talking about…. When did you ever care about my daughter, you fool!" Granny shouted. My father seemed only slightly embarrassed by the mayhem created; the only indication of his overt failure his bowed head and lack of eye contact.

"Arranged for a nurse and housekeeper to be at the house to care for Helena; I moved out, she and the kids need their home."

"Oh, so you think I give a good hot damn because you moved out? Lee, if it takes the rest of my life to see it, Helena is going to divorce you. You were an ugly wicked soul when my daughter married you and you're even uglier now. If my daughter wants to go home that's up to her, but you better keep your ass away from her forever if your plans ever include putting your hands on my daughter!" Granny proclaimed.

Pin drop silence, onlookers in disbelief on what they'd witnessed. White folks, unaccustomed to raw anger in Blacks took cover; maybe when enraged they feared retribution from the horrific deeds of their ancestors would trigger mass rage. When my grandfather was nervous, his English became so intertwined with Tagalog he might as well have spoken in his native tongue; everything was fast and fluid, you couldn't understand him, but there was one thing he did say very clearly to my father, "Stay away from Helena! Stay your distance, Lee, leave her and the kids alone; you had chances and blew it!"

My father stood at the elevator door just holding it, scared to move forward or backward. In that moment I realized my father was a bully; finally someone called him on it and he was a mouse; what a coward he turned out to be. The vision haunted me of my father breaking my mother's jaw day and night; I couldn't shake it, when eating dinner, walking or reading a book, flashbacks of blood spewing from my mothers' face, the choking, my reflective witness to her fear and pain. Hell yes, my father had gotten off easy.

My mother sat on the edge of her bed staring out, looking at the Santa Susana Mountains; she did not resemble our mother more a young girl taking her first plane trip alone, scared and longing for the security of home.

"Come on baby, your Momma going to take you home, taking the week off to be with you," Granny said. Mommy whimpered, unable to speak due to her mouth wired shut, broke my grandmother's heart, she perched her lips, swallowing hard, trying to hide her pain.

> "Amazing how God allows you to endure so much,
> yet provides enough joy and grace to make life bearable."
> Denise

CHAPTER NINETEEN

STRENGTH

January 1973 was cold, the dry morning air caused a shiver; luckily, the wait at the bus stop was not terribly long, our bus driver most mornings, Mr. King, fellow Pacoimian, always looked out for Poe and I.

Sheldon called often, but I was in no mood to share with him, sure people on Claretta knew something happened to my mother, but they assumed it was my father's usual crap and no further questions asked. Even Bev was out of the loop; shame and guilt contained me, unable to release the words needed to tell the story, regardless of the cruel vividness logged in my mind.

Granny explained to the nurse and housekeeper all of my mother's needs and, going over the preparation of puree blender meals, what to do if my mother choked, the removal of the wires to open her mouth in an emergency (Poe and I already knew what to do). Despite the madness, my parents pushed self-sufficiency—just in case they were not around to care for us.

"What do you mean you're not divorcing Lee? Helena, are you crazy?" Granny railed. "Helena, write what you trying to say, I can't understand you," Granny said.

My mother wrote something down which made Granny turn red. I thought she would have a stroke. "What do you mean, he's in counseling? That fool could have killed you! Don't take him back… please baby, I'm trying not curse on a Sunday!"

"Okay girl, you take the fool back, but the first time I find out Lee's hurt you or my grandkids, I'm going to kill him," my grandmother said, crying through her words in a voice filled with conviction. "Helena, I can't make up for the years I was drinking and not there for you, but know I went to work seven days a week so you could have all that life had to offer. Momma has always loved you, baby."

My mother could not speak but her eyes conveyed the need to hear these words from her mother, their embrace one that should have happened long ago.

As March concluded wires in Mommy's mouth were removed. Our mother had triumphed over the latest adversity with a two-inch wide scar on the bottom left corner of her mandible. Her eternal fluidity of beauty made finite; still beautiful but it was different; like tree rings which provide a record of seasons, the scar on my mother's face a record of a horrific time. Granny insisted on plastic surgery as soon as the baby was born to remove my father's tree ring of madness.

"Oh wow, my water broke!" My mother said to Poe; he immediately telephoned Granny and retreated to his bedroom, the many years of madness had damaged Poe, causing him to huddle into the shadows, unable to handle change or conflict. Each argument, fight or disturbance witnessed, Poe became invisible; Granny provided comfort for Poe, as he was able to channel the burden to her.

Once again, the creator graced us with joy in the face of all the sadness; amazing how God allows you to endure so much horror yet provides enough grace to make life bearable. My parents brought the baby home without a name, contemplating dozens of names from Hasani to Wallace, deciding on the name Matthew, one of Jesus' twelve disciples.

The Vietnam War raged on; it was no secret America was losing. Mr. Unger, my history teacher, said the U.S. military was not up to fighting such a war, that the United States of America didn't know how to fight a jungle war. All one had to do was watch the evening news footage, Walter Cronkite made the comment the United States should get out of Vietnam because we could not win. Cronkite was right, just like the college kids shot down in Ohio at Kent State.

My father said President Nixon would not stop the war because he was politically on the line with his own problems. Watergate began to dominate the news, Nixon was in crisis; his staff tape-recorded the Democrats' office at the Watergate hotel, Nixon could be impeached and stripped of his presidency.

The Babies began to change as well; all preoccupied with falling in love, what happened to our dreams? Deebie's party arrived, she'd invited all the right people to attend, and it was a certainty the party was going to be good.

Standing in my bedroom doorway, my mother said to me, "Ne, I know Sheldon is going to be at that little party, so you make sure you do right now, don't let him think you're weak," my mother said.

"Yes, Mommy," I said. Eagerly dressing to leave the house, my mother shocked me; she took my hair out of ponytails. I was wearing my hair down, my father looked shocked; what was wrong now?

"Ne, you look beautiful; your hair is so long, Helena, let her wear her hair down more," my father said, again throwing me for a loop.

"Alright, you make them boys behave, remember who you are, be outside by ten." Inside Deebie's den the lights were out, the glow of black-lights providing the only illumination. I looked to see if there were any familiar people; Smitty and Lulia had not arrived; I was alone with Deebie, all bets were off; I needed to get ready for crazy

125

to jump off, but this time I looked forward to her off the wall antics. "Ne—dang, I didn't know that was you! What's happening?" Deebie shouted, making her way over to me, amped up ready to go. This was old hat for Deebie; I had no clue about the party scene, Deebie, enlisting blackmail, forced her older sister on several occasions to take her to high school parties; she was a pro at the party scene.

"Hey, girl, Sheldon is here," Deebie said, so giddy it made me laugh.

"Where, I can't see anything in here," I said to Deebie, but before I could turn to search for Sheldon, he walked towards me, possessing a sparkling smile.

"Hello Denise."

Wearing cuffed and starched 501 jeans with that beige double knit shirt and three-quarter length black leather jacket, Sheldon seemed taller; he looked especially nice this evening. Reciprocally wide grin, I stayed in the corner the majority of the evening, wallflowering it, just watching all the drama playing out in front of me, fantasizing what a dance with Sheldon might be like. "Ne dance with me, common on please."

1974, Nixon resigned, Vice President Ford became President of the United States; immediately Ford began mopping up Vietnam, passively pulling out American interests in droves, causing mass chaos and destruction. Soldiers returning from Vietnam dropped back into society, scurrying about lost, what happened to America's promise for them?

Bev and Sheldon graduated from the ninth grade. On Claretta Street, Deebie and John began smoking weed, soon Lulia followed; times once again were changing and not necessarily for the best.

Shauna, as expected, was pregnant, as all knew she would be regardless if he attended Catholic school; her parents shipped her off to Oakland to have the baby; when the baby was born, Shauna stayed in Oakland while her mother raised her son. Oakland was a place of immense Black Pride; the Black Panthers called Oakland home. Shauna's mind exploded in self-discovery; she joined the Panther's youth program and never looked back. Shauna traveled with Huey Newton across California; Shauna was now a devout Black Panther. A few years later, Shauna lost her life in Los Angeles in an LAPD raid of the Symbionese Liberation kidnapping of Patti Hearst; the police burned down an entire block to the ground. I always wondered about Patti Hearst, seemed like (to me) *she found her* way into the movement. Shauna secretly mailed letters to Bev who shared them with us, the letters were always disguised and loaded with information. Bev never (nor any of the Babies) told a soul about the letters; after Shauna's death Bev burned all the letters but shared the contents with her parents (as we all did). During this time we did not believe (for a second) Shauna was an outlier or alone; one can only surmise that there were countless young people who sacrificed everything for our people. Joanne Reilly read to us "The Spook Who Sat By The Door;" all of the Babies sat motionless as though we were back in kindergarten on those small brown mats, attentive and engaged. My father's stint at Islam and Black Nationalism in a way prepared me for bad things that might victimize me, like the protests against police brutality at Hansen Dam and the arrests that followed. My father feared he might lose his job so he never went, though he always bailed out people who did go.

CHAPTER-TWENTY

BEGINNING OF A METAMORPHOSIS

My mother assured me she would allow me to wear a natural, at least for the summer. Styling my hair in "fro" was a good way for me to enjoy the summer and not have to worry about my hair. The best part of wearing a natural were my trips to Magnificent Brothers in Los Angeles on famous Crenshaw Boulevard; the *Shaw* was a happening place for Black people. Granny traveled to Los Angeles in full dress and white gloves; in addition to Oakland and San Francisco, Los Angeles was the hub of the African American experience on the West Coast.

Santa Barbara Boulevard (which would be renamed King Boulevard, as did every American Black intersection in major cities) vibrated with art, energy, beauty and wealth. The eastside had Central Avenue; Granny talked about the music, the gala of Central Avenue; from Ellington, Sarah Vaughn, Dinah Washington everyone came to Central Avenue for the West Coast Jazz sound. Granny's scotch and milk stories were deliciously paced and intoxicating for us. Everyone made their way over to the Black part of town to partake;

Central Avenue was Los Angeles's own version of the Cotton Club. Nevertheless, Crenshaw was a happening place for Black people; all the businesses were owned by Blacks, the people were Black and everyone looked good; stylish clothes were commonplace and it was immediately apparent that I was more than a little out of the fashion loop.

This trip, I would get the works, my hair cut, shaped and blown out, I kept imagining looking like Angela Davis or Huey Newton's wife Katherine or my all time favorite, Cleopatra Jones (on that one I was tripping because everybody knew her fro was a wig; I saw it at the wig shop).

Deebie ran away from home with some dude she met at Maverick's Flat Soul Train after party she went to with her sister. "I think the boy running over her really messed her up, girl," Lulia said for the thousandth time.

"My sister told me Deebie held some dirt on her sister Jackie and was hanging out in Hollywood at the Soul Train tapings, you know her sister was Johnny Conti's partner, you know the fine Puerto Rican Black dude who lives in the Terrace," Smitty said.

"Deebie hanging with that crew, you know John Oliver, Jay Kenney all those Pop Locking guys that dance with what's her name… Toni Basil, Deebie's out there, when she gets tired she will be back," I said to the group.

"My sister told me, that they don't even get paid on Soul Train, eat Kentucky Fried Chicken and no brand sodas for ten hours; and remember the Homers who lived on the corner house?" Smitty asked.

"Yeah, how did they fit into this?" I asked.

"Well, they moved to Thousand Oaks or someplace like that, their father was elected mayor. Remember their older sister who always had Nancy Drew books stuck to her face? She went on to become the publisher of *Right On* magazine. Her and Deebie's sister stayed tight, that's how they got the connection to the action, heard they hang out and some bad after parties!" Smitty shared.

Deebie returned home the end of September, Smitty was so angry she spontaneously expressed what an idiot she was.

Tuesday at Mommy's Bible study it was shared that the Garden of Eden was located in Africa; raising my hand, I asked, "If the Garden of Eden was in Africa, why do Adam and Eve look White in the drawing?" Brother Williams seemed miffed, answered, "It does not matter what color they are, the word of God and his son Jesus Christ is not based on his color."

After a couple of responses like that, I stopped asking questions for which I could not get an appropriate answer. Why not see the significance of Jesus, Simon, David and Solomon as what they were—Africans? The unrelenting pride generated by a large segment of the globe; Africans were directly linked to divinity and knew so little about their role in it.

"I'd been taken on a roller coaster ride without a safety bar,
the rules of momentum playing out in my soul."
Denise

CHAPTER TWENTY-ONE

JOSEPH

Not wanting to start school in the fall unfamiliar with what high school was like, opting to attend summer school at Pacoima's storied San Fernando High School. Now that I was in school with *adults,* I had to grow up become organized. Some students took care of themselves, working at Lockheed or Certified Grocers with union (Teamsters) cards like my father. Some had families of their own, baby strollers stacked parallel to classrooms and wedding rings; no high school was not a playground.

San Fernando High School was one of the oldest high schools in Los Angeles. San Fernando, a largely Latino community, possessed a relationship of conciliation between African Americans and Latinos, each experiencing oppression by Whites, Black ancestors of Africa through the slave trade and American Jim Crow; Latinos via the intersection of European exploration and religion.

Studying the course outline, trying to decide what classes to take for the summer session, suddenly I was knocked on my back by an unknown force; looking up at the sky was a tall, sweaty figure peering down at me.

"Oh wow, I'm so sorry, I didn't see you. I was late to Hell Week practice, I mean football practice, I'm so sorry," the towering figure said to me.

Sweat dripped off his suntanned caramel skin, the unknown giant's moustache was thick and real, his enormous Afro uncombed yet perfect. Best of all, his teeth were snow white and straight. The Goliath figure kneeled down, scooping me up like a fallen bath towel, quick and easy; I felt like a toddler staring into his deep brown eyes. I was mesmerized!

"Are you okay?" I realized I had not uttered a vowel or consonant sound and the Jack-in-the-Beanstalk giant probably thought I was injured.

"Yes I'm alright," I said, brushing myself off. Looking up towards his face he blocked the light of summer; this prince had to been six feet four or five.

"I'm so sorry," he repeated as his teammates laughed at the unfolding scene.

"I'm alright, thank you, no I'm truly not hurt, please, have to go!" I said to the giant, annoyed. Hurriedly walking away, embarrassed by why things always seemed to happen to me, I felt a hand touch me on my right shoulder.

"What's your name?"

Perspiration beads dripped off his massive chest and arms, insisting I stare at every ripple of toned flesh…damn, must say something!

"Denise Burelford." Two words, that's all I could gather my thoughts to say.

He stared at me and as if I were in slow motion, a voice said to me, "My name is Joseph Williams." His mouth seemed to call me out, inviting me into his personal physical space; I had never experienced such a powerful force. "Wait a minute, where can I call you?" Joseph said, taking one long step to my three tiny choppy steps. I stopped in my tracks but did not turn around, petrified with fear that I had no real street credibility.

"Hey, why can't I have your number, are you mad because I knocked you down? I said sorry like a hundred times, what more do you want me to do…I'll do it!"

I turned to face Joseph the Giant, a warm slight smile erupted on my face, "Here's my number, please don't call after eight."

A magical way to start high school, what was I to make of this? It was probably another Sheldon thing; this giant of a man probably had a ton of girlfriends. Standing in line to register I focused on the events that had just occurred, my heart racing as though riding the roller coaster without the safety bar, the rules of momentum playing out in my soul.

Mommy instructed me to greet both my counselor and college advisor. Mrs. Jones, my counselor, seemed very old and unconcerned about my academic future, looking a few years shy of a hard sixty-something. Discouraged I walked over to the next office in the main hall and met the woman who would expand my academic horizons, Mrs. Goodman my college advisor, a tall thick middle-age graying woman who professed Yiddish wisdom with the most fascinating metaphors.

Telephoning Bev that evening, sharing with her the excitement of meeting Joseph, she was elated; I had no clue that this giant figure was on the social landscape.

"Wait! Joseph Williams knocked you down and asked for your number? Ne…girl, what did you do next? You have all the luck!" Bev said.

"Yeah, Bev, he did."

Bev let out a loud yelp; I wondered why she was so emotional he was just a dude. "Ne, Joseph is fine! You gave him the number, right?"

"Of course I did, I'm not that square!"

"Well, now let's see what happens with this one. Ne, I'll bet you will end up going with him," Bev said.

"Don't know about that, but I do know one thing, I've got to get a job; my mother said I can't drive without insurance, Bev."

"Ne, I'll get you a job with me at Bob's Big Boy as a hostess, just get that learner's permit so we have a hoopty to get around in," Bev insisted.

The start of school I had forgotten about Joseph, truly looking forward to seeing Sheldon; regardless of my Plain Jane status we continued to talk throughout the summer. Making my way across campus scanning for Sheldon, someone tapped me on my shoulder from behind.

"Denise, how have you been? I tried to call but lost your number, your boy Sheldon wouldn't give me your number, so I figured I'd see you when school started for the fall," Joseph said.

"Sheldon wouldn't give it to you? Why didn't *you* look for *me* at summer school?" I questioned.

Joseph's laughter rattled with shame. He smiled and said, "Okay I'm lying, but I really want your number and I really like to call you tonight. Can I get you lunch?" Joseph asked.

Why did he want to buy me lunch when he had girls waiting behind and in front of us? I'd be a fool not to accept the offer. "Sure, where should I meet you at?"

"I'll come pick you up after fourth period."

Dang, I was going to have lunch with Mr. Fine; no one ever invited me to lunch and now I was having lunch with the dude that made my heart pound double time.

"So, where do you want to eat lunch? In the cafeteria or canteen?" Joseph asked.

"I don't care, you pick the spot," I sheepishly responded.

My nervousness intensified, surveying the lawn as couples embraced in long passionate tongue, deep wet kisses; this dude only invited me to lunch because he saw me as a dumb little kid who didn't know any better, believing he could get some really easy. Returning with round plates stacked with sliced white bread and turkey I went said, "Look, you think just because I'm younger than you and seem like a square I don't know the biz, you got me wrong, Jo!"

Hurt more than anger tempered my voice, Joseph looked dazed then laughed; everything seemed funny to him.

"What's so funny? Why are you always giving me that goofy 'she's a rookie' smirk?" I angrily asked.

Joseph's facial euphoria changed, sadness proliferated, "I don't know what I'm trying to say, all I know since I, well, knocked you down, you're all that I've thought about. Tried to get your boy Sheldon to give me your number so many different ways we ended up in a dust up. Even drove around this summer looking for you, yeah I was desperate… Just give me a chance."

What was I to do? Joseph was talking as though he was desperate, voice holding back sorrow, eyes glassy on the verge of tears; even my father wasn't this convincing. Yet all I could think about was my crazy-ass father, the master at making me fearful. Why should Joseph spend time on a date-prohibited tenth grader who had to have preapproved authorization just to telephone; nope not in the cards for me—again! "Don't bother, Joseph, I'll only end up being embarrassed and you'll end up making me the butt of all your square biz jokes, let's just leave this right here," I said dejectedly, unable to handle him and the heavy-duty lines he was trying to throw my way. Needing to be free of anyone really reaching out to capture my heart; I'd experienced far too much pain in my young life only to have my heart broken by a stranger. What right did he have to me? "No, Joseph, not this time, I am enjoying what my life is right now, I have a car, I can play my own eight tracks and sort of control me, first time of it, let me be. You, you have yourself, let me catch up."

"Denise, give me a chance, just because you see all those chicks around me doesn't mean I'm chasing them, it takes all my time just to keep my grades up and take care of myself. My mom died a few years ago and I live with my grandmother." Having no idea that his life had as many twists and turns as my own life, a shift in perception opened my eyes, reconfiguring good looks with good intentions and virtue of soul. Maybe a phone call from him and the impending upheaval from my father might be worth it—maybe. Leaving school, I ran into Bev, who noticed the far off stare of contemplation other than the events of the first day in my eyes.

"Ne, girl, what are you stuck on? Did you like the first day of San Fer?" Bev asked.

"Yeah, school was fun...I had lunch with Joseph, totally unexpected!"

"Girl, go get him on the first day!"

"Bev, got to catch the Mission Hills bus, got to go, I call you later." Poe would be on the three-thirty Mission Hills bus looking for me; unable to afford a mishap, as I crossed Truman, hurrying to the bus stop, a mob of students awaited me. As the bus doors opened the crowd pushed onto the bus, the bus driver yelled, "Move to the back," the door of the RTD closed, speeding off without me.

Damn! What would I do now? Poe would worry something happened and probably get off the bus looking for me. Even if I called my mother at Benny Slayton Realty, she had no idea the route of the bus; I had to fix this myself. As I crossed the street I heard a horn honking seemingly in my direction; the "Don't Walk" signal-flashing caution red, I presumed the person honking was trying to inform me of this.

"Denise, where you going?" Joseph shouted out of his driver's side window. Standing on the sidewalk in a dilemma caused by a missed bus, not allowed rides with people my parents did not know. Peaches White died when I was nine, riding in a car with a dude drag racing on Glenoaks and Arroyo. She was just eighteen at the time; Peaches was decapitated, forcing the rescuers to cut her out of the car. Pacoima parents never got over it, just like the Richie Valens thing when he was killed in a plane crash. The dude Peaches was with had been drinking Thunderbird, and Riche Valens' pilot was to blame; this was my weak-ass reasoning; I needed a ride, praying to Jehovah and Allah to keep me safe. It was only a distance of three miles, I'd keep my fingers and toes crossed.

"Can you take me to Sepulveda and Roscoe?" I asked, realizing I had just entered new stage in my life, somewhere between smelling myself and behaving illogically, I had no clue about the next move. Joseph stopped the car, jumped out of his steel blue fin-tailed 72' Chevy Impala coupe (Joseph and my father drove Impalas). Running to open the passenger door, the rear seat was just as big as that shiny red Impala at five; I thought about my parents cautioning me, and reasoned Joseph was not a stranger in the literal sense; something strange and wonderful in me wanted to be with him.

"Denise, what really happened out there? I saw you go to the bus stop a couple of minutes before the crowd got there; you got pushed to the back, uh?" Joseph said, once again laughing.

Why did I always end up being on the embarrassing end of the story? Joseph had already figured out that I was not use to dealing with hustling for bus space, I was faced with coming clean with the truth. "They really push to get on the bus, that's all."

Laughing at me, now capitalizing on my greenness, Joseph said, "You got pushed to the back of the bus because you forgot how to represent like you were from Pacoima! If you miss the bus in the future because moving to Northridge has made you soft, please let me know, I'll give you a ride. You just looked so confused watching the bus leave!" he chuckled.

As the light turned green and Joseph blasted the Isley Brothers' "Fight The Power," he was silent; nearing my stop there was a rapid burst of questions from him, as though an interrogation.

"Hold up! Do you want answers or not? You'll get to know me, it will take time."

"So are you going to give me that much time to do so?" Joseph asked.

"Thanks for the ride, hope you give me a call tonight," I said to Joseph while he held the car door open for my departure. What else was I to do? My knowledge of small talk was equivalent to that of a toddler, just babble.

"I felt a sense of safety and security in his arms."
Denise

CHAPTER TWENTY-TWO

FINDING LOVE

Between school, work and responsibilities at home, I really didn't notice much else; only intending to work a couple of months yet enjoying my own money, I continued working. By seven each night, Joseph called discussing life (as we knew it), our dreams and each other. Joseph was always waiting in the student parking lot to give me a lift, rescuing me from the throng of students who rode the bus; chivalrously opening the passenger car door, he would say with wide full grin, "You look better at the end of the day than the beginning of the day, wow!"

"Why do you always say that?" I joyfully asked, laughing yet puzzled by his daily routine and why his smile still glistened. Today though was a little different, our nervous laughter ceased, Joseph pulled me towards him and kissed me, his lips soft, wide and engaging. My heart raced, his touch causing a quiver without me knowing why or how. Everything my parents and Bev told me pertaining to men left me being cajoled in Joseph's muscular embrace.

"Joseph, I've got to go…you'll be late for practice, let's go." Face to face with something Joseph knew about and I nothing—desire, in a flash pulling away, startled by this strange new force.

The Dramatics' "Toast to the Fool" played on the radio. Joseph laughed and said, "Sheldon never should have let you out of his sight." Stopping the car, Joseph held me in his arms.

"Here comes the bus, my brother will see you and my parents don't know you…I've got to go," I said, quickly opening the car door.

Joseph screamed, "I'll call you tonight."

My brother always busted me; I could never get away with anything! He was like the FBI on the throat of the Black Panthers; no, Poe was J. Edgar Hoover, did his own dirt but always got you for your indiscretions.

I had to think fast, not seem shaken or else he'd know I was up to something.

"Oh, it's just Joseph Williams from school; I missed the bus he offered to take me to the next stop."

Poe looked at me as only a brother can and said, "That's all it better be or I'll tell Daddy!"

The Babies and I were traveling in different directions, slipping up on the importance of school, while Bev was seriously preparing for college, either Spelman or Hampton. Spending a great deal of her time studying or working, we did not see each other much; despite this, Bev was my joy; I looked up to her, striving to be like her—confident, intelligent and beautiful.

Winter break approached; Joseph's introduction to my parents had to occur. It was only a matter of time before Poe or the Babies busted me out. Preparing dinner, I thought about how to complete this unpleasant task. Would I share with my parents like some twenty-one year old I was ready for a man, or use the tactic of he was just a friend. What was I to do? Finishing in record time, I would have time to call Bev and ask her about this new thing. "Hey, Bev, this is Ne, what happening!" (I never called her before five in the evening, so she knew something was up).

"Why are you calling me so early, need something? Everything okay? It's not that damn Rochelle Standard bothering you again, I thought I handled that."

"No, it's not about that…Bev, can I ask you something?"

"Sure, Ne."

"Tell me about love."

"Oh my goodness, you think you're in love with Joseph?" Bev questioned.

"I don't know if I am or not. I don't even know what love is."

Bev, who expressed more excitement in the possibility of love than I, said, "Girl, I heard that he had a Jones for you, since you hadn't said anything, I didn't believe the gossip."

"Let's move on, what do I do about all of this?" I asked.

"Look Ne, follow your heart but don't give it up for a really long time. I'm talking years, as my sister Annette says dudes hit and run."

At dinner, barely able to eat, playing out in my head all of the possible scenarios, all the while strategizing on the best plan of action for bringing up Joseph to my parents. Unfortunately, all ideas I once thought great now seemed stupid. Remembering with pride the time I asked about the Jackson Five concert, how I simply spoke the words. Why was I having so much difficulty now?

Each time I began to speak, the words wouldn't come out of my mouth, finally as the seconds ran out I uttered, "Would it be alright if a friend of mine from school comes by during winter break?"

My father, still aggressively chewing his food, asked, "Who is this friend, Denise?"

"His name is Joseph Williams, he plays football for…"

I was interrupted midstream by my father, his strict tone lightened, "You know Joseph Williams? That cat is a hell of a football player, he's an All-American and just a sophomore. Sure, he can stop by, maybe I can go to a few games and see that cat play." Again, I was dumbfounded, that was it? No why or how? I could not predict anything with my parents, but I was not off the hook yet, my mother seemed overly concerned by my request.

"So how long have you known this boy, Denise?"

"Summer school."

"Is this your boyfriend, honey?" my mother inquired.

Dang! My mother caught me every time. I would deny this, at least right now, "No we're just friends."

"A friend that gave you a ride to the bus stop," Poe interjected.

"Ne, we told you couldn't accept rides from boys! Do that again you won't get to drive anytime soon," uttered my mother. Poe needed to be slapped; his ass was fronting me!

"Ne, tell Joseph and his parents to come to dinner Sunday, get him on the phone, I'll invite him," My father said.

"His mother's dead. Joseph lives with his grandmother on Pinney Street."

"Well, invite him and his grandmother," my father demanded.

Sunday my nervousness heightened, as my father being my father invited several of his friends over, I knew this evening would really be difficult for me. The doorbell rang, there stood Joseph and his grandmother. She was a petite woman like Granny, but unlike Granny, stoically reserved, possessing earned gray hair tightly held in a bun, waiting on her grandson's signal to enter our home. Joseph appearance older than a sophomore, even she seemed smitten with her grandson. As dinner progressed, men talked football, and I was glad when armchair trash talking concluded, everyone gathering in their respective huddles, surveying the room for the next round of activities.

"Get your coat, it's cold outside, oh you don't want to go upstairs because your mother and my grandmother want to skip to the fifth degree of questions right? Wear my jacket, Denise, I like your parents,

your dad really likes sports, he knew more about my stats than I did."
The setting sun and frigid breeze of a dry California December evening
crept up on us walking down the street. "Joseph, glad you and your
grandmother came to dinner, it really meant a lot to me."

"Why was me coming to dinner so important for you?" Joseph
asked.

"If you had not come to meet my parents, I would have been one
very sad and Joseph-less girl," I confessed.

Joseph pulled me close to him, "Denise, be my girl. I know I'm
older and you think I have a lot of girlfriends, but I want you and
only you."

"Why me, when you can have any girl you want?"

Joseph stared at me as though I had dropped the game winning
pass, "You are the best. How could you not know that?" His arms
enclosed me, looking into his eyes we kissed, and the chill of winter
disappeared.

CHAPTER TWENTY-THREE

Denise Burelford had her chauffeuring duties down to a science! I enjoyed picking up Matthew and Lee Jr. from preschool and Maclay five days a week. Cruising down Van Nuys Boulevard to the 118 Freeway, proud of my new tape player and selecting my own music, enjoying Parliament Funkadelics' *Flashlight,* happy in each other's company.

Arriving home, we saw our father's car. Laughter ceased, our smiles disappeared; rarely did he come home early unless something was wrong. Meaning he was sick or mad; exiting the car tiptoeing to the front door, holding our collective breath.

"Hey Daddy, why you home, are you sick?" Matthew said running to our father.

"Denise, go get me a quart of half and half, my stomach is acting up," my father demanded of me.

Driving to the store, I prayed that this would not be one of his long, drawn out sick periods, for all would suffer. "Please God let this milk be a quick remedy."

Returning home with his demand, hurriedly entering the den, I overheard my father talking on the phone in a low soft voice, his overt dryness removed, oddly replaced with laughter. Silently closing the door to the den where my father lay sprawled across the sofa to observe a bit closer; yes, something was amiss; perched as if he hit the slots in Vegas, his powerful voice purred, "Yeah baby, I'll be your way later on this evening, we'll go to dinner all right, stay sweet."

My worst fear had come true. *It* was back; we had lost our father once more. I truly did not know what to expect this time. Bitterly shaken, with no desire to pour the milk for him, what would happen to our mother, my brothers?

Thinking about fourth grade when Alice Jones's father shot and killed her mother in front of Alice, she was never the same. Last year the paramedics took her out of her grandparents' house in a straightjacket to Camarillo State Mental Hospital. I thought about my options, if I had any left. Flashing back to Granny telling my father he was the reincarnation of the Devil after he broke my mother's jaw. Tears rolled down my face, keenly aware the worst was yet to come; somehow I had to protect my mother this go round, cognizant of the signs of my father's hell-inspired metamorphosis, limiting the damage he could so swiftly inflict. "Denise, Matt and Poe, is your father home already? Everything alright?" My mother shouted, placing her purse and briefcase on the dining room table.

Pouncing on his prey, my father began his attack on my mother, eyes wide with anger, all too aware this look signaled full domination by the demons.

"Why don't you have on stockings? Been fucking around haven't you!"

"Mommy, leave Daddy now! We have to go, he will kill us all!" I begged my mother.

"Ne, I'm going to leave…this time I have a plan, I promise, I will not let him hurt any of us, believe Mommy!" My mother whispered. As expected, this scene freed my father to hit the street (as he wanted), quickly dressing, continuing his rant, exiting the front door.

Joseph sensed something was wrong, he knew that it had to be serious due to my silence. "My father beats my mother; before Matt was born he broke her jaw because she asked him did he take another woman to Las Vegas… he's at it again, everything is back—no more for me," I confessed, crying, feeling humiliation and shame; my family was supposed to have it all together yet no one knew what went on behind closed doors.

Sharing only a fraction of my father's madness with Joseph, aware if I told him all that we had been through on my father's account he would have waited for an opportunity for the infliction of physical harm to my father. Joseph had never gotten over his mother's death, leaving his father when Joseph was six after knocking out his mother's front teeth, working two full time jobs to care for Joseph and his sister as his father never did a thing for them, driving home after working a double shift, Joseph's mother fell asleep during an Indiana snowstorm. The car slid off the road into a creek, killing her; Joseph and his sister shuffled off to live between relatives and had not spoken in years.

"Ne, it's alright. He will never hurt you again. I promise on my mother's grave," Joseph affirmed.

My mother had obtained her real estate broker's license, opening her own real estate firm, though my father offered little in the way of support, jealous of her success, though it benefited all of us, purchasing an apartment building because of her efforts. My mother was a quasar pulsating with power, driven for her family despite the mad man at the helm.

My mother's plan was to move to Atlanta, far enough from my father that he could not make trouble; the hurdle to climb— implementation. Complete high school by June. Three college prep courses this summer, and two early morning courses, and if that was not enough of a push, my SAT exam was moved up to October. All this for a bid at Spelman or Clark, Atlanta, but I could do it, freedom for Black people always came at a hefty price. Mommy shared her plan in the privacy of my bedroom, my mind swirling, needing something to anchor on for support, my Nana's words. As children, Nana forced

Poe and I to repeat Ida B. Wells when she felt us weak, "One had better die fighting against injustice than die like a dog or rat in a trap." No, I would not be a rat in a trap; we had to go, anything was better than living in fear.

It was 1976, with Joseph experiencing another All American Year. Sport critics said he was good enough to play Division I football right now, some thought he could even play in the pros. San Fernando High School had a lineage of amazing athletes, Anthony Davis blazed the way for the likes of the Moore brothers, Manfred, Kenny and Malcolm, Kevin Williams, and Heisman winner Charles White, birthed from one little town called Pacoima. As young kids, sports blanketed neighbor streets, Pacoima become football and basketball fiefdoms, Pony League baseball and Pop Warner football kept children and adults affixed and protected. June concluded and our house was a time bomb with the fuse burning closer to detonation. Poe, now thirteen, began to stray. As expected, my father's madness was in full swing, frequently absent days at a time, each time we hoped he would not return. Sadly, this was never the case, returning like an alley cat after mating season. One morning the bomb detonated. Sitting on the living room sofa consuming the previous night's missed dinner stew sat my father nurturing rage. Making my way through the living room for school, my father gazing out of the corner of his eyes, still mechanically chewing a spoonful of stew said to me, "You can't drive that car today, take the bus."

"Why, did I do something wrong?" I asked, preparing to comply with his demand; my father hurled the bowl of misdirected rage, hitting me in the head, the bowl shattering. My pain minimized by anger, stew spattered on the walls and in my hair, warm liquid running from behind my ear, touching the spot, seeing blood.

"You always talking back, that will teach you, go in there and wash off the damn blood," my father nonchalantly said, snatching my purse from me. I had no way of leaving. Examining my head in the bathroom mirror, I cried, fully aware my father gone over the edge, unable to imagine what was in store for my mother. I couldn't leave her alone to this fate despite wanting to dash out the front door to freedom, Poe stood in the doorway of his bedroom like a deer in oncoming auto headlights; my brother needed assurance we had a way out of this disaster.

"Poe, calm down, it's going to be alright, soon as Mommy comes home we will never return here," I said to Poe, but seeing blood running down the back of my neck at the hands of our father was hard for my brother to shake.

"Ne, call Joseph, he will come and get us," pleaded Poe.

"Can't do that, someone will get killed, you know he will stomp Daddy into the ground, and Daddy will shoot him because he can't win the fight."

Despite my explanation, Poe would not let the issue go, we would have to ride this mess out, there was no way we could leave the house; our father snatched the telephone from the phone jacks and absconded with my purse; Poe and I were stuck. Thankfully, my brother always had a backup plan. In this case a phone, "Ne see this telephone? I made it in electronics class. I'm calling Granny and Joseph."

We'd become prisoners in our own home; the time dragged painfully slow, sleep unavailable, only fear, which began to take us over. "Ne, I called Granny three times, nobody's home, I called Joseph, his grandmother said he was going to church with her for revival."

"Why did you tell her about our problems, Poe?"

"We need help right now!"

Joseph's grandmother was closely linked in the elder's community of Pacoima; she too was good friends with Old Lady Stewardt, sensing something was wrong with Poe's call inquiring of Joseph's whereabouts, shared her concern during the Pacoima elders' afternoon high tea.

"Stewardt, Ma'Dear, that little Burelford boy Poe called looking for my grandson, the one going out with Mrs. LeAn granddaughter, something is wrong in that house. I felt it, that daddy, Lee, is real controlling. Heard how he broke her jaw few years back, hushed up because it was Mrs. LeAn daughter."

"LeAn and I go way back, nothing I would not do for her, promised her before with him breaking that beautiful girl's jaw, I wanted to kill him…I could not believe he was so damn ignorant, thought he was different from the rest of the family. Let me call Lil Stewardt, send him over there check on things," Old Lady Stewardt shared.

"Joseph does love that Burelford girl, his first real love, watching him real close, no accidents, I'm too old to raise babies, that's why I make him go to revival with me, keep Jesus as his best friend," Joseph's grandmother professed.

"Heard Reverend Broadus and Pledger were trying to have the biggest choir in Los Angeles that will be pretty hard, seeing Rev Crouch son got one of the most blessed voices in the world. That Andre Crouch been singing since he was in high school at San Fernando, beautiful voice, bring you to tears, he's sanctified. Ma'Dear, if you need Joseph we be at Reverend Goodman's Revival tent on Vaughn."

"Buster, take this ride with me, man, Ma'Dear called me to check on Jo's girlfriend's house."

"Brother, you still *boost 'in*? I told you to leave that shit alone dude," Buster declared.

"No man, something with the father, I don't know, I just gotta check, ain't telling Jo just yet, you know he's a little crazy after his momma and all," Lil Stewardt announced.

I thought about Claretta Street, David, and our struggles as a family, unable to comprehend how after all we had survived my father had not learned anything. He was a callous human being, overhearing Granny say, "he was a mean son-of-a-bitch," sharing my father stubbornly stood outside in a Nebraska ice storm refusing to come inside, frostbite almost cost him the loss of his feet. Most people thought our lives were so good, but I knew and lived its truth.

Festering deceit smelled; it was time for all of the Burelfords to stop living a lie and remove the rot from our home.

Slowly driving down the block of flawless lawns framing opulent homes, Buster and Lil Stewardt stood out like sore thumbs.

"Wait, this is the address right here; let's just park and wait till sunset, we cool, ain't nobody outside. Man, that's a big-ass house for Black folks; Ma'Dear told me pop's a fool though…I seen him hanging out at the Glenoaks Room back in the day, Nigga be at the house parties though. Man, why you get to have a father put you in a fancy house and show his ass, man they ain't standing in line at the park for government cheese and canned meat, what's the problem?" Lil Stewardt pondered.

"Here he come, oh I know him, that's the cat that works at General Motors, always keep a new car every mother-fuckin year, cruising down Van Nuys with the Standard's momma, oh shit what's the plan, man, quick!" Buster said.

"Let him go in and I'll get an earful, take it back to Ma'Dear, call her after that, man I got to remember this street," Lil Stewardt proclaimed.

My mother arrived home after our day of imprisonment, entering the living room; instantly my father started his, "where the hell have you been bitch," routine. Not wanting to argue, our mother apologized for her extended day and assured my father it would not happen again.

"Bring your ass into the room…I want to read something from the Bible," my father demanded.

My mother was reluctant but fearing what would happen if she refused. My father carrying a large Bible followed her into the bedroom. Poe and I stood next to their bedroom door, terrified, holding on to his every word.

"Helena, do you believe in God?"

There was a long pause, my mother's voice quivered as she spoke. "Lee, what have I done to you?" My mother sobbed.

"Put your hand on the goddamn Bible now!" he shouted.

Poe was ready to die defending the honor of his mother. "Wait Poe, if you open the door we will have to fight; maybe things will calm down," I said to Poe.

"No Ne, this is enough!" Poe shouted.

The door ajar slightly, our mother crying, her right hand placed on the Bible pledging alliance to God for a maniac, "I swear Lee."

"You are a lying bitch! Open up the Bible and I will show you what God told me to do to lying asses like you. Open it!" My father demanded.

Instantaneously, Poe opened the door, our mother sitting on the edge of their bed, our father holding a gun to her head. He'd cut the pages of the Bible in the shape of the handgun inside the hollowed book; for sure this man was evil.

"I want you to swear on the Bible that you were at work and not out screwing around, that is what I want," my father demanded.

"I swear Lee, please...Lee!" My mother begged, now sobbing for the torment to stop.

"Daddy, you'll have to kill us, let my mother alone now!" Poe declared to our father, who turned facing his son, realizing that he was no longer a little boy but a young man coming of age, ready to stand up to him, even if he could not win. Moving the gun away from our mother's head, striking Poe across the head with gun butt, the gun discharged, the bullet narrowly missing me, shattering the mirrored closet door.

"You'll never get the house, bitch," my father shouted as he exited the house so enraged he did not see the slim figure perched outside the door, the person now running full speed to a waiting parked car.

"Man, he's a crazy mother fucker, carved out a Bible put a gun to his wife's head, man, took and hit his own son with the damn gun butt...gun went off, almost shot his own daughter, man! Shit, not ready, no steel! Find a pay phone, call my grandmother on this shit right here!"

"Man, you telling Jo about this, right?" Buster asked.

"Hell nah, why you trying to get him in trouble? Stewardts have this!"

Old Lady Stewardt took the news directly to my grandmother who thanked her friend and began her assault.

"LeAn, let me handle him, never cared for them, all of them so mean; they were heartless, that yellow one stabbed my brother's son through the heart for no good reason, overdue for death them people. No chicken bones in the yard, hex everyone, just let me deal with Lee Burelford."

"Ma'Dear, thank you, I have this under control; you're right the whole family is meaner than hot coals on a bear; should have whipped his ass when he broke my child's jaw, all that metal, she couldn't eat, oh Lord...No more!"

CHAPTER TWENTY-FOUR

MOVEMENT

Gone for a month before his return home, the family was quite happy during my father's absence, unfortunately October 12, 1976 *he* appeared. Why *he* had was no mystery to us—money. Using the same old, "Baby I'm sorry, though I almost killed you and the kids take me back." Mommy devised an elaborate plan of escape, traveling to Atlanta several times, finding a home to purchase. While he was working, movers would load our possessions, fleeing to Atlanta, free of Lee Burelford's prolific madness, able to start our lives anew. School'd been arduous; however, I was determined to keep my grade point average up despite the madness around me.

Joseph was now the talk of the town, and his biggest decision was what college he'd sign a Letter of Intent with. His senior year, Joseph was leaning towards Stanford. Before my father's last round of crazy, I had considered Stanford, despite my parent's cries against it. Unbeknownst to Joseph we had less than six months to share, and the guilt of secrecy left me immeasurably saddened. April's prom provided an opportunity to share happiness with Joseph, prom a time- honored tradition, and San Fernando's prom was no different; guys enjoyed looking debonair in cummerbunds and polyester wide bell- bottoms, Flagg Brother platforms and massive Afros. Girls began in the summer to find the *baddest* McCall and Butterwick patterns, once in possession splurging to have your design made by one of Pacoima's finest dressmakers, going from zero to a hundred before the clock struck midnight, all the while the classic battle of chivalry versus *getting some.*

I took the SAT in October only scoring 1100, as anticipated math threw me for a loop, thank God for a 3.95 grade point average; hyper-focused in the completion of my college applications before the deadline. My father began to loosen up somewhat; I really think he believed we had forgotten that he had tried to kill us. As prom neared my mother shared she had not attended her own prom, seemed to really be into preparation of this event.

"Ne, I want you here by four, beat sunrise home. I know Joseph's graduating and, well, you know, but don't you sleep with that boy and ruin your life," my mother said.

"I want to take a ride to the beach," Joseph whispered to me as we danced, my mind ticking with scenarios and angles; everyone this evening was getting *busy. Busy* was not in my plan, so much was riding on me; regardless of how much I loved Joseph, my family depended on me to do my part.

"Joseph, I'm not ready. I love you, it just doesn't feel like the right time for me right now, so if the beach includes us together this is not my evening for togetherness."

"Do you think that's all I wanted to do this evening, Denise?" Joseph's eyes now expressed a different emotion, telling me I had misread his intent.

"I don't know what you want from me! One of the reasons I wanted to bring you out here tonight was to tell you I have signed a Letter of Intent to Stanford." The moon glistened off the Pacific Ocean, my heart dropped. Joseph did not know about the Atlanta move, I had betrayed him. Taking a small box out of his pocket, Joseph pulled me close, opening the small box, removing a diamond ring.

"Denise please marry me. I know you have another year of school left but I want you to marry me. I'll wait until you finish, we can get married in June right after graduation."

"Joseph I can't marry you. Should have told you the whole story earlier; just too scared for you and me. All those extra classes I struggled to finish, I had to so I could graduate early. My mother's moving to Atlanta, applied to Spelman. Didn't tell you because I was so scared my father would find out!"

"Why didn't you tell me? I would have gone to Georgia Tech just be with you."

"No Joseph, I know how bad you wanted to go to Stanford, I won't take away your dreams, it's just I can't now."

"We were leaving the madness behind.
We would be free to speak our minds without repercussions."
Denise

CHAPTER TWENTY-FIVE

LOVING JOSEPH

For Joseph this was a magical time, he had received a car from somebody at Stanford so he could visit his grandmother on weekends, pulling up in a brand-new shiny black 1977 Ford Mustang.

May was a good month for me as well as I gained acceptance into Spelman, but all that I sacrificed in the process displaced the joy of early acceptance: I'd miss what it was like to be a high school senior, more importantly no Joseph, all my hard work to pull this off seemed meaningless.

"Hey Girl, pull over for your man!" I always laughed at his command because he said it with such conviction.

Joseph got out of the car wearing shorts as sweat ran off his body. "Why didn't you turn on the air conditioner?" I asked Joseph.

"You can't go looking for a graduation suit sweaty like this, come on in and take a shower, you're kind of ripe!" I joked.

"But you love this ripeness."

Truthfully, I had forgotten my birthday, with all that was happening, numbness set in, intercepting any feeling of happiness. "I don't know. I'm leaving after graduation so I really don't want to do anything, just be with me—alright?"

Retrieving a towel from the linen closet for Joseph, who was showering, the staccato stream of water running as I opened the door placing the towel inside. There stood Joseph in the buff, the flow of water muted by the scene, I was unable to turn away, transfixed in the splendor of his being, every muscle glistening.

"Oh sorry, thought you were in the shower."

Joseph pulled me into his chest, an ache erupted from deep within me, his lips caressing my neck delicately, removing layers of clothing, tasting my breasts. Pleasures at hand and my heart racing at his touch upon my body powerfully conjoined as he gently caressed my thighs, water dancing off our bodies, together for the first time.

"You have skin as soft as a baby's," Joseph said, drying my back; I was somewhat embarrassed by his remark, unfamiliar, trying to shift gears, matter-of-factly said, "Get dressed, I have to pick up Matthew by five."

Joseph's mannerisms seemed so thought out, so deliberate, even buttoning his shirt seemed like a thorough calculation. "Do you think about everything that you do?"

"I guess I do, I don't have room to make mistakes. Never had anyone to fall back on when I messed up, got to get it the first time." Joseph said.

"Congratulations to the class of 1977!"

Students cheered wildly, Joseph's time with me fleeting, and tomorrow the Georgia move would conclude time shared with my newfound love. As hard as I tried to give one hundred percent happiness to this occasion sorrow rose in me.

"Well it started, were moving Joseph," I said.

"I told my grandmother I was going with you to Georgia. My boys Lil Stewardt and Buster are coming along to help me drive. Just can't leave me like this, I have three months to do nothing and I want to spend it with you…I love you."

My room emptied of belongings, Joseph went to help Poe and Matthew pack, my mother in a knot fearful of my father's early return home. Her action meant that we could not turn back, he would kill her if caught, and my mother's plan had to succeed.

By two in the afternoon, the movers packed the last of what had been home. I loaded Matthew into the car while Poe sat stoically in the back seat. Mommy emitting nervousness rooted in clairvoyance quickly jumped into her car insisting I follow, "Ne, get in the car right now, have to leave."

Buster and Joseph, both sequoias, were opposing figures; Buster was the mincing-looking one of the pair, outweighing Joseph by at least forty pounds. Known for his gangster lifestyle, everyone liked him, he was a teddy bear to a point—just do not step on his toes. Lil Stewardt on the other hand was a crazy dude, demure, standing just five feet six inches he took no mess, a sheer bantam rooster. Dropping out of school in the ninth grade, working at the cement plant on Glenoaks; Lil Stewardt had a link to me through Granny and he took his connection seriously.

Pulling away from the curb, the unthinkable happened—my father drove up behind the moving van, jumping out of his car in the middle of the street, sprinting full speed to the moving truck, "Where do you think you going, hell no! Stop!" My father demanded.

The White men, unfamiliar with his maniacal behavior and bulging eyes, froze as my father removed the gun from his waistband, quickly and willingly gave up the ghost, "Georgia, Atlanta to be exact, man, please get that gun out of my face, please!"

Pivoting, my father ran towards my mother, she was petrified, unable to hear my screams to drive, we had to go! This reign of horror had to end, no more! I had to tell my father; this was all any human should have to endure.

"Daddy please let us go, we have to leave, please," I begged, Joseph and Buster flanking the driver and passenger sides of our car.

"Oh, what's this little bitch, you your momma's security?"

Joseph pushed me behind him, Buster opening his shirt as any true hood exposing his own heat.

"Mr. Burelford, man, why you talk to your daughter that way in front of me? Naw man, you just can't do this."

"Helena, you were going to take my kids to Georgia without my permission?" My father knew that this was his only way to keep my mother trapped here. He didn't give a damn about his kids.

"Lee let me go…. Just let us go!" My mother pleaded.

He knew our mother would never do such a thing; this was his method of stopping the move. Why had he come early today? What was the force that he held over us? Were we destined to his subjection?

"Mrs. Burelford, get in the car, I'll take you to your mother's," Joseph said, possessing a look that said things would be all right, just believe in me.

"Ne, I'm going to ride with you guys, Buster and Stew going to stay right here with your crazy-ass daddy; he ain't gonna bother with them."

Shaken to her core, Mommy hysterically crying, how had her plan been foiled by my father? Granny herself in shock, confused as to why she was not heralding my mother's escape, Mommy through tears, said, "I didn't want Lee to hurt you too Momma."

My grandmother let loose, "What Helena, he going to do what, hurt me? I should have killed his ass a long time ago!"

"Momma, he knows under California law I cannot take these kids out of state, and I'm sure he's going to get an attorney to stop me, what am I going to do Momma?"

My grandmother never stopped to think of her plan of action, her reply instantaneous, "Helena, for years your grandmother and I have put money aside for you, we knew that damn Lee was a fool, I want you to move to Hidden Hills. The place has twenty-four hour security, he ain't coming in there and risk having the law and White folks come down on him, ain't nothing but a coward beating up women and children. Helena, Lee is to never come to you ever! I want you to forget he ever lived; this is your time to get on with life!"

We moved into our new house the following week, before the painters could even finish. My mother seemed more at ease living behind guarded gates and security; she began to get back to her dreams and desires, becoming our old mother again.

August arrived far too soon; Joseph prepared for Stanford and I awaited acceptance responses from USC and Stanford. Joseph was happy with all of it, praying he'd have me with him at Stanford, completing his plan for us to marry.

Despite how much I loved Joseph, we were not ready for the responsibility of marriage. Maybe it was more my fear than his, probably because most of my life was orchestrated and arranged for me. Now I wanted to experience life on my terms and marriage (now) would sanction the two of us, at least we'd share in the festivities of his going away party my mother planned. Everyone from Pacoima was making his or her way here.

Observing the discontent in the faces of security, knowing what security really wanted to ask, "Why in the world are all these Negros coming here? Is this a Chitterling party?" At seventeen, I realized that regardless of where you resided or how much one possessed in knowledge you were always Black—an outsider looking in, moving in real time.

Both Buster and Lil Stewardt planned to drive up with Joseph and "check things out," filled with pride in his accomplishments. Despite all of the crazy which surrounded his sidekicks, I was glad they were involved in this leg of Joseph's journey. Wishfully, hoping, Joseph behave a bit longer, keeping his groove thing to himself. Joseph had his own apartment, allowing Buster and Lil Stewardt to hang around a few days longer. Those few extra days turned into a few extra weeks, as Buster and Lil Stewardt awaited try-outs. Both, concerned Joseph would be red shirted his freshman year, stayed to be the cheer squad for Joseph; the very last week of scrimmage Joseph earned a starting defensive lineman position. Buster and Lil Stewardt assigned themselves the job of personal assistant (to Joseph) and stayed in Palo Alto. Both landed construction jobs, so as far as money went they were better off in Northern California.

Buster and Lil Stewardt spent time in San Francisco and Oakland's Black sections of town, learning about Jim Jones. Buster recoiled in fear at the mention of Jim Jones and the Peoples Temple, blocking Lil Stewardt from getting caught up in mayhem, "Dude talks all Black people in America being treated bad, let me help you fake-ass Tarzan shit, man the dude's deadly!" Buster prohibited Joseph to discuss Jim Jones and Jonestown, declaring Jones was a drugged up White man taking money and screwing the women; months into their stay, Buster sadly turned out to be right.

"Letter from Stanford came for you today," my mother said on 27th day of September; insisting I read the letter aloud, gingerly I tore the corner of the envelope took a deep breath and began.

"Dear Denise Burelford, we are pleased to welcome you to the spring class of 1978 Stanford University," excitement took my voice; my mother and brother erupted in celebration. "Oh Ne, one down one to go, you're going to have a hard decision," my mother said.

True, I did have a hard decision to make. What would happen if I did not get into USC? Then Stanford would be my only option, I was a bit nervous. Joseph on the other hand was overjoyed by this current turn of events, "Ne you can start in January and plan the wedding for June!" Yes, I was shaky, so much too soon.

The passage of time waiting for USC's response was like watching wet paint dry, painfully slow. First Saturday in October, the paint dried. Quickly sorting through the mail the final piece of the puzzle, a written response via the United States Post Office awaited me. Familiar autumn Santa Ana winds ruffled the letter as I fumbled opening the envelope fearful of my fate.

"Dear Denise Burelford, congratulations. You have been officially accepted into the spring class of 1978." Wow, tell me what to do God.

My great grandmother, (Nana) from our first colic cries filled mattresses for higher education; this eased my fears about college, as well as securing a full academic scholarship; I could stand on my own two feet. My mattress money (aka trust fund) would help care for the family while my mother reestablished her life; all of the joint bank accounts were currently in divorce litigation and money tight, even with my grandparents. Everything depended on what Stanford put on the financial table for me; Joseph was my everything but family always came first…still waiting on you God…

A week later the dreaded 'Award' letter from Stanford arrived, as read the words, the meaning strikingly clear, partial scholarship—no Stanford.

"Regardless of where we may go, I'll always be with you."
Denise

CHAPTER TWENTY-SIX

MAKING CHOICES

One thing my mother knew about her firstborn child was when I made a decision it was done! No amount of back and forth could change my mind, as my choices bore root in my heart. Curled at the foot of her bed with Saturday's ancestral sunrise of Minnie Ripperton and cartoons echoing throughout the house, "Listen, Ne, look outside, watch the morning through the song," my mother directed me. *Loving You* played sparrow synchronicity with Minnie Ripperton's whistle registry harmonizing as one, the horizon an array of soft corona yellow then orange, the sun gracious in gravity; I gasped in the crescendo of perfection, witnessing rebirth, our frailty given grace to try again.

"Mommy, I want to go to Stanford next weekend. Joseph sent a plane ticket, I have to be there for his first game, I must."

"Ne, I know you don't want me to go with you so I guess you're asking to go it alone—right?"

I hesitated, both uncomfortable and fearful this moment may snowball into one embarrassing event. My mother searched the

163

expanse of the room for guidance, appearing confused as to what and how she should respond in this critical mother-daughter moment.

"Ne, you're not a little girl anymore but you're not quite grown either. Who would you stay with?"

Now the discussion had gotten down to the nitty-gritty, she framed the "are you having sex" question.

Taking a deep breath putting all my chips on the table.

"I'm staying with Joseph."

My mother stared at me, appearing amused by my assertiveness.

"I take it you know about the pill."

"Yes, I do."

I could not believe what I just said. In an instant, my mother went from selecting my wardrobe and combing my hair to adult kinship in sixty seconds—too much!

"Alright, you can go but remember Ne you must be responsible for your actions, and I do mean you will be responsible. Please do not make the same mistake I made at seventeen." There, she had put it in the universe, "Don't get pregnant at seventeen ending up not following your dreams with a crazy-ass husband like me" speech. This was the dawn of our newfound relationship as mother and daughter. No words explicitly harsh about the failure of my father and her husband, no sadness about hardship, loss or late night laundry and fatigue all for her children to have better. In this moment I loved her more.

Taxiing down the runway, I began to think about Joseph, his smile turning me to mush, his touch that rendered seventeen-year-old me vulnerable and helpless. A flash of sadness engulfed me in the realization his magnificence was not mine to own or contain, I could not "render unto Cesar" what Joseph wanted of me now. He was entitled to happiness and love; I refused to block this; I had to be woman enough to tell him I would not attend Stanford and accept my fate. The chicks on campus were going to lose their minds. Why did life have to be so unbelievably complicated for Black people even in love; it just seemed stacked against us. "Put it out of your mind, Barry Evans didn't make it out of the Pierce Apartments in ninth grade," I told myself. Now that was something to have mercy on and have a, "*Go to God moment.*" He was a kid when the police pumped him with bullets, the Babies and Maclay Junior never got over his death— no, murder. I was present in the world. Joseph remained in my life. There was still the opportunity for love; life was good. Accept all grace bestowed and move forward, I surmised, as the plane took off over the Pacific Ocean.

As I exited the gate, I heard Buster's rough and ready voice. "Hey Ne... Ne, right here!"

This was how Buster talked to everyone; didn't matter if you were the President of the United States or the wino sitting on the crate in front of Glen Oaks liquor store, Buster never deviated in his verbal delivery, just buck wild and crazy like a fox.

"Hey girl, what's happening, taking care of yourself I see." Buster and Lil Stewardt had let their naturals grow so long their faces were almost hidden by their colossal bushes. I smiled, happy to embrace familiar warmth and love, my smile making it easy to inquire about Joseph and Stanford straight without deflection, let the bad be known right now.

"Buster and Stewardt, let me get right at you; you been taking care of Joseph?" I asked.

"Check you out, trying to play wife for my man already," said Lil Stewardt.

Looking around Palo Alto, I possessed some familiarity with the city; some of my father's kin resided here. The Burelfordss (as they spelled it) shared grandfathers (the one Helda and kids ran out of Omaha), so they were honest to goodness Burelfords (or Burelfordss as they spelled it). God gives us only what we can bear, and my first cousins of Northern California were the direct polar opposite of the South; they were thoughtful, kind and loving.

Joseph's place was located in the upscale part of the town. Lil Stewardt blurted out, "Ne, Jo made them put him up in the best, all the money in tickets and television air time he gonna make for them, that's the least they can do, you know!" I stared at Lil Stewart pondering why he always ended a sentence with "you know." Buster unlocked the front door, "Here you are, sweetheart, Jo said to make you comfortable, he left this note for you, we gonna run."

Opening the letter, a wide smile erupted from his words, "Hey Baby, I'm sorry I could not pick you up from the airport, practice is rough! Be there shortly...promise I'll make it up to you. I who has loved you from the moment I first saw you, Joseph."

Why did he love me? Why did I have to give him up? Nana always said the way to a man's heart was through his stomach, and cooking was something I did well; on the way in from the airport we hit Safeway to purchase a few groceries. Finishing dinner by four, I even had time to shower and dress. Bev kept me on top of what was hot and sexy and Sonia Martinez was both. All hip sophisticated sisters on the verge of defining their sexuality kicked around the poem Black Magic, the words rolled off our yearning tongues: *Magic my man is you turning my body into a thousand smiles.* I loved things full of old symbols, poetry and jazz where such things. Symbols fascinated me as a child, provided purpose and motivation. Hieroglyphics entrenched with symbols and meanings, which is probably why at seven I wanted to by an Egyptologist. Aretha's "Day Dreaming" played on the radio; humming the lyrics while emptying my suitcase, startled to see Joseph standing in the doorway smiling.

"Oh my God, I didn't hear you," I said, elated to see him.

"It's good to see you, Denise," Joseph pronounced.

Herculean, he could in fact hold the Acropolis; how did Joseph grow so strong, so large in a minuscule unit of time? Realizing just how young I truly was, Joseph seemed so much more mature than I did. Bending down, he gently kissed me. Why did he want to bother with me?

"Let me shower; I will be back, you made me pot roast?"

"Yeah, I did." I responded, like a ten year old who'd just baked cookies for the PTA bake sale; like a fish out of water, I needed to call Bev in Atlanta and ask her what was wrong with me. I realized it was going to be more difficult than I anticipated; emotions have the ability to put a different spin on everything. As much as I hated to admit it, my mother was one hundred percent right. Nevertheless, I was not going to let myself down, that was for sure.

"Ne, can you dry my back?" Joseph asked of me. I tingled inside. "Ne, I've missed you so much, I need you here with me. Denise trust our love," Joseph said, gently placing me in his arms, pulling me onto his lap.

The words of the acceptance letter ran through my head, swirling around my pronouncement to my mother of my decision, I had to tell him now, "I love you Joseph, always will, but I am not starting Stanford in the spring."

Joseph froze, displaying a look of total despair. "Why? I don't understand, you got in, why Denise!"

"Joseph, I didn't get a full scholarship; my mother is having a hard time and SC gave me a full ride, must stand by my mother right now with the divorce and all that goes along with my father's mess."

"No, you can live with me here, we'll get married it can work out, Baby, I need you right here right now, this is so hard for me," Joseph pleaded. Releasing me, quickly retreating into his bedroom, returning, scooping me into his embrace.

"What are you doing?" I asked.

"If we only have this week, I want you to remember it," he said gingery placing me atop his bed; I laughed at his silliness, myself intoxicated in his love. "Marry me, baby, delay your admission until next year and I'll have the money for school for you here. In a few years I will turn pro, money won't be a problem for us. Denise, I need you here, it's hard, I'm so lonely."

Joseph reached under his pillow and pulled out the same ring box he'd tried to give me exactly a year earlier. Spooned, I thought about this moment, how sad in its thunder it was for us both. The box did not hold the same small ring he'd proposed with in April. This ring was large, easily sparkling in the dimly lit room. I was always too early or too late.

"Joseph, I'm not ready... Let me grow up! I am not your responsibility. Must find myself, don't you ever forget I'm in love with you." Heartbreakingly confessing.

Eyes trained on one another, mouths joined, willing yet confused how my words, though tied to uncertainty, hid my burning desire for this man's powerful essence. Understanding my desire meant surrender, which could not be given back as Joseph's tongue engulfed my breasts; motions delivered with perfect orchestration caused a sudden wetness, detectable to his hands. Joseph's maleness powerful yet gentle meeting me, "I'll go slow." I moaned affirming trust in his words.

We awoke to sunlight and the summons of the telephone the next morning. "Hello, yeah, Buster, why you calling me this early, man, I don't have to be to the hotel until five tomorrow evening. Ne is here, man." Guys are just as nosy as women are, they just don't see themselves through the lens of being busybodies.

Home games required the team to check into a hotel a day before the game. Northern California's cold crisp air waking Joseph who got up close the window and turned on the heat.

"Tomorrow, I'm going to have three interceptions and run back for a touchdown."

Parliament Funkadelic's "One Nation under a Groove" played on the radio. "Ne, I can see the play before the quarterback snaps the ball, it's like right there for me to take it!" He continued the verse. "Feet don't fail me now!" Joseph said

"They say making love makes you weak and affects performance."

"Why did we make love if that's what you believe?" I asked.

"Because I don't believe it, that's why," Joseph said.

"Hey, man, you ready, we gonna drop you off at the hotel. Ne coming, ain't she?" Buster asked.

"Buster hush, you know good and damn well she is," Joseph said.

"Man, I know that's the one ain't it? I'm going to tell my cousin Mervin to keep an eye on her at SC."

"Man, it is a trip how they don't allow college guys to have women in the hotel the night before the game. I heard pros have all kinds of chicks in their hotel rooms. Man Jo, yesterday Stew and me went to talk to those Panthers in Oakland, man, the motherfuckers are no joke! Stupid ass Lil Stewardt tried to talk shit, and the only thing that kept them off his us was we dropped your name man… They say they looking out for you, say some White-ass chick put word on you… Man you mess 'in with some White trim up here, man? Why, when you got Ne?"

Buster just said things that made you want to slap the shit out of his fat ass. Was Joseph up here sampling…what was I tripping on? What right did I have to pronounce any concerns? As we drove I contemplated Buster's words, trying to accept the unavoidable.

Buster and Lil Stewardt asked me, "So when are you two getting married?"

"I don't know," I responded.

The stadium bulging at the seams with excitement, not an empty seat anywhere; I was truly in over my head.

Buster seemed let down, "You're mutha fuckin daddy really jacked things up."

"There he is, number eighty-two, Jo do your thing!" Buster screamed. Joseph started his quest for three interceptions, the third play of the game he caught a Notre Dame pass and ran it back for a fifty-yard touchdown. Stanford defeated the Fighting Irish 34 to 16; Joseph did have three interceptions and one touchdown and he was only a freshman. As Joseph drove me to San Francisco International airport, I prayed that time would be on my side and I would not lose him, but nothing is ever guaranteed.

The University of Southern California, located right in the heart of the Exposition Park area of Los Angeles was commonly known as South Central or the "*Hood.*" It was such a dichotomy the first time I saw the college, its physical appearance scholarly illuminating immense power. While the community possessed another reality— American dreams denied, marginalized masses of Blackness. Ironically, most of the students were either White or wealthy Middle Eastern and Asian foreign exchange students; parking lots held adult toy stores of dreams. Porsches, Mercedes as well as shiny new American muscle cars. Izod shirts and khaki slacks were standard uniform for many of the fair-headed lads with names like Heidi, Buffy or Chip.

My roommate, also a freshman, hailed from a little town in Iowa on a basketball and track scholarship. Opening the door, I was startled to see her standing in the middle of the living room taking imaginary free throws, having been informed at orientation she would not arrive until August. Golden brown, slender and tall with subtle muscularity, crowned with short brown hair in a curly perm, she turned to greet me, "I'm Courtney, happy to meet you and glad you is Black, girlfriend!" We laughed as minorities on campus, both aware of the horror stories of unsuccessful interracial rooming situations and neither desired to be a benefactor of such right now. This was not to say that Black folks could not be messy but at least you had some insight into your own madness.

"Let's flip a coin to see who get the bedroom with the park view; call it," I said.

"Heads," Courtney declared. "Tails, you lose," announced Courtney.

The choice act was a non-starter for me, going along with the coin toss thing because Courtney really seemed into it.

Weekends, I was off campus, either home or Joseph's for home games. During the weekday hours of library time, dedicated to holding onto my 3.5 grade point average—my scholarship depended on it. Far as campus life went, things were wild. Herpes the new sexual worry of the day. Before leaving Stanford I bluntly spoke late one evening, laying out his indiscretions, insisting his condom use. Joseph exuded accusatory anger, asking me if I was accusing him of screwing around. My response, "Where's there's smoke there's fire."

Most Thursdays I would pack up my laundry, heading to mom's for love and clean laundry. However, I wanted to attend an Apartheid divesture symposium in Von Kleisman Hall, returning back to my apartment, noise emanating from Courtney's room let me know she was "occupied" entertaining guests; I quietly entered my bedroom, opting to watch the boob tube this evening. Drifting off to sleep only to be awakened to the loud vocal pronouncements of, "baby it belongs to you" from the living room, my bedroom door open, participants oblivious to my presence. Intrigue filled me. Stealthily making my way to the source of my curiosity, Courtney sprawled across the sofa with the women's basketball starting point guard bearing down on her, the moment broken by my presence.

Both clutching the quilt uncomfortably, "Denise, you're here, didn't know, I would have never asked Joyce over," Courtney proclaimed, equally embarrassed and fearful.

Familiar in Courtney's shame, I knew better than most the consumption of shame, how secrets exposed smashed the soul. I lived in a world full of secrets and shame. Whomever Courtney slept with was her business, the Rochelle Standard thing in music class never left me. "Courtney, sorry for the mix up, should have told you I was home. The life I've lived is full of secrets; I know how it feels to have your private in the public—ugly, just a bad scene. This never happened, though you two were super loud!" I jokingly told them. That moment changed our friendship.

Bev was in Atlanta at Spelman, Lulia was hanging at Cal State Northridge, with Deebie and Smitty (who'd barely finished high school) struggling, trying to find a job. America, the world and the Babies were changing fast, caught in a tornado of change without a storm shelter.

Smitty was caught up in the "find a man with money thing;" 1978 was turning out to be a funky time for Black people. Conspicuous consumption and greed pushed for Black people unable to ascend to the nouveau riche, yet yearning for the cloak of prosperity, while struggling gave birth to the invention of *Ghetto Rich* to trick Black people into living beyond their means; cars, clothing and "fronting;" now even people in the hood could *play* the American Dream.

Educational tracking put a real damper on Smitty's life, what could she do with a G.E.D and no skill set but find a man with money to provide the illusion of "making it." Smitty was beautiful and there was no shortage of suitors—all disingenuous, she deserved so much more; Smitty just wanted to be loved and valued. Deebie was never right after her accident; she and Smitty were fire and gasoline together, always explosive. Learning both were hanging out with a well-known famous entertainer who had access to some of the Black Hollywood players, old ass-men troving for young fresh things. Traveling in different worlds and circles, I tried to keep in touch with all, passing on information to our leader—Bev. Bev remained our shot caller, but it was hurtful receiving the call out from the Babies, being labeled a "snitch."

"Ne you need to stop telling Bev all our damn business, we ain't little kids no more, shit! Mind your own business, if I need you I will ask for you help!" Deebie and Smitty angrily yelling in our phone conversation.

"Oh shut up, we are supposed to help each other! Why don't you guys look out for me, who helps me?" I asked, hurt by Deebie and Smitty's attack.

"Helps you? Unlike you, *we* had to leave our homes bursting at the seams. Price Pfister laid off two hundred people and I was one of them, Smitty's working part time at the can factory, we share a single apartment in Panorama City, I don't know what you're complaining about college girl! You were the one able to always get the summer job from the Urban League; Mrs. Pittman always helped your ass! We never could get our paperwork right before all the jobs were given out. You run 'n tell Bev everything you hear! Ne, ever had to have some old ass bastard high tell you take the money out of his pocket with a condom not for his sloppy old ass but for his friend and he watch? Ne, that is my life! So excuse my dumb ass if I have nothing worthwhile to share. The parties, my threads and shoes; all that I have, I've mutherfucking suffered for; we're only eighteen years old, his drumming pervert orgy loving ass knows it—shut up!" Deebie angrily confessed.

What could I say? Nothing. But I could support them through their pain; they were right, I didn't know shit. Checkmate.

The cold and stuffy halls of academia held the keys to the past and my future, but some of its truths did more to confuse than inspire. Each book opened undid every premise I knew on the development of Africa and its great contributions to the world, the loss of a continent and its people in the worst human holocaust known to humanity, the African slave trade.

Granny taught Poe and me about the African slave trade, one hundred million Africans lost, most perished before the tall ships reached land. Ships loaded with human cargo chained and shackled, packed like sardines in the ship's haul days at a time, Yellow Fever, Small Pox, unimaginable vermin ate away the human cargo. The dead chained to the living, stench that permeated miles downwind. If you did not smell the ship's arrival, the encircling school of sharks that followed the vessel informed all on shore of its approach.

Professor Ibana, my Ancient African instructor from South Africa, forever changed the way I saw the existence and history of the African in America and the world. The first day of class, professor Ibana passed out a seven-page syllabus and I wondered how in the world he expected me or anyone else to complete any work but his class. First on the list was a book by John Hope Franklin, "From Slavery to Freedom" published in 1947; I wondered what the big deal was on this book. This ancient text couldn't shed any more light on the global struggle of Black people. I was the embodiment of Afrocentric thought. Far as I was concerned, Franklin could not shed any more light on the oppression of Black people in America and the world for that matter. Besides that, he looked too much like Booker T. Washington who talked as though all Black people had to do was cease drinking and sitting around, claim themselves and achieve. Washington turned me off, yet the assignment was the assignment so I read:

During Tenkamenin's reign, the people of Ghana adhered to a religion based on a belief that every earthly object contained or possessed evil spirits that had to be satisfied if the people were to prosper. The king, naturally, was at the head of the religion. In 1076, however, a fanatical band of Muslims called the Almoravids invaded Ghana and brought them under the influence of religion and trade. They captured and killed all who would not accept the religion of Islam.

Wait, if this were true, then the natural religions of Ghana and probably a large segment of Africa had been lost due to the invasion of Africa by the Arabs. Mali and the great King Mansa Munsa bowed to the force of Islam. Yes, my interest piqued by the implication of forced will on Africa, now having read Arabs were bound to a scourge that wrought the soul of one hundred million Africans:

When Muslims invaded Africa, they contributed greatly to the development of the institution of Negro slavery by seizing Negro women for their harems and Negro men for military and menial service. By purchase as well as by conquest, the Muslim recruited Negro slaves and shipped them off to Arabia, Persia or some other land of Islam. Long before the extensive development of the slave trade in the hands of the Europeans, many of the basic practices of the international slave trade had already been established.

My belief system of Islam and justice for the Black community shattered, lost to words that oozed a horrible truth to the illusion of my so-called reality that Arabs, my brown brothers, were party to our enslavement, and if these words were truth, Arab Muslims were just as responsible for my people's genocide as Europeans; my head ached reading further:

It is to be noted, however, that slavery among Muslims was not an institution utilized primarily for the production of goods. There were no extensive cotton, tobacco, and sugar cane fields in Arabia, Persia and Egypt. Slaves in these lands were essentially servants. And their demand in large measure was seen as a symbol of wealth.

A new truth revealed, Arabs and Islam shared Africans with the European for profit and prestige; damn, what a historical distortion. The mission of Islam, maybe even the Nation of Islam and Elijah and Malcolm, was just wrong for us; moreover Islam needed to atone for their treatment of the African.

Pausing from my newly learned anger, glancing at the television screen, a segment on collegiate football players, Joseph's smiling face appeared; hurriedly turning up the volume he was the first freshman in Stanford's history to make first team All American as well as breaking three long-standing interception records at Stanford. Joseph worked his entire life for the success beginning to take form. As the interview finished, I dialed Joseph to congratulate and tease; instead I was confounded wondering why he was not answering his telephone Sunday morning. Concerned about his grandmother's advanced age, he always left the ringer high, so what was the problem, where was he? Hanging up, redialing the number only to have a woman answer, my heart sank. She was not there making muffins; she was there next to him in bed fucking. My mouth desert dry, eyes welling up with tears, what was I supposed to do, call back demand him to the phone and hold court on his ass, tell him that he was just like my father? Joseph proposed twice, begged me to marry him, I had refused; the blame on this conflated event was of my own making, I had to deal with it. Possessing no right to expect him to be the Wantu Wazuri Afro Sheen beautiful star athlete left navigating in a new and exciting space; no this was Adulthood 101, so painful.

For a solid hour my body sat stationary, frozen in thought, contemplating what life might have been with Joseph if this event had not been set into motion. It was time for me to accept life as it was and not as I wanted it to be. My phone rang; might this be Joseph in contrition mode? What else could be taken from me? I had hoped the knot in my throat still aching would disappear.

"Hello."

"Denise." It was Joseph; how would I handle my new reality, I had to put my big girl panties on deal with it.

"Hey, Joseph, I saw you on television today, congratulations on the *All American* thing." A gigantic pause of silence ensued.

"Joseph, are you there?"

"Yeah Ne, I wanted to explain about the chick answering the phone this morning…it was nothing, baby, I want you to know that." His words sounded like my father, I had to listen to him now; I would not let him ruin what he meant to me.

His voice seemed frantic and tense, breathing loud and rapid, present in fear, "Denise, baby, I have loved you from the moment I first saw you, that will never change, I want to marry you, have all my babies… This is just something I'm going through, please believe me!"

CHAPTER TWENTY-SEVEN

TWENTY

1978 and 1979, the silver markets exploded with speculation. The Hunt brothers of Texas played the silver market extensively. I did a great deal of listening, researching and praying when it came to playing the metal markets. Gold began to climb and all research on South Africa and political strife told me that it was time to buy and hold. The price of gold was going up, just as crude had in 1977 with the Iranian revolution. Mouth zipped, not telling anyone of my hunch. Figuring I had a few weeks, I held my breath. Waiting for loses to accumulate but it never happened. My two hundred dollars climbed to twenty thousand, when I got out of the speculation market.

To err on the side of caution is always wise. I decided to double major in International Finance and Education. If I could not find a job in financial investment, I could always teach. Completing finals June 1979, exhausted and happy the school year finished. Joseph and I continued sharing in one another's worlds; he was scheduled to come down for a week to visit his grandmother. Courtney hadn't met Joseph, though she'd taken his calls and seen him on television.

Having a roommate meant compromise; I suspected Courtney would not be happy with Joseph staying the same week as her girlfriend who was going home the end of the term and planned to stay with Courtney until her departure. Courtney was somewhat uneasy about Joseph finding out her lifestyle; to make things work, I arranged for him to stay at my mother's; she loved him too.

The 405 Freeway true to form was gridlocked. Exiting on Century Boulevard to LAX required great patience, reaching the United Airlines arrival terminal, suddenly I saw Joseph. Even at a distance, he was radiant and getting lots of play.

"Baby, open the door," Joseph shouted as I hurriedly shook off my Jones. "Baby, when did you cut your hair?" Sitting in the passenger seat, Joseph held my face in his massive hands, kissing me. "Still love you, when are you going to marry me?" he asked.

"Joseph, you really turned into the 'Mack' haven't you?" I said in a calm but concerned fashion.

"You really call out my stink, that's why when I settle down I'm coming back for you, from the very first moment a saw you I have loved you, girl."

A healthy attitude to possess about opportunity is that the appreciative person realizes that opportunity is never guaranteed. I had to make it happen; graduation was in sight, my mind linear in thought, maybe I could get Joseph back.

"Hey woman, what are you thinking about?" Joseph said, aware of my preoccupation.

"Sorry, you know how I am—thinking, that's all."

Joseph approached, consuming me in his strong embrace, and said, "Think about this."

"Hey! Stop all that! Hello there Mr. All American, I'm Courtney, man, this season was out of sight, looking at the Heisman huh?" Courtney shouted as she made her introduction.

Athletes, male or female, are motivated by challenge and conquest; Joseph and Courtney instantaneously had a far better relationship due to sports than expected. Joseph's homegirl was Bev (I often wondered if this was to keep an eye on me). He had attempted to fix her up with Buster until I told him he had lost his mind. Bev was not the least bit interested in Buster. Primary reason being Buster was too loud and rowdy, as much as Joseph hated to admit I was right. Why subject my girl to this munchies, weed-loving clown?

"Alright, Mr. Mack, we have dinner reservations for Harold and Bells, your favorite, guess we'll take a cruise down Crenshaw, pretend were really from Los Angeles, maybe that will change your vibe, cool brother."

"Come here, girl, give your man some love," Joseph said.

Lips swirling, greeting my breasts, fire ablaze while he in me. Unbuttoning my shirt, Joseph's hand raced down my thigh that he kissed with intensity that sent shivers throughout my body. I was lost in the moment, confused by its rapidness of my wetness. Here we were as though it were the first time, intense and fluid.

I'd begin my paid internship at Michaels, Josephs and Smith, a black brokerage firm in the fall. Selected out of a pool two hundred candidates, I was upbeat and ready to go. Making our way west on Jefferson, Joseph sang along with James Brown's Big Pay Back, pronouncedly snapping his fingers.

"Jo-Jo, you looking to pay somebody back for something or you just like the song?"

"Yeah, this song has meaning for me because I'm going to show all those folks who did not believe in me they were wrong."

"Why?" I asked.

"They tried to tell me I couldn't because my sixty-five year old grandmother had to raise me. Because she did day work and I wore secondhand clothes and hand me downs. I'm gonna show them just what time it is!"

"...White folks love the color of green
regardless of who it comes from..."
Denise

CHAPTER TWENTY-EIGHT

SERENDIPITY

If the fall of 1979 was any indication of what was in store for me, I was going to be one busy student. With zero time for anything else except school and work with classes back to back until noon, running to my car hustling to work at the brokerage firm, working until my bosses called it quits; all of which made for a very long day, waiving the white flag, I gave up on the party scene. The first few weeks of my internship were spent intensively studying reams and reams of paper, articles, documents and books on business capital investment. The crazy part about all of this I had no ideal capital investment was so involved.

Those with money to lend for venture capital endeavors sought to option the best financial advice on business; this is where my job came in, providing research on all possible venture areas for the best return for lenders. A new firm, MJS, made quite a name for themselves by turning White investors onto the power of the Black consumer market. White investors, uninterested, hadn't stopped to view the potential spending power of Blacks in America; starting the firm in

1970 by disillusioned Wall Street brokers who grew tired of turning away Black entrepreneurs in need of venture capital because brokers saw their business as risky and unable to generate profit. Therefore, Richard Michaels, Timothy Josephs and Robert Smith decided to start their own firm to assist Black businesses in need of venture capital. These men were not doing this just for good will; they knew Black consumers generated hundreds of millions of dollars a year, there was a bundle of money out there and they were going to get it. Unable to secure a business loan of their own, they saved a third of their salaries for five years, opening the first back venture capital on Wall Street in 1970. In one year, the firm made a profit of twenty million dollars. Matching White investors to Black companies by assuring them absurdly high rates of return, there was no way they could lose. White folks love the color of green regardless of who it comes from. Word spread on the street of their success; before long they had more investors than clients.

1979, President Carter was vilified by the ongoing Iranian hostage situation, high unemployment and inflation with oil and empire at the root of the matter. Carter's re-election would be close; White folks in America were leaning toward Reagan, a B-movie actor and governor of California in the sixties and early seventies. He was a terrible governor; before Reagan mental health services and education in California were forward-thinking; Reagan undid the mental health system, downsizing the services to a song, using well-meaning "activists" as a façade, in the process gutting mental health; no wonder so many disheveled souls crossed the city.

Reagan immediately began campaigning for the dismantling of unions; Affirmative Action and government assistance, i.e., welfare, insisting the time had come for people of color (who were often poor) get off their backsides and work. Assuming (wrongfully) the only reason they were unemployed was personal apathy, this was Reagan, completely discrediting the effect of four hundred years of oppression let alone prejudice. The world as I knew it was changing and not necessarily for the better. Black people once again were on the move, nomads relying on faith to take us through despite the many uncertainties that awaited us.

1970, William Morrow, a cosmetologist from California, invented a revolutionary Black hair care product called the California Curl. His product made Black hair form ringlets or curls that were smooth in texture. White beauty companies followed suit to get their share of the Black hair care wealth. Revlon and Alberto-Culver rushed in to make money on this capital builder. Black hair care for time immemorial was always arduous and difficult; at best any product that made the care of our hair less stressful and time consuming was truly a blessing.

MJS traveled the country looking for offshoot companies to develop and take public. Selecting companies needed capital, while making huge sums of money for corporate investors (White people) who invested in them; one firm in the curl business had a profit of five million dollars in six months with my firm's help, as corporations gobbled up these small Black companies. Black hair care products began my journey into *minority* product placement at warp speed onto main street U.S.A. If only I knew…

Lee Jr., now seventeen, decided to join me and attend the University of Southern California, on an academic scholarship majoring in Pharmaceutical Science. Being a Black male teenager and having to overcome the effects of a crazy-ass father to say the least is a challenging and complicated task, one that Poe was beginning to have trouble with. Daddy demonstrated such repulsive behavior, poor Lee Jr. (my brother) was confused. As much as he wanted to do right, he selected the wrong, courtesy of my father's destructive modeling. Poe began staying out late, drinking and smoking weed. The more the family tried to reach out to my brother the more he resisted. Poe arrived home late one Sunday morning after being out all night, our mother, worried senseless, called the hospitals, jails and police stations looking for him. "Lee Burelford where have you been?" My mother asked.

"Out."

Angered by his nonchalant response, she asked, "What did you say? Kept me up all night and you come into my house smelling like alcohol and marijuana and I'm not supposed to ask you anything?"

Poe, upright, his body language reminiscent of our father's, eyes bulged and nostrils flared.

"Look, I can do what I want to! I was with my father, he knows how you are that's why I didn't call you! Furthermore, I'm going to move in with him as soon as school is over, you get on my damn nerves!"

Horrified by his position, my mother now enraged with my father's sanctioning of Poe's drug use. Since beginning divorce proceedings, he'd really turned into a street urchin, hanging out with the hustlers, hoes and drug dealers in his recreational time; Smitty dimed my father was in with the Freeway Ricky Ross crowd.

"Poe, are you smoking and drinking with your father?" My mother asked.

"Yeah, we smoke together, hang out with friends." My mother turned and silently walked away; passing her bedroom, she sat crying, finally wanting an end to him.

More disappointing news rolled in November of 1980, with the defeat of President Carter by Ronald Reagan. President Carter's failed military plan to rescue the hostages in Iran eroded his support. Reagan's first acts as Commnader in Cheif was to dismantle the striking Air Traffic Controller's union, using his Executive Order power he fired hundreds of controllers who refused to work, attempting to replace them with non-union controllers. There were so few air traffic controllers, military personnel were used to fill the cavern created by the firing of union air traffic controllers.

Smitty was spot on, my father had fallen in with bad company; his drug dealing embarrassed me, chasing women all day and night, obsessed with his *Superfly* mentality; I was sorrow filled. Some of his ridiculous escapades involved my childhood classmates—God the humiliation. Nevertheless, the award for the most horrific father goes to his destruction of Lee Jr. My brother's first semester at USC, I really tried to shield and stay close. By December I'd lost my grip as my beloved brother slipped away from me, now tumbling in a rip current of depravity. I found a small vial of white powder that had fallen out of his pocket, keenly aware it was cocaine derived from my father, I did not share my discovery with our mother for I knew this would break her heart, electing to confront Lee Jr. directly and reclaim my brother, I'd go to his evening chemistry class and to discuss his change in behavior.

Disappointed by his actions, I asked Poe about the cocaine; he told me that our father had given it to him as payment for *rocking* cocaine, no respect for his son who dreamed of becoming a pharmacist. My brother now found the lure of street life more invigorating than academia, decided to take a leave from school in June, joining in what our father called the "*family business.*"

"What family business, drugs? Daddy does not care about you. What kind of father would invite his son into the drug business?" I asked.

"Business is business. Look at the Kennedys, old man was a bootlegger, snuck rum into the country during Prohibition, that's how the Kennedys got started. Ne, White powerful families have checkered pasts, alcohol, illegal activity and slavery before going mainstream," Poe rattled off.

"You're right but you forgot something in your analysis—you are not White, and the rules that govern them penalize and destroy us, Poe; nothing good can come from this."

What was happening to my brother? Was he succumbing to the pathetic rhetoric that filled far too many minds of Black men? Didn't he see that the rules that White people played by never applied to us? How was I going to tell our mother of Poe's spiral?

"Mommy, please hear me out, Poe's using cocaine, it fell out of his pocket when he came to my apartment; Poe's going to take a leave from school to help in Daddy's drug business."

"What did you say to me, girl?" my mother angrily demanded.

"Daddy's dealing drugs, your son plans to go in the drug business."

"What the hell is wrong with him, he's your father! This is not about money, he has it, he got the house and most of the money and now sweet Jesus he wants to destroy my child. Ne, I have to go!"

My mother fired the first shot; she'd let my father keep our home and money just to be free of him. Mommy would not have him sacrifice her love in Poe. Reminded how it was always me that created controversy by default. Pissed how shit seemed to blow my way, now I prayed that this would pass with a peaceful and above all safe resolution.

Granny phoned an hour later wanting a word for word accounting of my conversation with Poe. I feared her retaliation more than my mother's; for Granny knew the right folks to make things happen. I could feel my grandmother constricting in anger. Something was going to happen, the likes of which I did not want to focus on. One thing about my grandmother, her wrath was always swift, and this time was no exception. Poe called cursing and screaming about our father being cut out of the Douglass operation. Explaining they'd sent folks to get all my father's dope and cash, telling him he was out of business and to be thankful he was still alive. Immediately, I knew my grandmother had called in her marker to Old Lady Stewardt. My father was the benefactor of a fierce beating on top of losing all his money and dope. He blamed our mother for the takeover, promising "he would kill her." April of 1981, my father's demons resurfaced, this time however we felt relatively safe, able to continue with our lives. My father, defiant to the end, refused to heed the warning to stay out of the business, attempted to buy a kilo of cocaine for ten grand from a new Los Angeles source. When the Douglasses found out he was still in the dope business, a Molotov cocktail went through the window of his brand new Cadillac. Old Lady Stewardt visited Granny one family dinner night to share the news; Granny took Old Lady Stewardt to her rose garden to talk, her expressions told me something was about to go down, and I wanted to know; I shadowed the two elders. "Listen to me, Stewardt; if he puts one hand on my family you must end it, enough! All these years later he is finished," Granny said through a solemn sip of tea.

Mommy got a call from Poe, wanting to come home, he'd had enough and needed help shaking his crack addiction. Sadly, by the time Poe returned home, he'd flunked out of school and truly was a crack addict on the way to drug rehab. The moment Poe stepped foot in our mother's home, Granny was there with three Stewardt kin to deliver Poe to the drug intake desk at a high-end San Diego residential drug treatment program.

One afternoon in May, my father (who been injured during his beat down and on medical disability) snapped. Poe during his ill-fated stay with old Dad had disclosed our mother's new location. He'd probably driven out to the gates a hundred times trying to figure a way to get past the guards. Watching as contractors picked up day laborers to work on homes within the gates, he figured out how he was going to get in. Pretending to be a day laborer, my father rode through the gates to finish the job he had started many years ago.

My mother had just returned home from dropping Matthew off at school, sitting at her desk in her office upstairs, she heard glass breaking in the guest bathroom.

"Mommy, is everything okay?" I asked, making my way towards her.

"Something just broke." My mother opened her desk drawer, removing the .38, now cautiously hurrying to the scene of the breakage; there stood my father laughing at her inability to escape him.

"Bitch, everything I've tried to do you've fucked. I'm going to get you this time for all the bad that has come to me!" Approaching my mother with possessed eyes and clenched fists awaiting connection with her flesh.

"Lee, not this time, I won't have it in my house, do you hear me, just leave, please!"

He lunged forward; my mother raised the handgun under her blouse, squeezing the trigger three times, the force knocking him backwards off the balcony; he lay motionless in a pool of blood wounded by self-inflicted rage. In critical condition for weeks, with bullet fragments in his spine; if my father lived, he would never walk again; so much for madness.

Despite the cyclone, which now engulfed my life (once again), I was forced to move forward and live; there was no other choice. Nana years ago sat us down, sharing her divine destiny for our family, her visions as a young woman, and the adversities of life and how a prophetic dream's reoccurrence summoned her forward, never giving up. Visits to Joseph curtailed, deciding not to make the call of despair on the latest Burelford tragedy.

Offered an entry-level investor position at the firm, I was determined to be successful, sitting in my small cubicle, pondering how the eighties (with Reagan) became obsessed with the dynamic of money and power. A potent elixir creating euphoric happiness and a cavernous abyss and sorrow all in the same drink; how many young Blacks lusted for a Fortune 500 lunchroom rather than the workroom? Somehow, along the way, the process of being a plumber turned out to be a contemptible occupation.

Working late, watching the maintenance crew, the realization of what was in the midst was unsettling. Not everyone would be able to get a college degree (let alone make a six-figure salary). Black folks were on the verge of losing our community in a quest for more. My peers swore to remove grease and sweat from their brows, signing a blood oath to IBM or General Electric, jumping ship from the family building trades, leaving behind summer apprenticing required for trade licenses. Arguing against their stance, yet here I sat in the center in my *Buppy* job, party to this terminal transition. Every day, I took more than a few blows to the face, never letting my makeup run, cognizant at twenty-one how Black women in the professional arena had to be strong as cinderblock.

Graduating from Spelman, Bev returned to attend graduate school at UCLA; I was glad to have her return, our phone bills were astronomical, I needed my rock. Bev was stability. I tried to find solace with the sisters at school. The majority of our discussions centered on the brothers, now if it pertained to the get down on how a brother was in bed or what new lines he tried to drop last night at the club I was in good company. However, the minute the conversation changed direction and focused on us as women, how the world viewed and treated us through myopic lenses, sisters became frustrated, reverting to dishing the dirt; it was substantially less painful. Maybe we did not talk about ourselves out of fear. On the other hand, maybe it was that old long-standing practice of being strong women who sang spirituals and worried about the sale at Sacks or getting that new Gucci handbag. Whatever the reason was, as young intelligent and beautiful Black women, deep down inside we were cheerless, passive aggressively feeling blessed because we had it *so* much better than the sisters back in the *community* with two or three kids by different men receiving public assistance and living at home or in public subsidized housing—but we all ran from our common shared sadness of human devaluation. We were the firecrackers, feisty finger-pointing, get in your face, Angela Davis sapphire-wannabes who ate men and spit them out for sport, when nothing was further from the truth. We craved being respected and graced with chivalry-inspired men who protected and cherished us just once in life. We were the stolen American vessels who fed, clothed, and sexed others with little regard to ourselves, our powerful voice trying to scream from the highest mountain our existence, just wanting to be valued and loved.

Clearing my desk ending the day, thoughts of Joseph flashed in my head, thinking about what I may never have with him, and I was angry. Closing my eyes, feeling his lips on the bend of my back, he was there. Opening my eyes, realizing I was all alone, I had to call him, tell him I loved him, needing to feel before it too disappeared and left me.

The urgency to hear Joseph's voice made my drive home seem to take longer, reaching into my purse for my keys, minimally acknowledging Courtney, dashing to dial and hear his voice. Awaiting an answer as images of Joseph pulling out the ring his box prom night and freshman year of college encircled my thoughts, suppose life had moved on for us?

"Hello," Joseph answered on the fifth telephone ring.

"Joseph, I just wanted to hear your voice, I'm sorry I have not called you, things have been a little crazy for me…I want you to know that I love you, I always have."

"Ne, baby, glad you called, tried to call you a couple of times, the line was always busy, Buster's mom told me about your Dad's crazy stuff, what do you need? Lil Stewardt's people had the family protected, nothing was going to happen to any of you, I was getting a daily account. How is your mother? I was so worried, Buster and Stew's people gave me their word for your safety, did not want me to blow it here—Heisman nomination and my dreams, it's all I got right now." Joseph shared.

"I'm fine; Mommy and Matthew are in New York with her sister, Poe's in a drug treatment program; I'm working full time at the brokerage, going to school in the evening."

"Why are you doing that, Ne, you can't have any fun and I miss us, there's a sports party coming up next weekend, I was going to surprise you and visit, it was really the only reason for me to go to this thing anyway…Denise Burelford, I have always loved you."

CHAPTER TWENTY-NINE

FINDING MY WAY

Matthew, now six, was quite a different child in sprit than Poe and I, outspoken and keenly independent; it was strange listening to conversations shared between Matthew and our mother. He spoke his mind supported by our mother; there was no question if Matthew so engaged he was denied a response. Maybe my fascination hinged on jealousy at his freedom to say at such a young age whatever was on his mind.

United flight 148 was on time; finally, I would have my Bev back. She looked so beautiful and mature; Atlanta was good to her.

"Ne, look at you, you're gorgeous, what's happening girl!"

Laughing loudly at each other, tickled by our transformations, infatuated by our bond of friendship that had always been a part of our lives, waiting for Bev's baggage, listening intently as she talked Spelman and Atlanta on the drive back to SC; entering my apartment the aroma of culinary satisfaction filled the room. "What's that smell, it has the whole apartment stinking, I want to eat!" Bev exclaimed. Laughing at Bev's remark, in the kitchen stood Courtney finishing dinner; I took this opportunity to introduce Bev. "Courtney this is my Bev, Bev this is my first and hopefully only roommate, Courtney."

"Courtney, is Ne still stuck up in her room studying all the time when she is not at work? Do you have to drag her out to parties?" Bev asked.

"Girl, you have her pegged! The only time she can come out and play is when Joseph's is in town, she needs to go ahead and marry the Nigga." Courtney said, both laughing and high fiving at my expense.

Bev stared through my laughter and asked me, "So Ne, it is true Joseph still has your heart? Everything about you seems so different, you have a different center." Bev knew me, and she knew the difficulty I had with wearing my emotions.

"Joseph's at Stanford seven hundred miles away from me, it's not quite the same anymore, Bev."

"Yeah, right. You love the man, I don't blame you but I hope that you two can make it happen, you deserve him and not some groupie White chick looking for a rich Black football player with extended extremities," Bev said.

Bev and Courtney hit it off right away though polar opposites. Bev shared stories of Spelman sisters that made SC sisters seem like church girls. She asked Courtney about her man, remarking how being an All American basketball player and athlete was probably a plus in checking her man. Courtney (this time) seemed determined not to skate the issue of her sexual preference. Courtney paused momentarily, smiled, looking at Bev, picked up her bottle of beer and said, "Yeah, keeping my woman in order is a hard job, but I take care of business."

"You're a lesbian? Girl, I had no idea. Ne never mentioned it. Well, tell me about the sex."

I laughed at Bev's response and genuine desire to understand what being a Black lesbian was about. Courtney seemed shocked at her candor. Though we had been roommates for years, it hit me how ignorant I had been to Courtney's human experience as a gay Black woman. For the first time in our relationship, she freely put it out in the open.

"Bev, Ne is unusual; from our first uncomfortable experience she was cool with me being a lesbian. That is why I will always love her, for most of my life that has not been the case. Girl, you cannot even imagine the shame and fear I've felt being a gay Black woman. Think about it, what is worse than being a gay Black woman? Nothing. We are at the bottom of the barrel, living in the life, I exist in a world that never sees me, I am invisible; it is just too deep to explain in a day or a year, for that matter. Bev, we as Black people live in a nation that has oppressed us since our arrival. Stolen out of Africa in the millions, but what do *we* do to one another? Practice learned self-hatred; my people hate me because I make them feel more defective about themselves, we were taught this madness."

"Wow, Courtney, let's continue this after dinner, but Ne what about you?" Bev commented.

"Bev, I've always loved Joseph. He is the only man in my life that has loved me unconditionally. Just like the photo album you are looking through shows change, I have changed. Why can't I have a career and love as well? Bev, my mother sacrificed her journey for my brothers and me. Mommy's reward, beatings and disgrace, lost herself in all that she had given for her kids; now at thirty-nine she is trying to get a little bit of herself back; I am not going out like that. I love Joseph so much it hurts, but I have got to find out who I am first," I confessed. "Right on, Ne, you've always been so damn strong," Bev said.

If the sports headlines held true, Joseph was easily the hands-down favorite for the Heisman. It'd been years since a defensive player won the award, but Joseph wasn't the typical collegiate defensive player. Speculation began to mount about him not finishing school and turning pro because of his unbelievable talent and skill.

My employers could not conceal their interest in Joseph. Solely due to the potential he had to make money for all those associated with MJS, they went overboard to stay on my good side, discovering we were dating. Sports Illustrated, Time and Ebony magazines ran cover stories on Joseph on a regular basis as the media followed his every move, which became somewhat unnerving for him.

My flight up north was always quick, up and over before I got through the on flight magazine. Surveying the terminal, there was Joseph awaiting me. Eagerly turning in his direction, full of glee and longing, couture in a cream-colored, form fitting Yves Saint Laurent wool gabardine pant suit, blouseless, cleavage high position perfect, Charles Jordan pumps propelling me in a low-slung wide hip Caribbean girl stroll, sexy, assure of intent in every switch, when suddenly my thunder was stolen. As he peered at me, the crowd began to swell, encircling Joseph. Reality knocked the wind out of me; humbled to this new thing—Joseph was famous; the private life we shared now public.

Joseph held me in his arms, female voices conferred to one another, asking the question, "Is that his girlfriend? Damn, I didn't know he had one!" Suddenly feeling as if I was back in chorus again having another Rochelle Standard moment, fear must have been reflected on my face as Joseph quickly said, "Let's go."

Buster and Lil Stewardt waited outside as we got into the car driving away from the airport; again, that *green* feeling arose in me. "Ne, Baby, did all the folks rattle you? Ne, it's just like the RTD, baby, no big deal, you can handle it," Joseph said.

"Jo-Jo, is it this way all the time for you lately?" I asked.

"Yes, Ne, it's a trip for me. Glad you came up, my grandmother's heart well, you know, she doesn't travel much these days."

Buster and Lil Stewardt, on the other hand, loved all the attention; they'd become more raucous because they could get away with their antics. Well liked at Stanford and a good student mid-western suspicion kept Joseph's guard up, trusting only his boys, Buster and Stew. In addition to boisterous chatter, Buster wore a huge greasy-ass curl that hung down his shoulders, one crazy extreme to another.

Reaching the apartment, Stewardt and Buster mumbled their normal madness of, "Man she got you sprung, marry that so you have it on hand, be ready!" An abrasive exterior, Buster was quite bright, true to form they had looked after Joseph since childhood as kids playing in Pacoima Park; Buster had a team of attorneys and agents ready to go if Joseph went pro. Buster's ignorant bravado garnered no rise from me, more importantly, he wanted us married, how bad could he be?

Closing the door, the Joseph of old surfaced. Carrying me in his arms, wrapping my legs around his waist, jacket dropped, breast tasted, holding on, never wanting to let go, securely intertwined, falling forward on fire, exploring each other, his strength tempered by wetness in perfect ebb and flow, an ache both rich and forceful throughout the evening. Each thrust, my body trembled, thinking about nothing else but one another.

"Okay, here we go, Heisman, ready or not," Joseph nervously whispered to me; as he made his way to the stage, five other players joined him, all petrified in fear.

"The winner of the 1981 Heisman Trophy is Joseph Williams from Stanford University." The ceremony pure Hollywood; press, officials, of course the money; this scene had it all, and Joseph was firmly aware he was in elite company, the electricity in the room palpable. My head spinning, voices and conversations babble-like, incomprehensible weaving in and out of memories of Joseph's tribal celebration to "One Nation Under a Groove," confidently predicting in high school three interceptions in a game; reporters and moneymen huddling around us, both overwhelmed but focused; Joseph's long struggle to achieve had paid off, everything shared in confidence with me about his dreams and goals now a reality. The little boy from Indiana who survived on potato and egg sandwiches was the winner of the Heisman trophy— sometimes dreams are real.

No longer Joseph's cute bookworm girlfriend, I too felt the pressure to conform to the projection of an image others deemed I should be. Reporters volleyed questions while camera flashes bounced around the room. When reporters asked Joseph about the young woman standing next to him, he automatically responded, "High school girlfriend and part of my package."

"Mr. Williams, Scott Smith from the Los Angeles Herald Examiner. Are you going to enter the draft this year?"

"I'm scheduled to return for my senior year, thank you very much for that question," Joseph matter-of-factly answered.

"Ne, I have decided to enter the NFL draft, my grandmother does not need to work another day, and she can't pay to see the doctors; I must do this now, I want to play for San Francisco, win a Super Bowl."

Understanding that his life was truncated with a myriad of hardships, Joseph's decision was logical and clear, he had to enter the NFL draft. San Francisco, Oakland and Los Angeles all made multi-million dollar offers, great news for Joseph longing to stay in California to be near his grandmother. Marty Swartz, his agent, who represented many of the top players, expressed to Joseph that San Francisco was willing to trade several of their top players and future picks to get him, in addition San Francisco had a hefty signing bonus in the neighborhood of eight hundred thousand dollars.

Returning to Los Angeles, Courtney and Bev were waiting to hear the madness first hand. "Okay Girl, lay it out, we saw you on television with Mr. Heisman. When are you marrying the Negro? You two are just too damn cute!" Bev said.

"You have been my everything since I was six, so you know I'm not saying until I'm saying homegirl!" I told Bev. My New York weekend was the reason why assignments stacked three feet high on my desk, but my bosses uttered zero complaints. MJS knew I had direct access to Joseph Williams—potential wealth generator extraordinaire—and they weren't going to jeopardize this opportunity. I'd hunted down and researched several prospective investors ready to give small Black businesses the opportunity to take off and fly through sports celebrity product placement.

"Denise, while you were in New York we assigned the other trainees to cover your accounts, so how's Joseph Williams?" Mr. Smith asked.

Sitting down at my small desk slowly with a demeanor of being in the driver's seat, I answered, "He's absolutely perfect."

At USC, on the other hand, was not easy to get back into the swing of things, accounting and marketing courses were beating me down, if I had to get a tutor or do all-nighters, I was going to finish my classes with excellence; no Stanford for me this weekend. I had to hit the books or lose my scholarship to USC. Joseph was upset, I was aware he was under a great deal of business and panty pressure, but what choice did I have? Give up my dreams like my mother or hold on to the faith that we would work it out in the end?

As the NFL draft approached, I had to take a few days off and fly to Stanford, suspecting Joseph was beginning to run wild, all the women putting it his way; he was still only twenty-two years old, I needed to get my ass up the coast. Buster sounded relieved when I telephoned I was coming up, "Damn that's good, why did you stay away so long anyway?"

When Buster talked like this trouble was on the horizon, his tone made me immediately take the rest of the week off and fly up to San Francisco. Buster seemed annoyed, trouble was now in effect.

"Buster, where's Joseph?" I asked.

"Ne, he's with some White girl, her daddy's some big shot attorney in Frisco, Ne, it ain't nothing you can't straighten out." He seemed irritated with me rather than Joseph. I began to cry, his words pierced my heart, we had traveled so far and shared so much of each other and now just when we were about to begin our lives together—now this.

"Buster, how long has he been seeing this White chick?" I angrily asked.

"Girl, I don't know, not long! Just get my boy back, he misses you, should have never left him up here with all this trim in play; Ne, you messed up! A dude like Joseph needs you all the time—you're his strength."

Silence framed the rest of the drive back to Joseph's apartment; I envisioned how it might feel to walk in on Joseph and *her*, hurt and shamed that he'd not trusted our love and me.

"Joseph, I'm staying until the draft is complete," I pronounced.

Joseph, staring down at his black snakeskin loafers, never making eye contact until the utterance of my words. "I needed you...I'm so sorry. I will get myself straight...I promise."

The next afternoon Joseph and I drove to San Francisco. Eating crab and sourdough bread at Boudin's, people acknowledging he was one of the best things to come out of the Bay area in many years, even children knew who Joseph Williams was. He would be the perfect pitch man for products, putting his face behind or in front of a product ensured success.

Walking along the shore reminiscing, laughing at (my) missing the bus, our meeting and the first time we made love. The sun shined brightly overhead, the wind danced in my hair, cradled, watching the sun depart as the evening's chill sent us shivering, dashing to the car.

I loved sleeping in Joseph's arms; he provided me constant assurance and peace, something I had little of. Watching this man sleep I wondered why God blessed me in having his love. Joseph's eyes opened, scanning the room then me, "What are you looking at?"

"I'm looking at you, silly, that's what! I will never be as happy with anything as I am with us," I confessed. San Francisco selected Joseph as their first round number one pick. Signing a five-year, 2.5 million dollar a season deal; in his announcement to the press Joseph let his truth speak, "I must take care of the woman in my life who was always there for me, my grandmother." Joseph's grandmother's health was failing and he knew this was the only action which felt right. This was a good time to talk about my vision for Joseph before someone else came along and started him down another road.

Entering Los Angeles, Joseph waved to folks laying on their horns as he sped down the 405. Making our way past security, guards at the gate for the first time in three years behaved, performing their duties effortlessly, greeting us with respect because of Joseph Williams. Thinking to myself, what a shame their tired minimum wage asses had such a low opinion of Black folks unless you were *somebody*. The conditionality of how Anglos saw Black people was remarkable in its ignorance.

"I really need to lay low for a few days. I miss my friends and family, Pacoima will be good for me."

The sky foreign, the air stroking our faces possessed a different spirit fresh with a deficit. Our lives had changed but infused in the essence of Pacoima this little town still so sacred to us, yes the moment was senescent but in it our strength. Matt ran out to greet us, running full speed into Joseph's arms.

"Hey Boo, I'm going to stop you, little man," Joseph said scooping Matthew into his arms. "Joseph, can I go inside the locker room with you when you play?" Matthew asked.

"Yeah, little man, here's a jersey you can wear right now."

"Jo-Jo I've got a few small Black businesses that would really benefit from your endorsement: more importantly you would too. Black people spend lots of money on things yet we can never break into corporate America because we lack capital," I shared, snuggled in his lap. Joseph eyes twinkled, suggesting his interest aroused, "This time though, I've got venture capitalists ready to loan folks money, they now feel Black consumers a sure bet when it comes to materialism. Jo, what more do we love than fun, dressing well, all that comes with a modern lifestyle—all the things that have eluded us in this country. There is a little Mom and Pop restaurant with three hole in the wall spots with great food that stays jam packed looking to franchise. With you as spokesperson, investors would be on board immediately; first franchise then take the company public."

His smirkish grin disturbed me, worrying me I'd overstepped my bounds. "Why are you laughing at me Joseph? Alright I take it you don't like my plan, well I thought it was good."

Joseph pulled me toward him, kissing me, he sighed, "Be quiet woman, I love your concept, and I'm just shocked. I never knew how talented you were, that's all, I am just proud baby. Sure, I am interested; I will let my attorney contact your firm. Ne, you really are looking out for us aren't you? Ne, thank you for sticking it out with me, you should have kicked me to the curb but you didn't," Joseph said.

I wondered why this man felt as though he owed me a tremendous favor. Didn't he see in my eyes that it was him I needed to thank for being there for me? Joseph loved me unconditionally. Glancing at my watch, realizing I'd promised to bring Joseph to Ed and Betty's restaurant.

"Joseph, remember the party I told you about? I wanted you to attend with me."

"Yeah, what about it?" Joseph asked.

"It's tonight, are you up for it?"

"Yeah, tired, if you drive it's cool; you know you sapped my energy don't you?" he warmly replied.

Laughing as we dressed for the evening, our closeness turned me on, wrapping my hair up in a towel, Joseph seemed massive and

I demure, a swell of emotions filled my throat. I just loved him. Unbridled fear clouded my mind. Images of Davey, pain and loss, the disappointment and shame my father purveyed upon us, in each case both were my own flesh and blood; what was Joseph capable of? Hoping to believe that Joseph was different, praying that despite the twists and turns of my life he was the real deal and would not break my heart. The cleansing of my hands sent fear and doubt down the drain, where it needed to be with all the grime.

"You need to marry me right now, woman, I know everything about you, I'm *you're* man."

Thinking about my multiple refusals of marriage, a rush of adrenaline flooded in as a defense. Extending my arms, pulling Joseph close, now was the time, "Yes, I'm ready to be your wife."

"What did you say, Denise? I need you to say it again."

My voice was filled with joy as tears began to fall from my eyes.

"Joseph Williams, I love you. I want to be your wife and have your babies." Reaching into his bag, pulling out the same small box he'd possessed since senior prom, "Denise I have loved you from the first moment I saw you, that has never changed. I ask you right now to marry me, be my soul mate, lover, and yes have all my babies."

Joseph opened the box once more, removing a ring with such an enormous stone that even in the dimly lit room it glistened.

Patting the last bit of foundation and checking my pale rose lipstick, Joseph made his way to me, "Hey gorgeous, can you fix my tie?" I laughed; this was the one thing he could not accomplish on his own. Studying his face, Joseph's eyes moved rapidly in thought; I needed to be in on his plans.

"What are you thinking about, Joseph?" I asked. Joseph's subtle smile grew, sincerity sparkled in his eyes, "Thank you Denise, you have always loved me, throughout *all* of my madness."

Outstretched necks and telescopic eyes, laser-focused onlookers huddled, conversing about the young man exiting in the 500SL

Mercedes, proclaiming Joseph's identity, no longer a member of the faceless swell of Black men void of identity, his metamorphosis complete, no more Ellison invisibility. My plan of action for the evening included a private reception meet and greet before dinner; Joseph's attorney rushed to meet his multi-million dollar golden goose, pushing aside guests, now running towards us—he would have to wait, the Johnsons were first.

"Hello young man, pleasure to meet you, I'm Ed Johnson and this is my wife, Betty." Mr. Johnson seemed nervous, worrying me; Joseph hated people who seemed tentative about what or where they were going. Fortunately, Mrs. Johnson was poised and collected; she and I hugged, assuring the evening's success.

"Joseph, I made your favorites, tonight were going to have a red wine pot roast with twice baked potatoes, macaroni and cheese, greens and a wonderful crab and shrimp salad. Oh, I forgot, corn bread and homemade rolls."

The mood lightened, I knew if we could keep the focus on the product I could hit a home run. As waiters eloquently served each course, my stomach knotted, praying Joseph's intense delight would continue through all courses of the meal. A working dinner allowing Joseph's attorney the opportunity to talk to all three partners who were hands-on with the project.

"Mr. and Mrs. Johnson, how many restaurants do you operate?" I asked.

"We operate three restaurants in Los Angeles. On any given night we are overbooked, last year we had net profit of one million dollars." Mr. Johnson, now calm, began to speak with confidence. "If we can get the capital to open restaurants in Atlanta, New York and San Francisco, I know *Mamma's* can make it across the country; Joseph, with you as our pitchman, well, what can I say, we need you!" Black athlete product placement skyrocketed and Joseph was on everyone's short list of *must haves.*

The night moved on; with Joseph's plate clean silence erupted into gastronomical admiration when he asked, "What's for dessert?"

"Well, baby, I made peach cobbler and a lemon pound cake with homemade butter pecan ice cream," Mrs. Johnson declared. Two hours later we sat, tension heightened awaiting Joseph's answer.

Joseph chimed in, "I say yes to dessert and to *Mamma's*."

"Now this little ghetto hang from South Central
was in the big leagues."

CHAPTER THIRTY

The Johnson deal took off; when the venture capitalist discovered Joseph Williams was pitchman for the product, they were more than happy to drop an additional five million dollars into the expansion phase of the deal. Ten months later, restaurants in Atlanta, New York and San Francisco were completed, grossing more than a million dollars a month. I was extremely excited, yet nervous as phase two of the plan was in high gear, as *Mamma's* was about to trade publicly. If the public offering was successful, this South Central hangout was going to be the largest Black-owned restaurant chain in the country. Nervousness an understatement, on the plane with the team to the New York Stock Exchange, how did this all happen?

I was a kid from Pacoima standing on the floor of the New York Stock Exchange, terrified my eighties destiny was only imaginary and the stock offering could fade onto the market floor of dreams. Sleep deprived and fear packed deep down inside, the four Brooks Brothers suits I'd brought. Black people who, less than two centuries ago, were on the auction block at this very place, a prayer to God and the ancestors chanted as we made our way to the floor, "Creator of all please allow the strength of those who stood here first to protect me, Amen." We smiled, waved, awaiting the ticker tape opening; above read, *Mamma's*

Food MFC; all the noise of the room vanished, my heart pounded in deafening silence, I heard nothing as I watched the stock offering price set at twenty dollars a share, the number of shares accelerated from zero. The price continued to skyrocket from twenty to forty to seventy-five dollars a share; I began to hyperventilate; the shares of stock climbed over 100,000; now the little ghetto hang from South Central was in the big leagues. As the stock market closed, *Mamma's Food MFC* was worth more than forty million dollars; investors were loving collard greens and corn bread, the Johnsons earned a cool two hundred percent on their investment, which translated to millions of dollars plus their cut of net restaurant receipts; who said Black folks were not good for business?

All the excitement of the deal, I had not contemplated the change my life would now experience. Bev had taken a red eye to New York, awaiting my return to the Ritz Carlton (I guess Bev was certain I was in the big leagues). Riding in a limo, and my need for counting change for gasoline and standing in embargo lines was just about over—what a day!

"You're a millionaire, Ne, you did it girl, they all thought you were crazy, you made those jackassess rich because of your brilliant dreaming mind!" Bev shouted as I entered my hotel room, I had earned three and a half million dollars, exhausted and elated at twenty-one. Arriving back to Los Angeles, retrieving my 1979 silver Camaro from the parking lot, my family would never have to worry about money again.

This was just the beginning; I had four other deals waiting to take flight. A Black clothing designer wanted to mass-market blue jeans to America with an urban look. The jeans stylish, fashion junkies in L.A. came to his Compton storefront to purchase a pair; all he needed was capital and Joseph Williams in a pair. The office was ablaze celebrating our unbelievable fortune. The feeling I had the night David died returned, running in the cold air, not knowing where I would go, just running. I needed to be around the people who made that feeling subside.

"I just need a minute to take it all in, a little jet lagged and tired, I like to go visit some people right now, my family," I said.

The massive Chinaberry tree branches framed my home on Claretta; this house held so much of me. My mind drifted back to childhood, Maurice and Poe laughing at Mr. Hackmon, Poe hurling Chinaberries in his slingshot at all in his path.

As I made my way to Smitty's, the Babies in boisterous chatter, Deebie the expected loudest, I slowed to eavesdrop on their smack talking.

"Girl, did you see all those fake-ass Pacoima folk trying to pretend they all some big time folks at… *Back to Pacoima*?" Deebie said.

"Hell yeah, Ne was not there trying to show off, that's why she's my girl for life! Real as they get, you can believe her ass always could!" Smitty professed.

Every year at Hansen Dam there was a homecoming of sorts for Pacoima folk. *Back To Pacoima* brought out faces from long past. As kids Hansen Dam was breathtakingly beautiful, Hansen Hills and Lakeview Terrace homeowners had spectacular waterfront views. The dam stretched all the way to Tujunga (for which Black folks stayed out, fearful of the Klan), loaded with blue gill, perch and catfish. A replica miniature Southern Pacific Railroad train encircled a mile of the dam, which Poe and I rode once a month, along with horse trails and pony rides; during the winter, fun filled hayrides. The *Dam* was the spot for barbeques and drum circles; it was our African communal zone. There was Zulu-like combat as people had lost their lives as well. Nevertheless, it seemed that so much of what I loved about Pacoima was illusionary since the Army Corps of Engineers decided to dredge the dam and now it was no more.

Lulia and Deebie greeted me. Lulia worked part time to pay tuition at Cal State Northridge, her grade point average declined, placing

Lulia on academic probation; as a result, her financial aid was lost. A recovering cocaine addict, Deebie was doing well in her twelve-step program, studying to get her G.E.D. Months earlier, Deebie could be found holed up in one of Rick Sherman's dope houses, selling herself for a few rocks and a pipe; God intervened, LAPD equipped with a tank and SWAT team raided the house, arresting Rick Sherman and everyone in or outside the house. Deebie, unable to make bail, stayed in Los Angeles County jail for thirty days, long enough for her to realize she had a drug problem; Deebie went into a court-ordered treatment program and now had seven months of sobriety.

Of all the Babies, my heart really went out for Deebie, the boy running over her, the brain damage she suffered and the drug abuse; scum of the earth Rickie Sherman learned the business from my own father, this hurt me. Lil Stewardt said Deebie early on brought her dope from my father, Lil Stewardt made sure to put salt in the wound, surmising, "Ne, your Daddy turned out your homegirl and friends, what's up with that?" If there was contrition to make it was to Deebie, it was time.

"Hey, Ne, what's happening, why you stopping on Claretta today?" Deebie said, startled to see me.

As we laughed at our happiness of being together again, Smitty's four and five year olds cried, longing for their mother's undivided attention.

"Shut your damn mouths, I don't have money for the ice cream truck!" Smitty screamed, annoyed by their insistence. Smitty was losing it; her of all people should possess the patience of Job, as she was the most annoying amongst the Babies; Smitty's kids cried wildly in the background. Walking to the ice cream truck, I purchased a box of Big Sticks

"Ne you think you can come here buy my kids a damn ice cream and tell me how to raise my kids, don't you? Who do you think you are, Ne, oh I know you're the rich Black woman now, you always thought you were better than us!" Smitty proclaimed. Wow, I always extended too much patience, biting my tongue far too often. Not today though, I was sick of Smitty's ass.

"Smitty, what have you ever done since we were kids but talk shit? That's all you ever did and you know why? You're scared of failing; it is easier to put down everyone else, than try yourself. Guess what, homegirl, I am not taking your crap anymore. You talk to your kids like your broke down Momma talked to you. She had too many babies from a man she never loved and you are mimicking her in your life!"

As a break in the argument occurred, Lilia quickly announced to us, "Girl, guess I better get used to all this noise and confusion because my dumb ass is pregnant, the baby is due in August."

"Why, Lulia, do you have to be dumb to have a baby? If you lay down that is the intended outcome, you know the deal, child, even though that piece of shit man you have as a boyfriend is married, you're going to have someone to love," Deebie said to Lulia.

"I can't even have kids; when I got strung out on crack, caught every sexually transmitted disease you could imagine. Now I've got something...I keep a cold sweat at night.... Oh well, the Lord will work it out for me," Deebie concluded.

"Ladies, right now I need to discuss something with you; we can't change where we are but we can make the future better and now it looks like it is me that can help you this time.... But I'm counting on you in the future to be there for me, we've been together since kindergarten, a bit of good fortune came my way, have an apartment building in Van Nuys, all you are moving. No rent, stay as long as you want, just get your lives going again, we are family and family sticks together."

Deebie, Lulia and Smitty glazed over, stares reminiscent as children after David's death. They came to my aid in the only way they knew how, flawed yet gallant, still they came for me. Smitty's eyes began to well up, tears streamed down her face, her voice weak, "Ne, thank you, I did not know how much longer I could stay here with all the kids; I can't pay for child care and rent it's just too much…thank you." Deebie stood up from the table, opened the refrigerator, getting out leftover potato salad and cold fried chicken, refilling the jelly jars with lemonade, laughing and talking through intermit grazing about the old days, longing for their return.

CHAPTER THIRTY-ONE

September of 1982 really felt different to me, missing the invigorating Santa Ana winds of Pacoima, the simple pleasure of the wind greeting you while retrieving the morning Herald Examiner.

Days and nights stuffed with business while finishing school began to spill over in September; when I fell asleep driving home from an evening class, my car popped the curb, hitting a stop sign. Fortunately, I did not suffer physical injury, only damage to the front end of the car; I could not continue at this pace.

MJS finally made me a partner in the Black entrepreneurial capital venture game, *URban Clothing Wear* and *Mamma's* profits were in outer space; I put together five other deals for Black entrepreneurs ranging from the introduction of ethnic culinary delights to athletic shoes. Several athletes and their agents approached me to get in the spokesperson market, particularly in sports, as athletes and entertainers in the eighties now were the marketing tools of choice.

Young minority companies taken public within hours became huge multi-million dollar firms. Plain hard-working Black folk who'd nurtured ancestral crafts were now Wall Street CEOs. What I was doing was not new nor was it a big deal; White investors had followed this path for the last sixty years, and it was just business—business denied Blacks.

I as a young Black woman was garnered a limited "look see" each time a company went public, instantly amassing millions, making me feel as though I'd committed a crime. It was all so easy, so matter of fact. Unlike my parents who had taken their small checks, carefully counting all their pennies, culminating the end of summer paying off school clothes in layaway; with each deal completed earning millions this just didn't feel right; yes I toiled, spent countless hours researching, creating and compromising with the good, the bad and the foolish in making the deal. I was relentless, never giving up, looking for an angle, something that was unique. Still, regardless, I needed sweat, gray hair, a wide midriff that frequently accompanied the opportunity now in my path. A year and twenty million dollars later I had earned more money than all of my ancestors since their theft from native homelands.

As I counted my blessings for not being seriously injured, I made up my mind to take a leave of absence from school, through the end of the football season, giving me time to prepare for my wedding.

Passionate about helping the community meant improving lives of people. Not this generation of obscene fortunes, which did not seem to *trickle down* as Reagan predicted fortunes would be made in the market would. I thought about the brother who came to me as a simple cat from Compton who made a great pair of jeans for a fair price, a person who I believed in, racked my brain for. Yet, when his company went public and he became a multi-millionaire, instead of building the (promised) factory in the "hood," he moved his entire operation to Korea, not a damn person in Compton benefited from his great fortune—only the Rolls Royce dealer in Beverly Hills that ran his ignorant ass out of the dealership. Pounding head, maybe I hit it on the steering wheel or maybe the realization that too many of us wanted to emulate the White man, believing our own models defective.

Disillusioned by my gift, hearing Nana's words reminding me not to let my blessing become my curse. Now it was I helping far too many folks get rich who couldn't give a damn about the same people who took their little checks to buy their shit. The wrong lessons were being learned, my days of assistance were nearing a close…I hoped.

Courtney moved in with me, which was a great way of staying real, besides she needed to train hard for the 1983 Olympic trials; she could focus without confusion or worry. As expected, Courtney was between girlfriends (she was the *Schleprock* of romance), maybe being away from her hamster wheel of women would be good for her. Courtney and Bev had become fast friends, just what Courtney needed right now. I loved this new domestic situation which freed me up. Thursday evening I made it a point fly to San Francisco to be with Joseph as the whole process of being the "Million Dollar Man" was filled with immense pressure. Reporters and photographers followed his every move at practice, other players felt Joseph received an overabundance of press, jealously made it their jobs to make him look bad. Missed blocks or tackles always seemed to come into play when the press wanted to highlight him, but Joseph was no stranger to interlopers, he just worked harder and threw up the middle finger. Regardless of the pressure, Joseph had a will made out of stone, he would not be denied, nor did he brag; Joseph left it all on the football field. Our time together was to fortify one another with love, besides that the groupie train was running ten women deep, it was like the United Nations of "snatches."

Football season began in late September, Joseph's career was only getting hotter, his first game against the Los Angeles Rams he had two interceptions and one blocked field goal; if the first few games were any indication, Joseph might be heading for Rookie of The Year, and he felt pressure mounting. Buster and Lil Stewardt, keenly aware of the stress, strategized around the clock to keep Joseph focused and steady. My time at SC I'd seen more than my share of unbelievable riffraff. Orgies, women literally hanging from the ceiling, hell yes, I was glad Buster and Lil Stewardt were on message with security duty.

Entering the parking structure, tightness radiated across my chest, pressure intensified I had to get my game face ready. Walking onto the foyer, smoky marble floors glistening, hollowed echoes radiating my arrival in coded tribal drum fashion, notifying curious eyes, "here comes that Black chick who made all the money," the chameleon in me taking over, suppressing "Ne," becoming Michelle Wallace's *Super Black Woman*.

It was hard being a Black woman; you are damned if you do and damned if you don't. Working like a dog for everything, no one was there in client meetings listening to bosses taking creative license for my greatness. Having White men and women in negotiations speak to you in a third person voice, I fought tooth and nail to get respect, never losing my composure; Mr. URban Jeans himself had tried to grab my breast as though he were a lactating infant throughout negotiations, continuously forcing me to peel his ass off. Men drunk with power dominate the world of business.

Personally isolated and cut off, aware no one really gave two cents about "Ne." God always provided me with just enough to make it through. My professional *grace* or exception was my secretary whose life mirrored (in many ways) my own. I was blessed to have her on my team by default, the other Barbie-like twenty something women were taken. Mrs. Gaskin was a White sixty-something single parent of three. Suffering fifteen years of violence at the hands of her man until she snapped, killing him, convicted of murder, serving five years of a life sentence before the American Civil Liberties Union fought to have her conviction overturned. The testimony of her daughter told a packed courtroom how her father came home drunk threatening to kill everyone because the kids left their bikes in the front yard. Inebriated, he pulled a gun from his pocket, wobbling to aim it at the children, Mrs. Gaskin stabbed him with a large butcher knife. A slight southern belle of a woman possessing remnants of sandy brown hair that had all but grayed around her temples, on her desk a picture of her children and a copy of the Serenity Prayer. Mrs. Gaskin became my right hand; other *Caucasian* women in the office would have nothing to do with her trailer trash identity. She, on the other hand didn't give a damn about them; Mrs. Gaskin stood strong, resolute in purpose.

"Ms. Gaskin, the Serenity prayer, do you have an alcohol problem?" I asked.

"Baby, growing up I didn't own a real pair of underpants, my daddy was a sharecropper a piss poor one at that, our home had no running water or bathroom, just an outhouse. There were six kids, four boys and two girls; I am the oldest; we were always broke and hungry. The only reason we were able to get by was Miss Mary, an old Black woman. Miss Mary owned a hundred acres of land, allowing us to have a hog or two a year, eggs, milk, whatever we backwoods Hillbillies needed. My mother went to get some eggs and butter from Miss Mary. We was saying thanks to Miss Mary when an old White man my momma was smitten on saw us, my mother warmly greeted him, he asked Momma why she was talking with Nigger Mary. Told her they were going to burn the Nigger's place to the ground. Momma looked right at him and said it would serve her right! After all Miss Mary had done for us, my mother knew what was going to happen and did nothing! A few days later Miss Mary's husband was hung up on a tree, their home and barns burned to the ground; I never understood why she did this, my toothless slop-jar mother could have saved them; I was fourteen years old when I left home. I never spoke to Momma again. Denise, she cursed my soul; me, other Whites, are cursed by the evil of slavery and racism. We know it, one day all will have to answer.... God granting me strength directs me away from the things that block my freedom, they keep me from moving forward.... The courage to change the things I can." Wickedly intelligent, Mrs. Gaskin was a meticulous worker; every file was referenced, reports methodically inventoried and updated daily. In the midst of my presentation, her intuition was always on point, providing me with just the right selection of information. My notorious all nighters, she was right there with me. I would tell her to go home to her family, she'd reply, "Baby what my family needs right now is money, don't have that—so please let me work. Denise, I've watched you from the time you started as a little college girl, you work harder than anyone here and your heart is always in the right place. Mr. URban Jeans is nothing but a fool; he never understood what he was to do in the first place, honey. Do not stop helping folks, just listen to your heart a little more and watch how folks feel about life and people. Child, the way they treat their pets can tell you something, remember that…"

Joseph was named Rookie of The Year; through the excitement though I sensed fatigue, it was present in his sleep, his body no longer seemed responsive, just tired, his massive body bruised and worn, the 49ers not making the playoffs might not be a bad thing, Joseph desperately needed to recoup. Joseph was a gladiator, playing a game that meant capture and destroy for victory. One evening, resting in his arms, I asked Joseph why he tried so hard to seem perfect; he seemed baffled, not understanding my words.

"What do you mean, baby? I'm Joseph Williams the badass warrior that makes more than four million dollars a year, I have to be tough, seem strong!"

"Jo, honey, you're going to have to relax, football does not last forever, don't lose yourself to what people want you to be, you have to live with yourself after that uniform comes off."

"Ne, I'm scared. How can I be myself; everybody expects me to be Superman."

One thing about L.A. is the proliferation of celebrity; many public figures inundate the town, just one more (Joseph) was no big trip; as the chauffer loaded us into the car, the Joseph of old returned. Courtney was away for the Olympics, and I would need all the time I could to get my man back on solid footing.

"The man that loved me for myself."

CHAPTER THIRTY-TWO

March of 1983, I began to concentrate on my wedding with a fervor. Invitations mailed out, the wedding would take place in a small non-denominational church overlooking the Pacific Ocean in Palos Verdes and the reception would be on site immediately after the ceremony. Weitzman Investment months previously had invited me to lunch, attempting to entice me to leave MJS as director of their minority business unit. His offer was quite impressive at one million dollars a year; the job motive, much the same—bring in Black companies and product placement so we can get a slice of the Black buying power. I'd put MJS on the investment map; Weitzman wanted some of the Black dollar, who wouldn't with a GNP the size of a medium industrialized country? Face it, we had become the ultimate consumers who had very little product of their own, what a capitalist bonanza and Weitzman had figured this out. Now American corporations were chipping away at the folks in the community who knew how to fish, buying out community-based companies and their products was like taking away the fishing rod. Someone had to sell you the same rod you once made to catch a fish to feed yourself. The Weitzman lunch was fantastic, held at private executive club in the cockles of downtown Los Angeles. Our waiter, a sixty something white-haired African man, who could not keep his eyes off me, not for the physical but the fact that a speck of pepper had made their way into this secret society of power; flashed a warning to me. I wish I could have told him not to worry, that I'd never be disrobed Sally Hemming-style, and Weitzman would be denied the Thomas Jefferson experience with me.

The eighties unlike the sixties were motivated by things; people measured their worth on what they had and how much, and not what you worked hard to accomplish and the condition of your heart. That was the primary reason my circle of friends was slim; the lack of depth and sincerity that the eighties began to pilfer from people.

Lee Jr. put his life on track in a big way, completing a USC pharmaceutical degree and working at the university's pharmaceutical research program. Though his dream of opening up his own pharmacy was lost due to his addiction, Lee Jr. found a new love in drug research and development. My brother, free of drugs two years, actively attended all scheduled twelve step meetings; dating, Lee Jr. was entertaining marriage.

Standing in my closet deciding which suit to wear this morning, surveying my guilty pleasure of clothing, able to encircle all of the couture my heart desired. At the last Fashion Fair show, braggadocio testifying I could wear whatever my eyes desired, I was proud of my family and myself. Selecting a pastel yellow cashmere sweater and skirt suit, suddenly the vivid yellow jacket triggered a flashback of my father taunting my mother, the bright yellow flash, sirens, her crying hysterically, a pool of blood dripping onto the lawn below and knowing he had finally gotten what he begged for after all those years of abuse.

Flash frozen, the sweater resting atop my head shivering in the stark vividness, engulfing me, images of my father in a wheelchair covered with a pale yellow blanket, sunken eyes and broken spirit. Crumbling into a withered ball of flesh weaken by remembrance, my father's soul troubled since childhood. Festering just below the surface, widening its entrenchment as time marched forward. My fetal stance channeling the Fourth of July, the plastic bat Poe and I coiled like dogs. Grief traveling from all stages of loss in seconds, anger rising in me, for as much as I hated that my father was only a shell of himself, it was all of his own making. My father cheated my mother out of a husband, robbing her of self-esteem, causing her to age before her years. Yet, I still mourned the loss of his myth; hell, who was I kidding, maybe I sent him five grand a month because it freed me; freedom truly was not free. Despite all, I deserved to be happy; I had tried all my life to do the right thing, never deliberately hurting anyone, and today I was determined to make the day and my yellow suit beautiful without guilt or shame. I'd board a plane to Joseph's in six short hours, luggage packed, driver scheduled. My spirit needed Joseph more than ever. I was ready to give all this newfound fame up, the hell with it.

Boarding the United flight to San Francisco, something made me want to arrive right away, as though I needed to be there, the forty-five minute flight seemed endless as the pilot circled San Francisco's International Airport several times. Having lost count at the number of times I'd made this trip, sometimes I would get up in the middle of the night drive to LAX just to be with Joseph, yet this evening as the plane landed anxiety permeated in me.

Exiting the plane, gleefully searching for Joseph's face, reconnaissance came up empty. Maybe he been detained by some fan wanting an autograph; he was probably making his way up to the gate running late, spread too thin. Reaching the departure gate, Joseph was nowhere in sight; he was late. If he was going to be late, without fail, Buster and Lil Stewardt were expeditiously dispatched to meet me; both their asses waited for me at the luggage turnstile. Circling the luggage carousel, collecting my suitcase, finding them would not be difficult because Buster was rowdily boisterous and Lil Stewardt always thought Buster a damn comedian, finding his jokes gut-busting funny. Singularly concerned, I gathered my luggage, having still not seen or heard Lil Stewardt or Buster pimping towards me. What was happening?

Searching for a telephone, dialing Joseph's house, there was no answer, which meant that he'd probably not arrived home, where was Joseph? Dialing Buster next, now irritated and more than a bit concerned, Buster's number continued to ring; had the tide changed for me? Had Joseph grown tired, just wanting me to go away, or had he found someone else, a new Baskin and Robbins flavor; was German chocolate crunch out?

"Hello."

"Buster, it's Denise, do you know where Joseph is? He's supposed to pick me up from the airport and he is not here."

Buster did not seem worried, the racing in my chest subsided relieved as Buster was never a good liar, and he did not give off a lying vibe; this was good, Joseph was just late.

"Oh girl, that dude is so caught up in a breaking his record he set last season his ass is probably just late, look here, you fly'in United right, give me your flight number I'll be there in twenty minutes."

Moderately relieved Buster had not lied about Joseph's whereabouts. There was a first time for everything, this was his first time being late, and I was sure it would not be his last. Waiting for Buster, the cool Bay area air wet and heavy, I hated Frisco evenings, smoky and cold. Through the fog, I saw Buster's Suburban pull up, "Hey girl," said Lil Stewardt, looking worse for wear, his shirt smudged and dirty; both had convinced Joseph to purchase a gas station. He made them both partners in the venture and if looks were indicative of happiness and intent, both really loved what they were doing.

"Buster what's going on with Joseph? Is he tripping out again, it's only March!" I said as Lil Stewardt shut the rear door of the truck.

"Nah girl, you know he really is doing this so he can get more money for yawl's future." Why did we need more money? I had made enough to last a lifetime; then it hit me, it was *my money*. Men were men and Joseph was a man, he needed to feel like he was the bread-winner of the family, the creator of our fairy tale ending…. I would have to learn how to tuck my ambition. Buster rattled on, speaking with immense pride about the gas station, how good it felt to work for himself, in the darkness we were illuminated in the light of joy, laughing about the old days, how square we all were back in the day, nevertheless all longing for that space once more.

Joseph's front interior lights shined brightly from the sidewalk as we emptied out onto the parkway. Now I was mad. Joseph was home, the question was why he had not picked me up from the airport; detecting my pissed off sentiment, Lil Stewardt and Buster allowed me to go ahead of them as they collected my bags, realizing Joseph and I needed a long private moment to work this hiccup out. Walking up the massive used brick walkway, music blared from inside his home. Decisively quick, placing my key into the front lock, the door silently opened. Entering the dark blue marble entry, I could see Joseph standing in the dining room, behind him reflective in the large mirror, a woman, very blonde, much the same age as myself, holding a handgun, sobbing then screaming at Joseph.

They had not noticed my entry. Paralyzed with fear, what was I to do? I had to get help, silently and quickly back out and get Buster and Lil Stewardt; at the base of the door, a panic button I triggered, backing out of it. Running, my legs weighted as though saddled with three-hundred-pound weights. Her screams intensified as I reached Buster and Lil Stewardt.

"Why did you leave me, you can't marry her Black ass!"

Joseph was fearful, his tone flat and eerie, he said in a low voice, "Why are you doing this, Susan, it was over a year ago, please put the gun down, we can work this out, don't ruin your life, please don't do this, oh God!"

"Buster, the White girl you told me about is here, she has a gun she's going to kill Joseph, please stop her, Buster, please!" I said running towards him.

"Goddamn! Stew, we gotta rush her, man, we can't give her a chance, that fool snapped, she's going to kill him, come on, man!"

Darting up the stairs, dropping to their knees, silently entering the house, Buster signaling fingers for Stew to rush on the count of three, I stood terrified watching the scene unfold, Joseph begging her to put the gun down, eyes large as silver dollars, hair unkempt as black mascara ran down her pale white skin.

"Joseph, I loved you, if I can't have you no one will, I just can't live without you!"

The gun moved from her side to waist height, the barrel pointing directly to Joseph's chest. Three flashes of light and M-80 blasts sounded, Joseph fell forward onto the floor. Buster and Lil Stewardt simultaneously lunging forward, tackling the woman, Lil Stewardt now laying motionless atop her, blood pouring from his head. Racing towards Joseph, I was too shaken to cry, only wanting someone to help me keep him alive. Opening his shirt, two holes had pierced his powerful chest, dark blood pouring out of his chest indicating that a major organ or vessel had been ruptured. Aware this was not good, applying pressure to his wounds, trying to slow the flow of blood as Buster stood crying on the phone for help. Holding Joseph in my arms, he was conscious though weak.

"Honey, hold on, the season is just few months, don't you want to break your records from last year?"

"Just hold me, I love you, Ne, I always...." Suddenly Joseph's hollowed eyes stared motionless at me; he was still.

"No, Jo, please don't leave me!"

Starting CPR, covering his nose and breathing into his mouth, Buster compressed his chest between breaths as blood entered my mouth, continuing CPR as the paramedics came in, moving me out of the way. Huddled and bloody in the corner of the room, shocked but aware my gift, my love, was no longer a mortal. Joseph was dead, his spirit borrowed from the creator taken back too soon. My world ended in three flashes of light; life, as I knew and prayed for was over. Lil Stewardt was killed trying to rush the fool, Buster broke down, Joseph's outstretched limp body, his eyes open, holding him in my arms as my mother had David so many years ago. Still warm, I wiped the blood from his face, I loved his mustache, kissing it and him one last time; Joseph was only twenty-four years old and now he was gone. I could not breathe; I was running in my head to Mount Boom Boom from horror, that piercing pain which is the finality of death.

"Why didn't I marry you the first time, why didn't I go to Stanford, I'm sorry so sorry baby…so sorry," I yelled.

Within hours of this horrific tragedy, every television and radio station in America reported Joseph's murder in his San Francisco home at the hands of an old girlfriend. Every agonizing detail discussed as news crews surrounded the murder scene to get that last parting picture of Joseph's body being loaded into the coroner's vehicle. Buster held me close, covering my face, pushing the press out of our path, blinded by pulses of light from photographers.

"Ne, baby, I'm going to take you back to my place, Joe's attorney is waiting for you, there are things that we have to do, you gotta hold it together for Jo now."

We drove in silence, Buster and I sobbed, lost in the magnitude of our loss, numb; nothing made sense. Life is a bitter pill and justice fleeting, all Joseph had done his entire life was provide compassion and good, all acts of divinity and now some crazy privileged White woman who couldn't have her way killed him.

"Buster, if that bitch does not get life I'm going to kill her."

"Ne, don't say it, if that trick ass bitch don't get life, she's gonna want to! Her life won't be worth a dime, she is already dead. Word already been delivered! My only regret I should of wipe her ass up myself!" he sobbed. Blood on my face and hands now dry and caked, the beautiful pale yellow suit no more, life force liquid that once pumped vigorously through Joseph's body now void of life, dull and brown, saturated my beautiful yellow suit. Eight short hours earlier I had stood in my closest with my biggest worry contemplating what would drape my body. Now that drape entombed me with the blood of the only man who loved me. Yellow must be the color of life, Ra-like energy hard to contain, defiant of control, my father and his yellow blanket, now Joseph and my bloodstained suit.

March in Indiana is dreary, dark and cold but I felt nothing. Eulogy and verse emitted from the minister muted until the realization of finality. Genesis 3:19, "Ashes to ashes, dust to dust." Joseph now entombed in cement, lowered into the ground, his earthly journey concluded.

"Joseph loved you so much, baby. He wouldn't want you to give up, he'd want you to push on, live each moment to your fullest," Joseph's grandmother said to me in our grief, pulling an envelope from her Bible. "Buster found this note in the house the night Joseph went back to God."

As she handed me the letter, her worn gentle hands touched my face as we spoke to each other for the last time, "Baby don't grieve too long."

My Dearest,

I thought I would fill our bedroom with roses because you are the wonderful one. There is not a moment in the day I do not think about you. Denise, in two months you will be my wife and have my babies. From the first time I saw you it was love and I had to be with you. Baby, you have been with me since the beginning and we've shared so much in our young lives that at times I have to pinch myself.... Nevertheless it is real, and we have made our dreams come true in a big way. Ne, that is why I know we were meant to be together, No matter what I achieve, you are a part of it and me; I love you for all time.

I Remain In Love With You Forever As Time, Joseph

"That which does not kill you will make you stronger."

CHAPTER THIRTY-THREE

FORWARD MARCH

Leniency for White people in America is an endemic assumption that we as non-Whites must face; the woman responsible for Joseph and Lil Stewardt's murder, upon the advice of her expensive legal team (courtesy of her daddy) went for the insanity defense.

Joseph's grandmother and I knew it would be an uphill battle to get a murder conviction; realistically, the best we could hope for was manslaughter. Her family attempted to post the one-million-dollar bail, public disgust resulted. Holding a press conference, I insisted that the crime be seen as a cold-blooded murder of a young Black man in America, as a capital offense and not insanity. My statement heralded public outcry and argument, bail was denied, she was held pending the preliminary hearing in May.

In a dark and depressed mood for months, oblivious to all, just staring at the ceiling, unable to remove Joseph's face, his eyes still, finite, and his last "Okay." Praying for strength to move on with life, to have the courage and strength to get off my knees, lifting one foot at a time, slowly raising my head, wobbling against gravity, the very force partnering against the living; no, I had to stand upright, feel the breeze on my face, be brushed with the Santa Ana winds. Once again perusing my closet, fearful yet driven to pick up the pieces of my life, I dressed for my first Monday back to work, glancing at stacks of newspapers and magazines dealing with Joseph's death, the media was fixated with his death. Was it the Black aspect of it? Maybe it was America's fascination with murder, usually of the African persuasion.

"You must move on, Ne; I came back from Europe to help you not hurt you, your little ass in New York; I slipped the doorman three hundred bucks to get you out of the hotel bar, wow you something else! This one, the power suit, your favorite, wear this today, no better time to move forward, shoot the three-pointer my love."

"Why move forward…why did you come back for me? Hollow, I have nothing left; shit, I understand my grandfather words. Um, I tried really tried to live the fairy tale, life for us Black people's always hard, maybe that's why we are oblivious to every goddamn thing but bullshit. Why put up with the wreck of a mess I am—why?" I asked the silk-pajama-clad figure coming my way.

"Because Denise, you are in me, have been since college, cared for me when I didn't care about my damn self; I always have loved you. Thought Joseph was your soul mate, I have to admit I was a little jealous, but Denise, baby, I unconditionally love you, and Joseph was your one, I pray there is one more left out there for you. Regardless, Denise Burelford you are my one, I can't shake you, you're what everyone desires; abounding beauty, intelligence and your gentleness; for that, my love, as long as I have breath I will be there for you," Courtney said to me.

"You're right, time to move on."

Selecting the navy blue pinstriped suit, today I needed all the help I could get; as I put the jacket on, the rhythm and routine of work returned. At least by working there was a focus, something I really needed right now.

Making my way south on the 101 Freeway my focus began to change; I was no longer driven by meager recognition nor was I invigorated by hyper-success. The fact of the matter was that after all the madness I no longer felt confident in the things of my creation; all I was certain of was I kept folded in a trunk; a blood stained pale yellow cashmere suit covered in the blood of the only man I had ever loved and believed in. Joseph was gone and now I had only myself to bounce things off, and I was scared shitless.

Buster began to make things work with Bev, and the surprising part about it was that this time my girl seemed amicable with Buster's advances; now they were seriously dating, and I was single again, forced into finding my way in a world that had dealt me several bad hands.

Through the lobby, Joseph's voice spoke to me, "Regardless of your feelings, Denise, always give them your game face and call their bluff." Yes, Joseph was beside me, preparing me for what was coming my way, a storm or ray of light—something was coming but I was not fearful because Joseph was *in* me. Time to put my game face on, time to smile widely, hold your head up and give the illusion of business as usual.

Hugs and waves, the shaking of a multitude of hands, a contingent of strangers all delivering odd-sounding condolences, exuding the courage of a gazelle in the midst of lions on the Serengeti, believing speed safety, yet emotionally empty as a public swimming pool in the winter. The elevator ride up to my tenth-floor office was eerily reminiscent of David's hospitalization. Walking into the office, my bosses cautiously made their way towards me, sensing my tentativeness. Searching for Mrs. Gaskin, who I knew would be supportive without making me feel weak; she stood patiently waiting inside my office, Jasmine tea in hand. "Well honey, you look a bit better these days.

Nevertheless, I see you did not eat any of the meals I took to you, you look awful thin, but that's to be expected, darling. Here, sip on this, you are trying to get through the day and that's what worries me. You have an entire life and must feel free to taste the future."

Placing the tea on my desk, falling forward into her arms, I sobbed; how was I to go on, so much pain in my short time on the planet, I just could not escape it. All I'd intended to accomplish was help; instead, now I was part of the new wave of drama spreading like wildfire in our community; money, power and things, what the hell happened? It was true, no good deed goes unpunished—damned if you do and damned if you don't! Acclimating myself back into this world, sitting at my massive desk with panoramic views, inventorying the businesses I had assisted in taking public, I grew uncomfortable, my blouse seemed to tighten around my neck. Four hundred years later not much had really changed; one fact still remained true, "You got yours and I got mine…. God bless the child that's got its own."

Where was the commitment of people to one another? From the looks of *URban Jeans* and *Momma's* not in the hood, the Black community spent millions of dollars with little return. My rage was further fed by the influx of cocaine and the myriad of gangs that sought wealth at the expense of our community; Lil Stewardt probably was right with his conspiracy theory mind-trip, COINTELPRO rhetoric, of the government's involvement in the cocaine thing. Crips and Bloods sought power and control through slinging the White man's dope, making mega-millionaires out of folks who did not give two cents about us, what Black person owned jets and super sea tankers? Unbuttoning my blouse, still absent air, I was just like them (street gangs); I too was a purveyor of pain and abstraction, the only difference, my actions were not intentional. Beautiful Pacoima's seams continued to unravel. Young adults (a vast segment that I personally knew) lined the streets without souls, eyes channeling the emptiness of failure. URban Jeans could have been a ray of hope to the young; no, I did not sell dope, but was I any different?

Now I would accept Weitzman's offer, allowing me to concentrate on helping those who really wanted to build the Black community, not just sing, dance and floss. Money was now inconsequential; I did not give a damn who viewed my decision as reactionary and foolish, a vast world of experiences awaited me, far more important than making money, and I needed to discover them. Epiphanies, awakened to the realization youth was not only for frivolous endeavors but painful, laboriously painful. As a child, the dinosaur dream played on my fear of anything outside my comfort zone; I knew how to avoid being in the mouth of this prehistoric reptile by staying hidden, and when my brother suffered through cancer, I stared down Tyrannosaurus Rex, insisting that he go to hell, as there were far bigger beasts to slay—the dream never returned. Once again, I had beasts to defeat, the monster of greed and money unraveling our community coupled with inopportunity that despite everything with this new American Prosperity raining down on Whites only sprinkled the Black community's way. No, I would not miss the trappings of this place I hid for comfort in, no more red-eyes to New York chauffeuring off to Club 54 and its decadence and fluidity just because I could to dull my pain after Joseph's death. I stayed drunk for a week, anesthetized, hung out with the art crowd, met a dude whose art was all over the city, Basquiat gave me an oddly shaped piece of wood with his artwork affixed to it, he was high, I was drunk; I'd gotten lost as well; there were bigger monsters to stare down.

The worst thing about tendering my resignation was I did not want the firm to think I was unappreciative or a sellout. Nothing could have been further from the truth; had it not been for the MJS, odds are I would have never gotten the opportunity to excel in such a quick linear fashion; this was true but I had made them unbelievably wealthy; rock... paper...scissors, they still got the better deal. Part of the Weitzman offer included my assistant Mrs. Gaskin; luckily for me she agreed to accompany me on this new adventure; had she not signed on board I would not have moved, this woman was my oracle.

"Unfortunately everything is a trade off…"

CHAPTER THIRTY-FOUR

STARTING OVER… AGAIN

Weitzman's brokerage firm was enormous, office doors passage to mazes; massive offices took up entire floors in the Century Plaza towers. My fifteenth-floor office with Pacific Ocean views was far more pleasing than the hustle and bustle of downtown Los Angeles. Unfortunately, everything is a tradeoff, and with all Weitzman's firm offered me, my heightened senses already detected the planets were not aligned.

Weitzman prided himself on being an equal opportunity employer, and it was true you did see diversity; however, on my way to the Wizard, once the curtain was pulled back I realized I had been duped! The problem was they represented what I hoped to escape at MJS; brothers and sisters wholly committed to the promotion of self-economic advancement and nothing else. One of the Black female brokers in the office made a point to befriend me; I initially appreciated her action, but soon it became apparent we had little in common. LaDawn Thomas was intelligent and beautiful, she enjoyed her job and the financial rewards it provided, unsettling was her hedonism, preoccupied in living and looking the part and the hell with everybody else.

We shared a *minority* project, another public offering that LaDawn was to assist with, which was part of Weitzman's plan to expand his foothold in Black business. She was a meticulous and thorough worker yet void of a pluralistic vision of the future for our community. LaDawn's vision of the future included massive stock sales and mega commissions for herself which did not include the masses of Black folk housed in the hood scraping by; no, they had to find their own way, she truly was a Booker T. Washingtonite. As LaDawn's saw it, "Hell, I made it out, so can they, if they (Black folks) don't want any more than the bullshit in front of them that's on them!"

LaDawn laughed nervously, unsure of my stance regarding her beliefs, which I purposely refrained from sharing with her until the end, as not to upset the already tentative deal. Mrs. Gaskin had this chick pegged right away, as she constantly hurled jabs my way about LaDawn reminding me to "distance" myself from her.

LaDawn soaked up my knowledge like a sponge; she was an excellent student, I give her credit for that; by the time the company went public she was so wrapped up in the process I thought she'd have a heart attack. After the barbecue and smoked meat company from South Central sold their first thousand shares, LaDawn fainted; she earned a cool six figures; I saw LaDawn's greed elevate; it was crystal clear she could not be trusted. Confusing how she was quick to call Black folks in the office "Uncle Toms" or "whitewashed" as she sought only to stuff her own pockets with little regard for the community LaDawn said she was down with, reminding me of junior high school, being called a White girl because my mannerisms not deemed Black enough for others. LaDawn categorized other Black folks as sellouts and did not see that being *Black* was not just street proficiency in shooting the breeze in *hood lingo*; no, this did not give you your Black pass—to the contrary we possessed no labels, categories insufficient. This tightly held truth kept secret like an illegitimate sibling, too ashamed what others might perceive of them. A brother with an MBA from Harvard was just as essential as the brother toiling as a gardener; we needed each other to survive.

The more I shared with LaDawn, the more arrogant she became, professing within a few short months to be the master of all the knowledge of venture capital and public offering. Mrs. Gaskin waited for me in my office, pensive and concerned something was amiss.

"Good morning, Denise, I can't bite my tongue anymore, you better watch LaDawn, she never really liked you, kinda saw you stuck up, I bet she's dangerous, cut her loose now, let her fall on her own weight."

LaDawn was a snake and I knew Mrs. Gaskin was on message. Recounting the story Nana told Poe and me a hundred times about an old woman living alone in the middle of a vast forest; one winter going out to the woodpile, she found a snake freezing almost dead. The old woman, filled with compassion, took the snake in, warmed and fed it, nursing the snake back to health, the snake and the woman spent many a winter evening cuddled close. Holding the snake one evening, the snake bit the old woman who was dazed in disbelief by the snake's behavior; she asked the snake why it had bitten her after saving the life of the snake. The coiled defensive snake reminded the old woman of its nature, I am a snake. Yes, I had to let LaDawn crash and burn on her own accord or she would destroy me.

The Barbecue and Smoked Meat Company agreed to build a 50,000 square foot facility in the Florence area of the city, but rumor had it that the CEO planned to contract the smoke meat portion of the business out to a firm in Vernon. If this were the case, she had to know as well, so this would be my transition out of the deal; she knew I would not have any part of their alternative plan to increase their wallet sizes, always a buster of a brother who would lie on Jesus to make a dollar. As expected, LaDawn was aware of the change and in fact encouraged the move to close the deal.

"LaDawn, what was the point of breaking our asses for the little-ass smokehouse if they never intended to help the community? How much is enough?"

"You think you're so down with the Angela Davis manifesto, bitch! If they want to give their business to the Ku Klux Klan, that's their goddamn business!" LaDawn shouted.

"You make me sick, you've been at this firm for what, five fuckin years and White folks never turned you to any real money making ventures, because you bitch were never supposed to have a piece of their pie! I've been here just a few months, assisted your ignorant ass in making more money than you're ever going to make here.... I'm out of the deal, finish it yourself!" I angrily replied.

Within a month, the company began to receive dissension from community organizers such as the Urban League and the Brotherhood Crusade, a boycott loomed if *Barbeque and Smoked Meats* did not build their facility in South Central. Stock prices fell and shareholders were not happy campers, the firm demanded that I work to save the deal before stock prices fell any lower; LaDawn's ass had no idea how to clean up the mess. The facility was built in South Central despite LaDawn's greedy ass; I never worked with her again.

Eight months since Joseph's death, my heart ached for him, returning to complete my degree, needing just one class to graduate, was a needed diversion from the train wreck I called life. October of 1983 was an uneventful month, a hole ripped out of my heart; I stopped expecting anyone to make me smile.

"Hey, Denise, good to see you. I'm so sorry about Joseph."

"Alan, right?"

"Yes, you have a minute? Can you join me for a cup of coffee or tea?" the voice asked of me; remembering him from my freshman days, which seemed like twenty years ago.

We walked, noticeably relaxed and comfortable, Alan sharing the politics of dental school and the stress of making the grade in a system that expected Blacks to fail. Beating the odds seemed to be a way of life for all Africans in America; there was so much to overcome, at times I understood how people would refuse to accept the challenge.

After months of legal wrangling, the trial commenced, Susan Holly Ashland, the face of evil who murdered Joseph and Lil Stewardt finally underway. As the trial began, maneuvering by her legal team was in full unlimited-money effect; Susan Ashland planned the murder tracked Joseph like a dog, and with the reinstatement of the death penalty, she deserved to die. Her legal team was going to have a hard-ass time, though, showing a pattern of illogical behavior when Susan was actively involved in a host of leisurely blue-blood events, ranging from polo to fashion shows, all on the arms of the most desirable *White* men in the country.

The day opening arguments began, Ashland's legal team sensing if they took the case to trial their client (given public outcry) would face conviction, entered a plea of guilty. The district attorney's office, as usual in high profile African American cases, dropped the ball. Susan Ashland was sentenced to twenty-five years; she'd serve ten years (or less), and the spawn of evil would be back in her privileged world. Buster was right; he should have killed her the night she shot Joseph and Lil Stewardt.

"So, Alan, no longer into medicine?"

"No, I'm in dental school. Completed my undergrad degree three years ago, at this rate I'll finish in another two years, because I just can't complete as much coursework, have to work, all good though, I'll finish."

"Keep the faith. Hey I've got to get back to class, thank you."

I was so glad this was my last seminar; it was awkward sitting in a lecture hall listening to an instructor employed as an entry-level consultant at my firm, reluctantly to avoid recognition I hid out in the nosebleed seats while he inflated his worth.

Making my way to my car, I ran into Alan again, "What's up, Denise, you following me?"

"Oh, I think you have it backwards, you're following me, all you guys are alike, big heads think you're wanted!" I joked.

"Oh, you want to be a comedian now, right, I'll admit it, I was following you, call campus police on me," Alan laughed.

Looking for distraction in the midst of my profound pain, Alan served as such, right or wrong things were what they were. Alan was a handsome enough guy in a different kind of way, six-foot-three, slender, coffee with a little cream, pencil thin mustache and goatee, brown eyes round and large.

"Denise, would it be a' right if all asked for your number? I know I have very little to offer you right now but I will—more to the point though, I don't want anything from you, I'd just love to share a little bit of the space that surrounds you," Alan inquired.

"A little bit of my space, well I can do that," I responded.

Casually dressed, not wanting to send a presumptuous signal this evening, I opted to play down all that had become my life, giving one final look in the foyer mirror before opening the front door.

"Hello Denise, these are for you," Alan said, handing over a bouquet of yellow roses.

"Alan, is something wrong?" I asked.

"No, it's just so nice, your place," Alan said. "Man, that's a beautiful statue. What type of wood is that, mahogany?" Alan asked me. He was somewhat uneasy about this new scene, I moved immediately to gain his comfort.

"Yes, it is, I got it last year on a trip to Africa; it's an ancient fertility deity, and natives of Senegal say it makes you fertile."

"What are trying to tell me?" Alan asked.

I laughed, realizing that Alan thought I was deferring to him, stupid on his part, here we go with the uninformed. "Alan, you have a real good sense of yourself, don't you. I purchased this with Joseph, and we were going to put it in our honeymoon suite, hoping that it would bring us children right away."

"I'm so sorry, you think I'm a fool, maybe I should go, I really have a lot to learn and I will, you are incredible!"

I decided to give a New Year's Eve party primarily because I did not want to think about the previous year and the present without Joseph, my wound still open, bleeding profusely, begging that the dagger in my heart be extracted; the ache of New Year's Eve was back, I hated this time of year.

"Ladies and gentleman, I'd like to introduce Courtney Williams, Ms. Williams made the Olympic Women's basketball team. I expect Ms. Williams will bring home gold. Let's congratulate and wish her well this evening!"

The party was packed, I did not care, seeking to forget about my year, this was the perfect distraction. Enjoying watching Courtney receive mass accolades, thinking back on the intersect which brought us together, how she'd become an integral part of my life, and now Courtney's unbelievable effort and hard work had earned her a spot on the American Olympic team. Courtney, in her enthusiasm, made me proud and envious at the same time; Courtney briefly glanced over, peeping, my stare disengaged, slowly making her way to me.

"Why you try 'in to jinx me, Ne?" Courtney said humorously.

"You're a whole lot better athlete than you are in love, what is this number three, why can't you keep a steady piece?" I joked.

"Ne, it's so hard finding a woman who loves me. I think not being able to validate your relationship when you're gay makes it so temporary, no long-term commitment…. Besides that, well, they can't seem to duplicate you."

I'd not meant to rattle Courtney's chain; she lived in a world that expected her to find happiness and love but did not grant her full acceptance. She hid her relationship from most, suffered silently in pain, and by the looks of this new woman in her life, Courtney would be alone in the future once again; the women were more impressed with being in the L.A. circuit than a long-term relationship.

"Let us butt in the conversation ladies," Buster and Bev asked.

"Ne, wanted you to be the first to know, were getting married in April," Bev shared.

"You're getting married, I'm so happy for you both!"

"Yeah, Ne, I feel so blessed, you know I've been in love with Bev since high school," Buster pronounced.

"Yeah, fool, if you would have cut the big greasy-ass Jeri curl off earlier and stopped being so loud, you two would have had a couple of little ones now, Buster."

Regardless of the time it took for Bev and Buster to get together, it happened; what a blessing they were to each other.

"…being gay or having AIDS meant that you'd finally found a way to be worse than being Black in America…"

CHAPTER THIRTY-FIVE

SPRING

Bev and Buster married in April. All of Pacoima attended the wedding at Calvary Baptist Church, and it felt good to be back with the people who'd been so much a part of my life one more time; watching Buster and Bev, a tinge of sadness flooded in, aware of my loss.

The opportunity to have such a love gone, unable to change anything in my life regardless of money or access, coming from Pacoima in the sixties, our time was like that of sand in an hourglass—fleeting. Vowing to cherish what images lay in front of me, smiling at those that graced the room, though graying, slow in step, these people were the essence of my life. Granny and her friends talked about the good old days, for with their departure a way of life and culture would surely die. My uncle, now a Civil Rights attorney practicing in Washington D.C., came home for Bev's wedding, somewhat heartbroken he'd held a torch for Bev for years, oh well, you win some and you lose some. Lulia had earned her B.A. degree in Liberal Studies and was finishing her teaching credential. I was so proud of her accomplishment; there was nothing as important as the competent education of Black children; as children, the Babies were a fitting example of disparity in education, unequal and disproportional. In June, Smitty would be a registered nurse specializing in cardiac care; finally, she would be able to care for herself and her kids. Despite many setbacks, Deebie had a will of steel, obtaining her G.E.D, and now was a U.S. Postal worker. Deebie had come down with a terrible cold, losing a considerable amount of weight, which worried me. Sharing a table at the reception with Deebie, we made our way out to a beautiful white swan-filled pond at Sportsman's Lodge, chuckling at the guests made uncomfortable at the site of so many African Americans congregating a stone's throw from them. Drug free for three years, Deebie evoked the most empathy, knocked down at such an early age, yet kept fighting, but tonight she was a shadow of herself. Her skin dull, eyes absent of sparkle, breathing labored; AIDS was now a reality in America, no longer just affecting gay men in the eighties.

"Deebie, we've known each other since we were five, I know when you're not feeling well. Tell me how long have you been sick?"

"Too long, Ne, but I just put it in God's hands, I go to the doctor and they can't find what's wrong with me. You know I just got my health insurance two years ago when I went to work for the post office, thank God for that. Even when I'm dragging I've got to go to work to keep my health insurance."

Monday morning arrived not a moment too soon; arriving at Deebie's apartment, weak, she'd crawled across the apartment floor, high fever and weak. David been dead for fourteen years, it felt like sickness all over again, I could sense catastrophe as we sped off to the hospital.

"Are you here with Deebie Wecks?"

"Yes," I said.

"Ms. Wecks has AIDS, she's is in critical condition, I don't know if we can help her," The doctor said.

"Did you tell her she has AIDS?" I asked.

"No, not yet, I thought it would be better to have a family member with her."

Once again taking the dreaded ride up the hospital's elevator, the same stale Lysol smell, but unlike before I was truly alone I had to be strong. Reaching the tenth floor, all patients were like Deebie, young people knocked down in the prime of their lives. Her face covered with an oxygen mask, when I entered the room she raised her hand to greet me.

"How you feeling Deebie? Can you breathe better?" I asked.

"I can breathe now," Deebie struggled to speak as her doctor entered the room.

"Ms. Wecks you have AIDS, your T-cells are very low, that's why you've been so sick, we're going to give you a medication, AZT, hopefully give your immune system time to fight, Ms. Wecks I am so sorry," the doctor said.

Sitting hours watching Deebie, remembering our childhood, her breathing painfully labored, forehead covered with black blotches, in the same place as the accident when we were in kindergarten at five beginning our journey together in life. Now, instead of blood oozing from the spot it was covered with something more terrible and permanent, this thing engulfing her entire body dooming her fate.

"Ne," Deebie said, motioning me closer. I placed my right ear next to her oxygen mask. "Get my mother and father here, I'm tired."

"They're on their way, hold on."

Her parents, wrought with sadness, held their child's spindly hands, stroking thinning hair, the circle of life playing out before them, the pain of burying a child out of sequence, their child was supposed to bury them.

Deebie's eyes opened as she smiled, "Momma, Daddy, I'm tired, it's all right now, I'm ready, I got myself together," Deebie took her last breath. Deebie's parents in denial, unable to accept she died of AIDS, told people she succumbed to cancer. Black folks had a thing about AIDS and gay people. Being gay or having AIDS meant a person finally found a way to be worse than being Black in America. As angry as I was, I upheld the secret; however, most people did not buy the story of cancer, and in fact did know what really killed her. The tentacles of AIDS was now tightening itself around Pacoima, with residents believing Ronnie Smith, Pacoima's major down low drug dealer who'd served time in jail (and had unprotected prison sex), was the vector for AIDS. Both his common law wife and child succumbed to the disease and now Ronnie was sick; Ronnie needed to meet his fate; he singlehandedly put the HIV infection rate on an all-time high in Pacoima.

I'd lost Joseph and now Deebie; it was time to move on with my life as nothing was guaranteed. Alan and I spent more time together; he was sensitive and caring. When I came down with bronchitis, he made me chicken soup; stripped naked of cover, exposed, I had no one to plug the gaping hole in my soul, I needed something or someone. My spirit felt old, stale, despite the vibrancy of youth Denise Burelford's star was fleeting; I needed Alan now, right wrong or whatever.

A sweeping metamorphosis began preparing for the 1984 Summer Olympics, the city abuzz with a new energy. For decades, city government insisted they could not clean up the Coliseum, but today the city did just that. Old or vacant buildings vanished overnight, new businesses put in their place, and everything got a face-lift, while the seedier side of town just disappeared. Darryl Gates, Chief of the Los Angeles Police Department gave them an early vacation as they checked into Los Angeles County Jail or were given one-way Greyhound bus tickets out of town. LAPD and the city of Los Angeles instituted American Apartheid, always the easy answer—get rid of us. There was some good associated with hosting the Olympics; the Amateur Athletics Association (AAU) provided millions of dollars for programs and jobs in Los Angeles.

CHAPTER THIRTY-SIX

FOR A MOMENT

Alan moved in with me, unsure where the relationship was going, but I was ready to begin the journey—regardless. Alan would never replace Joseph's fullness, but his truncated space was in an odd way enough; if Alan ceased to exist or chose another, I could and would survive—shamelessly well. That age-old story Nana shared about things which did not cause the end of your mortal existence made you stronger was true.

"I need some gut soul to tell you this. My yesterdays were blue dear before I met you dear. Denise, I love you, I want you to be my wife, I'll make you happy and provide for us, please marry me, what do you say?"

"Yes, Alan, I will marry you. I wouldn't want you to get use to this anyway—why buy the cow when you can get the milk for free?"

One thing about money, it forces you to take precautions that one would normally not take, and marriage was no exception. My attorney drew up a lengthy prenuptial agreement, protecting me from what I had witnessed as a child when my parents divorced; I was advised to give Alan two hundred thousand dollars and call it a day, no property, no cars, just cash.

June 1984, Alan finished dental school, meeting his family for the first time I was taken aback by their madness; so glad about the prenup! These people were far more interested in how he was going to help them back in Chi-Town where the family home was in ill repair and they needed help—right now!

Alan's mother, pygmy short and rotund in appearance, expressed a murkiness of the soul that said to me, "Are you as rich as they say in Ebony? You look better in person, though, I gives you that! Not to say you's ugly, cause you really pretty, but you look better in person, how much did you pay for them shoes?"

"I didn't give the interview, so I don't know what it read, but I've done all right for myself," I responded.

Her snake-charmer stare baited me as if blows would be her response as the words were released from her mouth, "I needs to have few thousand dollars until my husband goes back to work, eating salt pork and mustard greens can't last forever, the kids need some meat, you my daughter, help ya momma!"

No wonder Alan never spoke of his family; they were truly Chicago-hustling me. Quickly writing a check, I told his mother, "This is between me and you, Alan is not to know."

"I gotcha, thank you," she said as she stuffed the check down her bra, waddling back to her seat, fanning fiercely in the June heat, salt-pork-laden perspiration spewing from her face, indicative of her life. They'd made the trip to California by train, Alan hadn't the money for eight plane tickets, but after my introduction to these dark, liquor-guzzling, gold-tooth smiling folk, there was no way in hell they could stay with us; instead, putting Alan's family up in the Valley Hilton—my treat. So glad to get these people out of my life, purchasing eight first class airline tickets days earlier than planned, they had to go! Alan was angry with them; more importantly, his embarrassment drew him to silence, stoic in his disappointment.

After Courtney's Olympic victory, she told her mother she was gay, that she had been in a relationship with her current girlfriend a minute; funny, her mother shocked Courtney with her reply, "I know… I've always known baby, and Momma always loved you for you."

Truly Courtney's gold medal win was worthy of a celebration; with little left to celebrate, Courtney's success became my passion, having grown into the role of spring-boarding athletes into mainstream business avenues, simultaneously resurrecting memories of Joseph's triumphs. Maybe I was trying to hold on to him, recognizing I would never have him again, but I had a major surprise for her this evening. "Courtney, you know I'm proud of you, more than you'll ever know, girlfriend, I've got a client already salivating, ready to hire you as their spokesperson; you'll be the first female athlete with a sportswear clothes line and a half million dollars a year and stock," I eagerly told Courtney, her eyes stoic, her left eyebrow frowned, quickly her hands tightened around my waist, simultaneously pulling me into an empty room, slamming the door behind us.

"What's wrong, Courtney, did I upset you?"

Tears welling up in the corners of her eyes, flowing down her cheeks, Courtney lowered her head onto my shoulder, crying; what had I done or said to cause this rather sudden physical response?

"Quite the opposite, Ne, you have done so much for me and the only thing I ever wanted I can never have—that's you."

"Courtney, life's dealt me such highs and lows, you are a beacon of light in my life, nothing else matters but knowing you remain a part of my world. It's time for you to see yourself worthy of blessings coming your way now, and I'm really digging the new piece out there, I think she's in for the long haul… I'm going to Woodland Hills; make this place work for you. You'll be stateside until some European team offers you a contract." I professed, trying to hide my heavy heart.

Moving to Woodland Hills would be the next leg of my journey, truth be told I'd purchased this house as a tax shelter working at MJS, never planning to ever live in it, my new home San Francisco with Joseph—why was life for Black folks such a juxtaposition of fate? Waiting hundreds of years in America, praying for just the moment I had achieved, yet jinxed with a plethora of horrors, keeping a goddamn monkey on our backs, still lifting that damn cotton, when would it end?

Ready to start my family at twenty-four, ready to be a mother, ready to leave Weitzman and become a full time mom and wife. Alan wanted to establish his practice in South Central Los Angeles, worried how he was going to raise the capital yet determined to do this on his own. One evening during dinner, Alan finally shared his story of dejection; after his tenth bank refusal I had enough, "Alan, baby, you don't have to worry, let me give you the money as your partner."

Alan opened his practice in the fall of 1984, making a huge splash in the Black community. Alan and four other dentists worked in his flourishing practice, so much so that Alan opened up another office in the Crenshaw district. For the first time in years, Black people could visit a dentist without a month-long wait. Receiving recognition from the mayor and city council, Alan became a member of the A-list Black social arena; this meant a lot to him for he had achieved this exclusivity on his own (sort of; well, no), without the public assistance of his rich and famous wife—that was our storyline. I said little to toot my horn; just happy Alan was so enthusiastic and proud. Bev and Courtney were pissed but refrained from commenting other than their demeanor of disdain, both believing if Alan made me happy after all I had been through they'd zip their mouths; what Bev and Courtney did not understand was that even though I was twenty-four years old, I felt fifty, beat up and tired beyond compare; I wanted a family, there was nothing else for me to believe in.

The ebb and flow of my life always reverted to a low point after high pulses of brightness. I began to worry that my journey into motherhood would again be delayed, as Mrs. Alan Robinson's womb seemed to be a low priority for the good doctor, my desire to start a family put on hold, with Alan insisting he was not prepared to be a good father because of his growing dental practice. My grandmother and mother, still enamored with Alan, began to focus on him differently, their lenses changed; witnessing firsthand the plight of my mother, Granny was in pitch perfect form to tell me a thing or two.

"Denise, Alan is unusually boastful right now, and I don't like it, child, the wise person realizes the divinity of the gift and does all one can do to cultivate it, do you feel that Alan sees you this way? Reminds me of your Momma and Daddy, I told her then and I'm telling you now, you two ain't got nothing in common, baby you just wanted someone to love you, but my first-born grandbaby, he's not it, praying I am wrong. Denise, your Granny can't take anything happening to you." Leave it to my grandmother to deliver the sting of truth.

Alan built a thriving dental practice, but was beginning to change, demonstrating a newfound arrogance unfamiliar to me. In one year, the sensitive, loving man I'd fallen in love with had changed and not for the better; shamelessly enjoying all the trappings of his newfound social circle, the power, the money and the drugs. His appearance and behavior soiled and ugly, he seemed irritated from morning to night, his weight declined, his mood sour and brittle.

"Alan, why aren't you eating breakfast, I made your favorite, salmon croquettes and grits, what's wrong?" I asked.

Alan angrily stared at me, his eyes constricted, full of rage, "I don't have to eat every time you decide to cook for me, do you have a problem with that!"

Shocked in his response, the feeling of complete sorrow immediately overtook my person, caused a seizing and tightening of my vocal cords; I refrained from engaging Alan. "No, I apologize."

Driving to work a sense of panic came over me, a flashback of my father coming into the house explosive because of a missed card game with friends; no I was not my mother, I would not take this madness, I had to address it now, I would when I got home this evening, just had to!

"Good morning, Mrs. Gaskin, just got into my office, there's a note from Weitzman, what's going on? A mass of folks in front of the water cooler outside, what does he want with me?"

"I'll be right in honey. Denise, Weitzman's secretary told me at lunch he wants information on all your clients from MJS, insider info."

Immediately turning up the radio in my office, KJLH blasting the Gap Band, needing to speak freely, undetected; now the cat was out of the bag, Weitzman hired me for my knowledge of companies involved in public trading. Shaking my head in disbelief in my own idealism (more likely my ego-driven foolishness), how could I have not seen the obvious? Ivan Boesky, father of greed and America's financial mystic, heralded in the excess revolution, claiming genius parlayed his monetary dominance in the millions. Boesky earned more than a quarter billion dollars when suddenly the rug was pulled from under his feet, his genius not the result of divinity but inside corporate knowledge. The Federal Trade Commission led the charge against Boesky; his stock market house of cards crumpled, the country in sheer disbelief as "perp walks" played out all over the United States. The gawking public looked on as Boesky and Michael Milken took heat on insider trading; I should have anticipated bullshit, but recent events in my life were responsible for my huge lapse in judgment.

"Does he think I'm going to jail behind his tight ass? That would be the dumbest thing in the world; should I just put a gun to my head and pull the trigger because he's asking me to blow my own brains out! How could I have been so naïve and stupid; I was purchased for my knowledge, shit, with all the mergers and buyouts all of the companies taken public, I was ripe for the picking, and who better to set them up than me? I'm done!"

"Calm down, Denise, you've got to think your way out of this, please!"

How was I going to calm down when I had been set up to self-destruct, small firms were now the target of hostile takeovers and mergers by greedy stock barons, and now I was supposed to roll over, give up the ghost, be glad to have been allowed to live the life for a brief moment in America after three-hundred-sixty years of horror? Hell no, I had to fight my way out this scene right now!

"Mrs. Gaskin, start taking my files off my computer; if I'm correct Weitzman's already been in them, he's probably taken most of them; hurry, let's go load the disk," I demanded.

"He's already taken them, oh this does not look good, baby!"

"Mrs. Gaskin, take the day off, go home, wait for my call at noon, have to step out of the office, low blood sugar, just can't think straight, let them know I'll be back in an hour." Needing to downplay the avalanche coming my way, if my office was bugged there was limited time to save my ass, leaving my office a short time after Mrs. Gaskin's departure to strategize and pray. Joseph was no longer here to protect me; I was alone, exposed and vulnerable on the auction block, eyes hyper-focused with inspection. My throat Saharan-desert dry, the only Nephilim to call on was Granny; I could not call my mother tell her that I the wiz kid on the cover of People Magazine was now on the precipice of being deemed a criminal. Granny got an SOS call from me as soon as I cleared the building, strategizing, remembering I had a client who lived on the twentieth floor. I could use their phone and not be detected; Granny and Bev had to be informed and part of my plan. I thought about all that I'd been through this past year, exiting the elevator, quickly knocking on the door, suppressing panic and shame.

"Felippe, I need your help, please, just invite me in quickly," I begged. "Yes, yes, my dear, come in, are you all right, what can I do to help you?" the startled slight man said, ushering me through the front door.

"Felippe, I'm in trouble, so sorry to come to you, forgive me, I must call someone now, I can't tell you anything, please leave me, you cannot be a part of my madness!"

"Si' mi amore, I go away, anything, anything you need I get for you."

Felippe Soledad lived in grandeur, sweeping views and fifteen-foot ceilings cascaded against the downtown landscape; having found his way to the streets of American gold through me, taking his Mexican cuisine company public. Starting as a street vender selling tacos, Felippe parlayed his love of Mexican food into a twenty-million-dollar company with me heralding his public offering. This petite man from the shacks of Tijuana, orphaned at ten, who survived by selling chewing gum and small key-chained sombreros, never had to concern himself where his next peso was coming from, swore on the soul of his beloved mother that the Soledad familia would always be there for me. Right now, though, I needed Bev; there was no time to waste, I had to put my plan in motion right now if I was to survive this storm's growing darkness on the horizon; dialing Bev, praying she would answer, on the third ring her voice cascading in my ear.

"Bev I'm in trouble; I don't have time to discuss any of the craziness with you, please just help, please!"

"Ne, okay, tell me what to do," Bev said, her voice constricted with my fear.

"Go to my house, on the east side of the garage, the potted begonia, my house keys, go to my office, get my computer, take every file box in the file cabinet as well, give them to Buster for safekeeping. Bev, I don't know if I can beat this! In record box seven, there's an envelope with your name on it, you're one in a million, you changed my life I love you.... Bev you must go to Granny, tell her Weitzman's duped me, hurry."

"Ne, what the hell is going on? Let me help you."

"You are helping me, can't talk, just do it, please Bev, go! Don't call me on the phone, it could be tapped," I pleaded with Bev, studying my watch.

"Felippe, is your car on the street?"

"Yes, Denise."

"Felippe, drive me to First and Main, I need to take care of something, wait around the block for me."

Fifteen minutes remained, money had to be secured before my accounts were frozen, I'd worked hard to build a world and life for myself, presently worth thirty-million dollars, most of which I knew would be untouchable by sundown. My heart raced in horrific fear of not being able to complete the task of transferring ten million dollars from the bank.

My heart pounding so hard, my chest hurt as I reached the bank officer's desk, sitting quickly, my words fast and deliberate as I handed him what looked like a bank robber's demand note, "I would like to transfer all of the accounts listed into the account listed on the bottom please."

Perusing the account numbers, the bank officer looked at me, wondering why I was taking millions of dollars spread over ten accounts into one.

"Well, this is different, Miss Burelford, is there something we can do to serve you better"

"No, I need to consolidate funds," I said, watching the transfer being completed.

"Miss Burelford, your transfer is complete, ten million dollars has been transferred into the accounts of Helena Burelford."

Quickly making my way back to Felippe's car, he drove like a madman down Olympic, weaving in out of traffic, yet cautious not to draw attention, clearing his throat, he spoke, "You can disappear right now if you need to, mi amore, Soledad's protect their own." Ten million dollars would have to last, maybe my lifetime, hectically running back to the office, Weitzman was waiting in my office with three men I did not recognize.

"Denise this is Mr. Smythe, Mr. White and Mr. Brown from the Federal Trade Commission. You know the FTC. Have questions they like to ask you," Weitzman pronounced.

"Mr. Weitzman, I need to call my attorney."

"I'm afraid, Ms. Burelford, you are in serious trouble."

My office door opened, two federal investigators staring at me, "Denise Burelford, we have a warrant for your arrest; stock manipulation and conspiring to sell stock trading information."

The other shoe had dropped and, as usual, a Black person was to fall on the sword, caught up in someone else's madness. Mirandized and perp-walked as though at a children's Halloween parade, making my descent into purgatory; oblivious to jeering and stares, I began to shift gears, focused on the pig slop I was knee deep in, through the eyes of onlookers, who seemed to be in a state of disbelief about my enormous turn of bad luck on my elevator descent to hell.

"Tell me this, how did you get yourself into so much shit at your age? Take the next elevator, official business!" One of the officers uttered from the rear of the elevator, laughing at my human tragedy.

"You know how it is, these people get into business that's just over their heads," said the FTC investigator next to me.

Staring at them, these middle-aged, balding nondescript White men in navy blue suits and white dress shirts; representing White America's suspicion of the competency of Blacks; regardless of our academic or economic level of success, Caucasians viewed Black America with myopic lenses of their own creation, prohibiting them from ever seeing the degrading manifestation of the African in America; they were responsible for our misery, our mythology, our pain. "Hold on Denise, I'll get you out, I'm right behind you, baby," Herman Winston looked on, distracted and angry, versed in what was unfolding in front of him, helpless as a Black man in Tulsa Oklahoma in 1921.

Reassuring words, but I knew I was in real deep trouble, the likes of which Black folk really hated to cross—White men and money. Why had I not seen Weitzman for what he was, a trader of souls, barren of morals and principles, motivated by unmitigated greed? In my rush to help others I had lost sight of protecting myself, easy to do with so much loss in my life, yearning to see happiness, craving to be valued and loved; now I prayed Herman was making bail for me as I was manhandled and shoved into the back of an unmarked car.

"Hey little girl, how did you get yourself into this shit? Why don't you do yourself a favor and lighten your sentence, tell us who was in on this with you because a little colored girl like you couldn't put this together by yourself."

Terrified and angry, I fought to suppress rage, as only a marginal excuse was needed to beat my ass. Sitting on my handcuffed and numb hands in the back of a police car, trying to anticipate and prepare for the next round of bullshit coming at me.

"Hey, nigger, did you hear them talking to you!" The investigator angrily shouted at me, as though his words and the octave of delivery would shock me into confession about a crime I knew nothing of.

"All right, you want to play hard ball, smartass bitch, here we go!" Opening the rear passenger door, dragging me out by my jacket, the sound of the seams and blouse tearing, my wrists bleeding and bruised, focused on Nana's words about looking fear in the eyes in Coushatta, Louisiana with the Klan, this was my moment, my test. Mumbling to myself, "God has a ledger of the White man's deeds, just live through his sickness to see him suffer, but you can never give in, summon the creator to snatch back your soul and die in truth."

"Okay bitch, you want to play the tough-ass soul sister revolutionary game, here we go!" Dropped onto the asphalt on my back, cuffed hands still behind me, hogtied, I whimpered, refusing to cry, I'd lost my bearings of space and time, unsure where I was and what was next, focusing on Nana's words over and over again.

"Not so tough now, are you?" as I felt a blow to the back of my legs.

"I want names! Millions of dollars have been spent on this investigation, you piece of shit, just give me the goddamn names!" One of the feds angrily demanded of me.

"I don't know anything!" I shouted, tears streaming down my face, now I wanted death, make it sudden God, please!

"Mutherfuckas, we see your damn dirty asses, we see you!" Voices shouted from the distance, the assault on my body abruptly stopped.

"Call for another car take her to the locals or we'll call the news, got pictures, dirty bastards!"

A police car arrived within minutes of hearing the angels that had saved my life; Nana's prayer had spared me. Reaching the station, no one seemed unnerved by my disheveled appearance, as if it were normal to have a thousand dollar Yves Saint Laurent suit torn to shreds.

"Hey, were bringing in that Denise Burelford, you know the stock trader, the rich one, she won't be for long, that's for sure!"

"Your attorney posted bail, damn how did you get two hundred grand so quickly?"

"Oh Ne, let's go, I got to get you to doctor," Herman said, tears falling down his face.

Reaching Herman's car, in the rear of the station wagon was my headscarf and sunglass-wearing grandmother, and next to her Dr. Washington.

"Oh my God, Herman, gade nan ti bebe mwem an, look at baby! Yo pral peye, they will pay!" Granny shouted.

"Hold on, let's take her back to the hotel where I can examine her, take her straight to General if need be," Dr. Washington shouted to calm down my grandmother; disturbed by the contusions on the back of my legs, I was secretly taken to a small hospital for a CT scan and lab work using an alias. Released the next morning with no internal bleeding or injuries, I awoke groggy yet blessed to be alive; sitting next to my bed was my mother, staring out the hospital room window as she had when I was ten years old.

"Ne, I will never leave you, Mommy will never leave you."

"Where's Alan?" I asked my mother who seemed angry and saddened at the same time.

"Denise, I couldn't get Alan, I tried…. I'm sorry, your grandmother felt you would be better not having that much exposure with him, well, you know, these days he could be a liability, right now you have to focus on yourself, this is the biggest corruption case since the Columbians and cocaine, they're trying to bury you!"

"I want to get you the heavy hitters to defend you, this is your life, I'm not what you need but I'll be there to oversee your defense, Eric Rosenthal comes highly recommended, he's the best when it comes to corporate big buck deals, I called him and he's is willing to represent you," Herman shared.

Staring at Herman and my mother as I sat on the edge of the hospital bed, trying to analysis his response, was he about to abandon me?

"Denise, there are ten counts of inside trade violations, if convicted you're facing fifteen to twenty years, I won't have that hanging over my head."

"All right, Herman, set up the meeting."

The drive home seemed long; I was rudderless, floundering in the water; my grandmother kept a low almost inaudible conversation going with Herman, finally Granny's head turned towards me and my mother.

"Denise, I must tell you this now, when Joseph and Lil Stewardt were murdered, Old Lady Stewardt and I began to hear things from Buster, crazy things, had to get to the truth of it…. Sometimes Denise the truth is awful to bare, like what I am about to tell you. The White girl that killed them both was introduced to Joseph intentionally by her father."

"That's no secret, I know that Granny," I said.

"But what you don't know is why. Her father ran the country's largest commercial insurance firm in the nation; he targeted Joseph because he knew who Joseph was and the exposure and power of the NFL, her father was on the verge of getting to the commissioner using Joseph, Joseph and her father were scheduled to meet with NFL officials a week after he was killed, had the deal gone through they would have earned one hundred million dollars a year rolling through their purses," Granny shared with me.

"Granny, what are you holding back; as horrible as that was, I feel you're not telling me the whole story."

"Mr. Weitzman sits on the board of directors of the insurance company, all this time Weitzman and her damn father have plotted to keep Joseph and you in their front pockets. Weitzman, like the White girl's father, put nothing in front of money and conquest; both you and Joseph were destroyed and no one lifted a finger to steer you from the madness, child it is so difficult to break free from the grips of racism and oppression; Black people are still the moneymakers and White folk's the takers."

As we pulled into the driveway, I looked for Alan's 635 BMW but it was absent. Alan had not arrived home. After all that I had been through; walking towards the staircase, on the banister was a note, "Denise I'll be home late, going to Mount Olympus." Wherever the cocaine was, Alan was there, who was I kidding? His crack problem and my denial of it was a non-starter at this moment, needing to shower and prepare my defense with Eric Rosenthal. Our bedroom felt large and empty as our marriage, no Alan needed to go, he would never be Joseph and I could not get on board with his madness. Entering our bath, turning on the shower, contemplating Alan and my innocent yet naïve idealism about poverty which had damaged our relationship, just like "Good Times," Alan was stuck in Cabrini Greens, the byproduct of poverty. Despite having made it, Alan was traumatized by poverty, the insecurity of never having and the mere thought of losing it injecting so much fear into his being that Alan had become a monster.

CHAPTER THIRTY-SEVEN

HIGH NOON

"Denise, this is Eric Rosenthal."

"Herman filled me in on the matter this afternoon, I need to know the truth, I can't help you if you don't."

Rosenthal's face was small and delicate, his blue eyes pale and, more importantly, I sensed an air of doubtfulness from him regarding my innocence.

"Mr. Rosenthal, I had no involvement in any of the allegations. I do not have a clue. Weitzman asked me four months ago to share my client information. I know what that means and I refused."

His eyes widened, sensing my anger, "Calm down, Denise, I have to ask you these questions. If you didn't share the information, who did?"

"Mr. Weitzman accessed all my client records from my computer, he ripped through my files late at night, he used me to get information on Black firms going public," I responded.

"Are you telling me that Weitzman set you up? His firm is worth close to a billion dollars, why would he want to risk his career on, please forgive me, but a few Negro firms. Your story, Ms. Burelford, it's just not believable. Why didn't you step away from him sooner then?"

"Look, I'm very cautious about everything. There was no way I could have prepared for this."

Rosenthal paused briefly before giving me the *fact of life in America if you're an African* look, "Denise, in corporate America, White men don't extend the hand of friendship or hand you an olive branch freely. I don't care if you're the best in the field, it's that thing of inferiority and doubts of Blacks, and I guess you forgot."

He'd shared a plain and simple truth—I forgot my place in America; money caused me to behave in a delusional manner; I'd been set straight by this arrogant bigot.

"All right, Mr. Rosenthal, you made your point, but I did nothing illegal, no client financial information, nothing, and what I will not become is Weitzman's sacrificial lamb."

"Denise, I will do my best by you, at present with no documents to support your story you're rather, how can I say this, dead on arrival, and I strongly suggest you cut a deal. Maybe plead guilty to a lesser count of accessory, serve a year or two in federal prison, the time there is, well, pleasant, not hard time, pay the two million dollar fine and get on with your life."

What was he taking about! Was he out of his mind; do jail time be labeled a felon, millions in fines? I would fight this; Bev secured my client records, they would never find them, I had time to regroup and bust this case wide open.

"No, I won't plead I'm guilty. I was paraded out of my office, beat up and assaulted, and you want me to plead guilty to crimes I did not commit? No, I don't think so."

His pale blue eyes filled with smoldering fire, "Well you sure better come up with something in the form of proof in the days ahead or you're looking at some serious time; my fee is seven hundred thousand dollars to take this case through, and the retainer is two hundred fifty thousand…are you prepared to pay today?"

"Yes, my mother will write you a check."

Concluding small talk and sensing Rosenthal's desire to cash his check, things wrapped up quickly; I saw the look of worry in Herman's and Granny's eyes, she did not like him, but I had no choice as worry filled every wrinkle on her face.

Four the next morning into my tragedy and Alan had not returned home, my heart was broken; it was bad enough being made Weitzman's scapegoat, now left to fend for myself absent the husband I had always supported. The truth about his heart revealed he was no different than his mother and family, Alan was incapable of authentically loving me, only what I represented. As the sun rose, Alan decided to come home, his footsteps unmetered and sloppy-looking as though he'd not eaten in months, his six-feet-three-inch frame shrunken and gaunt as an Ethiopian famine victim. I was saddened in his presence, choosing my words carefully, speaking in a calm but deliberate tone.

"Where have you been? I called you today all over town to tell you I had been arrested, they took me to jail roughed me up, I…"

Alan lunged forward after me, "Look, bitch, that's your goddamn problem; all I want out of this marriage is the house!"

"Alan I won't argue with you, I had this house before YOU existed in MY world, but if all I mean to you is a house, then have it, you're dead to me now."

His eyes bulged, Alan clenched his fists, began swinging wildly at me, bobbing as we danced around the room, grabbing me by my throat, dragging me like a rag doll into the bathroom, trying to force my head under water in the bathtub, biting his hand long enough for me to break free and run. Alan yelling at the site of his own blood, too high to run right after me, grabbing my purse and briefcase at the front door, praying I would make it out of the house to my car, placing the key in the ignition and the gearshift in reverse, never looking back, pleading one more time for angelic oversight as I made my escape from madness, again, locked in a parallel universe, unable to escape upheaval, it was the red Chevy all over again.

Making my way down the 101 Freeway to Courtney's, anger rose in me, why now with this ignorant fool? I had to divorce Alan, one more dinosaur to slay. Courtney was in shock at my sight; hair wet and matted clothes soaked, she stood petrified at my appearance, I had no words or sounds to provide her.

"Oh God, my love, they die," Courtney professed as I fell into her arms.

Numb as I had been the night Joseph was killed, Courtney patiently removed my wet clothes, wrapping me securely in a blanket while she gathered dry clothing, carefully combing out my matted hair as though this were a sunny Saturday visit to my hairdresser, brightening my dreary spirit.

"Ne, I should have never let you marry him, leaked a story to Jet or the National Enquirer he was a con artist taking advantage of your broken heart, as much as they begged for stories…. I could have saved you. Alan is a low grade punk-ass hustler, I just didn't have the heart to take what little happiness you had away, and I knew you had a solid prenup, he couldn't take anything, despite that he hurt you, Ne, I'm gonna beat his ass!"

The eleventh of July, I filed for divorce, forced to beg Granny and Old Lady Stewardt not to kill Alan, as mad as Granny was this was not time to exact revenge, within days of departure from my home, Alan turned the place into "Party Central," while I worked quietly at Courtney's to salvage my life.

July 15th, a day shy of my birthday and my life torn apart at the ripe old age of twenty-five, my stomach a lake of fire, unable to eat without regurgitating my meals, plagued by the presence of ulcers.

Bev arrived daily with care packages containing my records, I would methodical turn up the volume on the television or radio, providing her a list of task and records to bring to me, returning the previous files, nothing was kept in the house, Buster kept everything safe, I prayed my plan would work. I had not shared with Granny or my mother about the files, fearing involving them, based on what had been done to me I did not want my family hurt and the best way was not to provide any information. The next morning the Feds came with search warrant in hand looking for evidence, everything was turned upside down. I had no way of knowing if my phone had been tapped or the house bugged so I watched everything that was discussed.

As the trial date loomed, every document needed was assembled, now it was up to Rosenthal to prove that all the information Weitzman obtained was done illegally from my computer files, each transaction carried a transmittal number that was time stamped and dated. There was one more piece of information needed to eliminate all doubt—a copy of Weitzman and Associates' appointment ledger documenting client meetings and their comings and goings. The only person with access to this information was Mrs. Gaskin, who as a matter of business copied every page of the book as a safety precaution. I knew the appointment book would disappear when it was asked for in discovery, but what no one knew was that there was a copy of it. If I asked Mrs. Gaskin for her copy, I would put her at risk, she was close to retirement and I would not jeopardize her future. I contemplated asking Mrs. Gaskin for assistance; having lost twenty pounds, which in a twisted way gave creditability to the media's story of me falling apart, allowing me to work on my case without notice.

Alan telephoned three weeks before the trial was to begin insisting that I sign divorce documents, I was hesitant in doing so knowing that his descent into hell was in full gear. Moving from freebasing to crack use because he was broke; both dental offices were in disarray, his partners meeting to buy him out before complete financial ruin, Alan taken out a two hundred thousand dollar loan against our home without my knowledge by forging my name. Now he was behind on the loan payments, foreclosure was the next step, and he was frantic in getting the fifty grand we had in a joint account. Dialing Alan, anger rose in me, laughter and music in the background.

"What's happening," Alan said as my throat tightened in anger, he was high as a kite.

"Alan, its Denise, got your message about the divorce papers, I was wondering if I could meet you somewhere down Ventura Boulevard?"

"Why can't you come here and sign them! Look, all right, meet me in Encino at the Chart House at four-thirty this afternoon."

Not wanting to drive to Woodland Hills to sign divorce papers, fearful of what may happen, Buster would accompany me, no more negative press before the trial, I truly had enough. Meeting Alan in a public place, he dare not act a fool—I hoped. Wanting to look especially nice for my own ego despite my weight loss, desperately needing to believe I was not the failure talked about in newspapers and magazines, that my spirit had not broken, selecting a soft white linen pant suit and white snakeskin slingbacks, I pulled my hair into a bun, painstakingly applied my makeup, and headed out to finish this chapter of my life. I thought about the things that I had wanted for myself and Alan, the babies, all the happiness that would never be.

Glancing at my watch, realizing I'd been waiting over an hour, it was now five-thirty and Alan was nowhere in sight. Six o'clock and the dinner crowd arrived, people began to recognize me, some seemed supportive but most White folks had that "it figures" look on their faces.

"Don't like this, Buster, too many people and faces, let's drive out to Woodland Hills."

I'd drive out to Alan's, he probably was there sucking on the pipe, afraid to leave it. I thought about the fork in the road I had met, yearning to get back on the main highway of life, no more back roads for me—I prayed that I could. Reaching Valley Circle my heart began to pound, racing with the history of not only Alan's acute madness but that of my father. "Ne, you don't have to go in there alone, I'll be right behind you," Buster said as I got out of the car.

Ringing the doorbell, music played but no voices, maybe Alan fallen asleep or he was in bed with one of his dope whores. Removing the key from my purse, unlocking the front door, there were no guests present, just music blaring, maybe Alan was upstairs.

"Anyone home?"

Walking up the stairs, I called out, "Alan, are you here?" Marvin Gaye's "Got to Give It Up," Doppler reverberation, pounding bass line, this the reason why Alan had not heard me, he must have been outside.

"Alan, coming to you," I said.

Making my way through the French doors of the family room, calling Alan's name again, walking toward the pool, my heart stopped, a quick glance, eyeballing a body floating face down, it was Alan. Jumping into the water to reach him, praying he was still alive, struggling to pull him out of the water, my lungs ached as I fought to pull him out of the pool. Turning him on his side, trying to empty the water from his lungs, hoping he would wake up, but he did not, frantically beginning CPR as I had with Joseph, fighting to catch my breath while Buster compressed his chest.

"Ne, he gone, he's dead, stop!" Buster demanded.

The coroner's report revealed Alan was full of cocaine and alcohol when he tripped over a chaise lounge by the pool, hit his head on the corner of the pool, and drowned. As much as I hated all the baggage that came with Alan, I still felt an overwhelming sense of loss—again. The timing of Alan's demise could not be worse, the press had a field day, which was the last thing I needed now, but this just seemed like the way things went for me.

Alan's family was more concerned with any money he had left than his death. Herman tried to explain to his mother due to her son's drug addiction he was heavily in debt, Chi-town mom knew about the fifty-thousand-dollar insurance policy and wanted the money wired to her immediately, Herman telephoned with their concerns, I was not surprised, providing him the fifty thousand dollars. His mother wanted the funeral in Chicago; I agreed, not wanting to share the same air with them, shipped Alan's body to Chicago for burial. Deciding not to attend the funeral, we'd said our farewell poolside, wanting to cherish the memories of him I held, not what he had become.

Mrs. Gaskin came to pay her condolences, she sensed something was troubling me.

"Denise, is there something you want to tell me?"

I stood silently next to her needing to ask, yet knowing I should not risk her security for my own.

"Damn it, girl, what do you have to say!" Mrs. Gaskin asked again.

"I need Weitzman's appointment book and phone log it will help me prove that he met with prospective clients and not me, no I shouldn't ask, you only have a year to retire, if you say…"

"Hush child, made you a couple batches of fudge and brownies," she leaned forward, whispering in my ear, "I came to give you the log, there in the fudge box. Honey, you helped this old country woman when no one else would, you are the reason I can retire next year. You're the best person I know, got a heart of gold. That annuity you got me three years ago when we left MJS is worth six hundred thousand dollars, I'll be alright." I cried in Mrs. Gaskin's arms, my joy intense, for all of society's confusion and hatred, Mrs. Gaskin represented all that was possible in America.

The eve of the trial, Rosenthal stopped by to suggest I plead guilty and cut a plea deal. It gave me great pleasure to substantiate my innocence, positive that half a million later this asshole thought I was guilty.

"Eric, I told you I will not plead guilty to something I did not do."

"Well, Miss. Burelford, my investigation points to you as the link; I told you that then, and now after reviewing the discovery."

I looked at Rosenthal then lowered the boom, "You know I entrusted my life with you, pointed you in the direction of truth, and you turned your back on it, electing not to do a damn thing about the obvious. What's the real deal here, you really believe I am guilty, right?"

"Yes, I do." Rosenthal proudly exclaimed.

Laughing at his smugness, signaling for Buster to bring in my defense files.

He looked in odd disbelief at all that I possessed. "What is this?" he asked of me.

"Eric, I have the records of every client I have ever serviced, each computer record carries a time stamp denoting the time of entry of each file, checking all the time stamps and the appointment log of Mr. Weitzman, I have solid proof who the inside source was and it is not me. You know, Eric, you're a huge disappointment, you could have least gotten the phone log from the firm. Whose side are you really on?"

He sat crumpled on the sofa, having been exposed for what he was, a man who operated with erroneous assumptions of every person of color. Speaking in an almost inaudible voice, he replied, "You'll have your retainer back in twenty four hours, this is pro bono, just don't sue me."

"Eric, at this point it is not about suing you, it's about exposing the bullshit of a person you are. To you, every Black person in America is guilty of a crime, you are both our judge and jury, listen, who died and made you God?"

Herman coldly stared at Rosenthal, "I'll take over the case, but I want you there."

"No problem, Herman, I understand."

The day of the trial, my family gathered at Courtney's, ready for the war, knowing that we were all that each other had. Covering open sores, preparing for battle, my father, never looking at my mother, took off his sunglasses and spoke, "Helena I'm here for our child, I was wrong, I cannot undo what I have did to you or my kids, I am sorry. This wheelchair reminds me every day how wasteful a man I was, I am flawed and apologize for all that I did to you."

Bev, Smitty and Lulia would meet us at court, Buster and his crew (most of Paxton and Louvre Street) met Herman at his office to escort him to court. We did not know where Rosenthal stood, so we behaved as though he was the enemy, and with the knowledge of my records he could have passed on the information to Weitzman, Buster took evasive measures to keep him off balance.

Reporters lined the halls of Division 10 of downtown Los Angeles County Superior Court. Buster and Herman guided me through the swell of lights and cameras, as Buster had with Joseph just a short time ago. A feeling of malaise came over me as flashbacks of that terrible night flooded in. Turning around to pan the sea of humanity crammed into this small space; directly behind me, left of my family, sat Bev, Courtney, Smitty and Lulia.

"All rise, court is in session, the honorable Judge Dyane presiding."

Herman leaned over to Rosenthal, "I'm moving for a dismissal right away." Rosenthal, stoic, watched for his lead, as Herman stood to address the judge.

"Your honor, I possess evidence which supports my client's innocence. May I approach the bench?"

The judge appeared baffled but quickly responded, "Yes, both counsels approach the bench."

Their conversation lasted for what felt like an eternity, the prosecution looked startled as though led into a wind tunnel, the judge irritated as to this new direction of the trial.

"There will be an hour recess, counselors see me in my chambers now!"

As the court cleared, Bev and the Babies gathered around me, all of us silent, Granny insistent that we pray. "I can't move, can we all just sit here together one last time just a minute more, please?" I asked. An hour later, the bailiff notified us court was back in session.

"After a review of the documents submitted into evidence I am dropping all charges. Miss Burelford you are free to go."

Staring coldly at Weitzman, certain his days of luxury were ending, the government was going after him like white on rice. Walking over to him, I said in a deliberate voice, "How does it feel to be on the other end of the stick? This is not over, you stole everything from me, you took Joseph from me, you and the bitch's father, I will come for you both. I know what you two did, harm anyone that I know and everything you both have I will destroy." Within months, Weitzman's firm was dissolved, he faced thirty years and millions in fines. I felt no pity; his greed, his demise.

Herman worked long hours restoring my financial portfolio attached by the feds, and above all I had my freedom, I looked forward not back at the next leg of my journey, needing to make sure that those who'd been there for me would be alright. Despite all of my tribulations, I was still standing, what a blessing. Time to celebrate, deliberately toss around some dough, experiencing the fragility and rapidness of life, money is no good when you're cold and done. I wanted to party, hit the streets with my girls, they wanted Carlos and Charlie's and Mickey's, clubbing with the beautiful and famous, the glistening neon of the Sunset Strip and hanging out with my *Hollywood folk*. Not me, I wanted Claretta Street, fried chicken and biscuits, excited and full we'd make a schoolyard run up Mount Boom Boom where we could cackle like hens and slumber-party giggle about which Jackson was the finest. Yes, I needed to go home.

It was August of 1986 and things in my hamlet were crumbling as all the other Claretta Streets in America had. General Motors and Lockheed found greener pastures, deciding to leave the San Fernando Valley; thousands of Blacks and Latinos lost their chance to grab the brass ring of the American dream. Crack cocaine no longer just lingered in the cervices just beneath the skin of Pacoima, now it poisoned the landscape. Claretta Street of memory was under siege, families contemplated battle strategies and simultaneous evacuations, where to go and what to do. Most talked of plans for moving to the

Antelope Valley where the dry high desert kept the boogieman of cocaine away, yet for this brief moment in time I wanted one more look at what had been in my life.

Mount Boom Boom now rested atop the new 210 Freeway, to shoot the breeze and laugh about the good old days, in my Jeep, we spoke about Deebie, desperately missing her wild ass, we laughed about Mr. Hackmon drinking port wine and spitting snuff in the front yard, and I felt whole again. Sitting on the ledge, looking out over Pacoima, watching the twinkling lights, we were silent. Besieged with grief with the new world outside of our small town. Absence of words an agreement of our shared beloved possessed past, and the uncertainty in a world that daily bombarded us with a multitude of challenges, we prayed that we could meet in the world outside of our little place that could—Pacoima.

"Well, we can't bring the old days back, but we can fortify ourselves for what may lay ahead."

"Hell yeah, we have to because things have just gotten crazy, shit, bring back the Dramatics!" said Smitty.

We laughed at her remark, but in our laughter we knew she was right, the comfort our community was gone, stripped and sucked of its love and nurturing, it was just a shadow of its old self. Now filled with faces void of life, just looking for the next hit of the crack pipe.

"Look, I don't know where the world will take me or you but I want us to make it, we are from Pacoima, all we ever needed was a damn chance!"

Reaching into my purse, I handed each an envelope, "Open um all, y'all."

"Oh, what the hell, Ne!" Lulia and Smitty yelled.

"Everybody has three hundred grand to begin again, for the first time all three of you are equal partners in the apartment building."

Talk of old fortified and warmed us despite the chill in the air, the same way it had the night of David's death. Frigid, that evening as I looked out over the city, the warmth of David's being filled me, removing my fear. There was something about the spirit of Claretta Street and its people that has always nourished me, and I prayed it would continue to guide me on this journey called life,

I remain,

Denise 1986.

HISTORICAL FOOTNOTE

Pacoima or the Entrance as translated from Tataviam, (the language of Pacoima Native Americans), were Pacoima's first inhabitants. By 1797, Spanish colonial control set foot-on-head of Pacoima's first settlers, as occurred to countless indigenous cultures which were destroyed or contained.

1877, California state senator Charles Maclay purchased 56,000 acres with a loan from United States senator and industrialist Leland Stanford (founder of Stanford University). Pacoima labored on as agricultural land, the indigenous population pushed off sacred land, making way for corps and cattle, forced to exist with indentured laborers in shacks, no paved roads and only dirt and dust.

World War II, Lockheed Aircraft, needing housing for its Burbank, California workers, began to arrive at the Entrance. 1950, and Pacoima morphed at once into a gateway of hope for African Americans who were not barred from homeownership by racially discriminating housing covenants.

1960, more than ten thousand African Americans lived in the greater Pacoima area as the great migration continued. Pacoima was the pulse of African American life in the San Fernando Valley, with more than ninety percent home ownership. With the passage of the Fair Housing Act of 1974, African Americans of the Entrance began the exodus into the vast San Fernando Valley, Pacoima's brief acceptance of African Americans held firmly in the hearts and souls of its decedents scattered to the west in Woodland Hills and into the Antelope Valley towns of Palmdale/Lancaster and other communities to the north.

ABOUT THE AUTHOR

Claretta Street is the first novel by Colette Barris. Claretta Street is the story of Pacoima a bustling Black pride-filled town of the Civil Rights era.

Pacoima's story is one Colette Barris shares having grown up in the San Fernando Valley. Pacoima provides the foundation for Colette Barris's remarkable life and journey to author. Colette Barris is a graduate of the University of Southern California.